Praise for *Taking Time...*
a Tale of Physics, Lust and Greed

"Mike Murphey's novel is a masterpiece, from the gorgeous writing to the sophisticated characters, it delivers entertainment at its finest."
—The Book Commentary

"With dynamic characters and futuristic science, the story is a sci-fi lover's dream! And just as the cover promises, there is just a little physics, a bit more lust, and a ton of greed to help round out this exciting novel. The pages are filled with manipulations and mysteries, but also a healthy dose of humor to keep the whole thing from taking itself too seriously. *Taking Time* is a slightly satirical and entirely entertaining twist on a time travel tale."
—Steve Quade for Indies Today

"*Taking Time* puts the mechanics of time travel front and center, showcasing what's possible within the laws of physics yet explaining matters in a very accessible way. The process sounds plausible and scientifically sound, with Murphey devoting a fair amount of the narrative setting up the parameters of this historic breakthrough. It's easy to get swept away into the story, as the characters hurtle headlong into strange universes while dealing with ethical dilemmas, psychological trauma, and murderous enemies hiding in plain sight."
—The Online Book Club

Praise for *Wasting Time*

"…Quirky side characters, like Cecil the cat-waxer and owner of Cecil's Margin Service, wander in and out of the book, adding color and a mischievous tone to the tale. The action is lively and WASTING TIME is never dull for a moment–not even in the middle of a Congressional hearing. Mike Murphey's WASTING TIME is a quirky, enjoyable novel with some interesting speculations on the consequences and possibilities of time travel, lightened by a playful sense of humor."

—Indie Reader

". . . The female characters that Mike Murphey created were very empowering . . . I loved that the women were able to own their sexuality . . . Romance lovers should also gobble this up like the most delicious pie. You don't come across many books that skillfully mix science, drama, and romance like this one."

—Online Book Club

Praise for *Killing Time*

". . . In what I've come to look forward to and expect from Mike Murphey, the pulse of KILLING TIME is the easy flow of sharp wit, insolent humor and prurient curiosity … Satire and subterfuge are paired flawlessly in this wildly entertaining and unexpectedly heartwarming piece of futuristic fiction."

—Indies Today

KILLING TIME

a Tale of Physics, Lust and Greed
— BOOK 3 —

Mike Murphey

FROM THE TINY ACORN...
GROWS THE MIGHTY OAK

Killing Time
Copyright © 2020 Mike Murphey. All rights reserved.
Printed in the United States of America. For information, address
Acorn Publishing, LLC, 3943 Irvine Blvd. Ste. 218, Irvine, CA 92602

www.acornpublishingllc.com

Edited by Laura Taylor
Cover design by Damonza
Interior design and digital formatting by Debra Cranfield Kennedy

ISBN-13: 978-1-952112-86-7 (hardcover)
ISBN-13: 978-1-952112-43-0 (paperback)

This book is dedicated to the memory of Miss Mae Gilbert who died at the age of 102 after teaching generations of students at Portales High School to love the written word. Her encouragement made me believe I could become a writer. She would probably be shocked at my content, but she would love to know I write books.

This book is also dedicated to Nancy who really did save me from an ordinary life.

1

MARSHALLING THE FORCES

SEAN BRODY HAD LONG CEASED WORRYING that strangers ringing his doorbell might be psychopaths determined to club him to death during Wheel of Fortune. He assumed the front desk folks at Brookhaven Assisted Care screened out psychopaths. And sure enough, Marshall Grissom was not a psychopath.

Marshall, Sean would eventually decide, only suffered from some milder form of insanity.

April 1, 2046
Brookhaven Assisted Care
North Phoenix

Sean rocked back and forth a couple of times to escape a chair that had become the de facto center of his life. This gentle rocking built momentum so prosthetic knees could propel him to a standing position and drive those first stiff steps toward his front door.

The doorbell's single hollow ding caught Sean snoring as he again tried making headway reading *Atlas Shrugged*.

Ayn Rand's preachy, interminable soliloquies were the most effective sleep aids he'd ever encountered.

Sean, who didn't expect a caller, took a quick mental inventory. He hadn't forgotten a doctors' visit, he was sure. Liam hadn't said anything about stopping by. Probably just the Jehovah's Witnesses at it again. Even though proselytizers were not allowed through the main entrance, the more persistent Witnesses sometimes sneaked through a side door. And seen through the distorting lens of Sean's peephole, this hallway stranger certainly looked goofy enough to be a religious zealot.

The peephole revealed Sean's visitor as not just tall but towering. The man's frame appeared so thin he might not tolerate a strong wind. He had a full head of black hair and wore a light sport coat that—even on an April Phoenix morning—he should be glad to shed. His tie was knotted a bit off center. The peephole's fisheye lens converted his pointy nose to a bulging prominence dwarfing other facial features as he leaned to punch the doorbell again.

Sean smiled. He enjoyed messing with the Witnesses.

He jerked open the door. Before the stranger could begin his spiel, Sean thrust Rand's fat paperback at him. "You ever read this book?"

The man, whose unmagnified nose still looked a little outsized for his face, jumped back. "Um . . . Mr. Brody?"

"You ever read this book?" Sean demanded again, waving the volume in the man's face.

His visitor seemed lost.

"*Atlas Shrugged.* Supposed to be a classic. Dry as dirt, though."

The man offered his own helpless shrug.

"Come on. Ayn Rand? *The Fountainhead?*"

Sean snapped his fingers and tapped one foot in a sloppy rhythm while reciting,

"I been Ayn Randed, nearly branded . . ."

The odd-looking man brightened. Grinning and, stomping out the same rhythm, replied,

". . . Communist, 'cause I'm left-handed . . ."

Sean laughed and slapped the man's shoulder.

"Paul Simon, right?" the man asked.

"Correct," Sean said. "*A Simple Desultory Philippic (Or How I Was Robert McNamara'd Into Submission)*. Decades before your time, though."

"We had a bunch of old records in our attic when I was a kid. I listened to the ones I thought were funny," the man said. "But I'm sorry, I haven't read your book."

"Just as well. A friend gave it to me months ago. Said it's one of those books everyone should read. I've been trying ever since."

"Well . . . okay."

An awkward moment of silence intervened—filled only by the glow of Sean's muted television set—before Sean's guest said, "Wow. Wheel of Fortune. I watched that as a kid. I didn't know it was still on."

"Well, it is," Sean said. "Pat Sajak is even stiffer than he used to be. I can't decide if he's had one of those Cyborg implant things, or if his continued role as MC is the result of some really clever taxidermy."

"Taxidermy?" Marshall said, appearing a little startled. "Well, I don't think they could—"

"Yeah," Sean said. "I don't know how they'd make his arm mobile enough to spin the wheel."

"Um ... I'm sorry to intrude, Mr. Brody, and I know this will seem strange. My name is Marshall Grissom, and I hope you'll have a few minutes to talk with me."

Sean found himself liking this fellow, and he certainly had a few minutes. At his age, visitors were rare enough that he welcomed an opportunity to talk with pretty much anyone, even the Witnesses. Oh, sure, his sons came by when they could. James and Russel lived out of town, though. Liam had his own life and children with which to deal.

Sean stood aside and, with a sweep of his hand, invited Marshall in.

Two chairs formed the focal points of Sean's living-room. A big chair—the one his sons had bought when they moved him to his one-bedroom apartment at a north Phoenix assisted living facility—reclined, rocked, and rotated through a full three hundred and sixty degrees. A comfortable clutter of magazines, bills and junk mail spilled off a small table onto the floor. An old fixed-screen laptop computer sat dark beneath a table lamp.

Sean directed Marshall to a worn recliner that swallowed Marshall in its failing springs.

Sean dropped into his own seat. "So ... Mr. Grissom, is it? What flavor are you?"

"Flavor?" Marshall asked.

"Denomination. If you want me to attend your church, I need to know what my ultimate destination will be. I have no interest in reincarnation. Too much of a crap shoot concerning what you'll end up with. And if you want a contribution, well, I'm afraid—"

"Oh ... No. This isn't about church, or religion. I just wanted to ... I need to ask you some questions."

"Ask away. I'll warn you, though, I won't confess to the murder."

"Murder?" Marshall asked displaying an expression of shock.

"I was joking."

"Um ... okay. Well, how's your health?"

"Good. And how's yours?"

"I'm fine," Marshall said. "So, you're ... well?"

"Considering nowadays they can pretty much replace your parts and keep you going until you just get bored with it all, yes. I suppose I am. But I'm ninety-three years old, you know. Another ten or fifteen years and I'll be done."

Sean thought Marshall seemed a bit apprehensive as his visitor asked, "Do ... do you have many of those ... replacement parts?"

Sean gave a little snort at the question. He often pondered the contrast between himself as a robust, athletic young man, and a person marked with the afflictions of age—his height compromised by a stoop declaring onset of osteoporosis, thick dark hair reduced to sparse wisps of white, age spots spattering his arms and hands, a face gaunt from his inability to maintain weight. Not to mention a missing hunk of ear sacrificed to careless years of unheeded sunshine. He hoped casual observers would not yet describe him as frail, and that his eyes retained their spark of fascination with the world around him.

"Knees. A heart regulation system—one of those little plastic and metal things they stick right in your heart to keep everything steady. And I got those new visual implants. My surgeon installed a control pad here," he displayed his left wrist. "Lets me adjust the focal length, so I don't need glasses to read or see at a distance. Which is great, because I love to read in bed, and you can't lie on your side wearing glasses."

Now, Sean's guest seemed clearly dismayed.

"Is this what you do for fun?" Sean asked. "Visit strangers and ask about their infirmities? Are you selling some kind of insurance?"

"No. I'm not selling anything. I asked because . . . because I—and some friends of mine—need a favor."

"Who are your friends?" Sean asked.

Marshall appeared disheartened, the wind spilled from his sails. Sean raised his eyebrows as encouragement for Marshall to continue.

"Marta, Elvin, Gillis . . ." Marshall said absently. "And some others. Marta runs things now . . ."

"Do I know these people? And this Marta, why didn't she come herself?"

"What? Oh . . . the thing about Marta is . . . while she's this really great lady, she's, well, she's Marta. And I guess she thought asking about this favor is the sort of thing that requires some degree of, I don't know, *charming*? Marta really doesn't do charming."

Marshall sighed and seemed a little more lost.

"Have I disappointed you somehow?" Sean asked.

"Oh . . . no . . . it's just that, well, implants . . . knees and heart systems . . . never mind."

A nagging spark of familiarity picked at the back of Sean's brain. "Do I know you from somewhere?"

"That's a difficult question to answer. I think a more appropriate question would be 'do you know me from *some time?*' And the answer, technically, would be yes, although it doesn't do us any good right now."

Uh, oh, Sean thought.

"I do know a few things about you, though," Marshall continued a little more brightly. "For example, you and I are both alumni of New Mexico State University. Go Aggies?"

"Okay. My health. Where I went to school. It's time to tell me what this is about."

"As I said, we need your help. We need assistance from someone who lived in or around Portales, New Mexico, during the late 1960s. Someone who might still be willing to take a risk..." Marshall paused and adopted a somber tone. "... a bigger risk than we'd hoped, I'm afraid."

Sean had lived in that desolate eastern New Mexico community from the year of his birth, 1953, until his graduation from Portales High School with the class of 1971. So, he fit that part of Marshall's profile. The thing about taking a risk, though... Sean's greatest regret was that he'd burrowed too deeply into his comfort zones too often and hadn't been willing to make a few critical choices that might have steered his life on a different course.

He rose, walked to a set of sliding glass doors overlooking a compact patio where he enjoyed sitting in the cool of early morning and tossing seed to birds eager to greet him.

"I'm afraid my risk-taking days are behind me."

"Not... not necessarily," Marshall said. "Your days, I mean."

Sean turned from the glass panels and studied Marshall with renewed intensity. "I don't mean to offend you, Mr. Grissom, but you are an odd man."

"Um... I'm really not."

"I worked as a newspaper reporter for many years, and I know something about intruding on strangers, trying to convince them they should answer my questions. What I usually said was, 'I'm a reporter with the *Chronicle*,' or the *Herald-Republic* or the *Sun-News*. I didn't begin like that, though, when I knew they'd kick me out—once they learned I was a reporter—if I didn't soften them up a little first. In those cases, I'd be somewhat vague or deceptive before we got to the truth. You haven't told me a thing about who you represent, Mr. Grissom. You, sir, are trying to soften me up. Why don't you just say what you want?"

"Oh, trust me, Mr. Brody, you're not anywhere near soft enough for that yet. Um ... would you mind telling me about Portales? I've never visited eastern New Mexico."

Sean retraced his steps, sat again, and considered for a moment cutting off this inquiry. Sending this character on his way. He felt intrigued, though, concerning whatever Marshall might be after.

"Okay, Portales. It's a town of about twelve thousand people, thirty miles or so from the Texas Panhandle."

"Your family is from there?"

"You want the history, huh? Well, I'll warn you, old men like to talk about where and who they came from."

Marshall grinned.

Sean rocked out of his chair, walked across the room, and picked up a photograph displaying a frowning, hollow-cheeked man with slicked-down hair, holding a wide-brimmed straw hat at his side. A small, weary-eyed woman sporting a bonnet sat in a chair beside her husband.

"These are my father's parents, circa 1920 or so. My mom and dad were children of homesteaders, who lived hard-scrabble lives during the Great Depression. Eastern New Mexico and West Texas are located at the heart of a plain called the *Llano Estacado,* where trees are nearly as scarce as rain. On the rare occasion anyone finds a tree, they install a picnic table and call it a park."

Marshal chuckled at this image. Sean felt encouraged to continue.

"Mesquite bushes, tumbleweeds, a few hearty grasses and the occasional prickly pear cactus are the only things that volunteer to grow there. Farmers trick peanuts, sweet potatoes and some cotton to grow with irrigation from deep wells."

"I'm from eastern Arizona," Marshall said. "I know about the desert."

Sean dismissed him with a wave of his hand.

"Son, your Sonoran Desert is a garden compared to the high plains. At times, I'm tempted to feel sorry for my forebears . . ." pointing at more ancestral photos lined along the bookshelf. ". . . for all the sacrifice it took to domesticate that hard place."

He shook his head, feigning sympathy. Then amended regret with accusation as a spark of mischief lit his hazel eyes.

"Then, I always conclude it was their own damn fault. They were homesteaders, for God's sake! A few more weeks, and *they* would have made it to Arizona or at least southern New Mexico and the Rio Grande Valley. If you were stopping someplace, why would you choose a place without water and a population of tumbleweeds?"

"Sounds pretty bleak."

"Oh, eastern New Mexico has its beauty if you squint a little bit and know where to look. The locals seem to like it. You've never smelled air so sweet when it finally does rain. On the best summer days, cumulous clouds pile up in the distant western sky with these tongues of lightning—well, it's close to indescribable."

"Times were tough? Economically, I mean?" Marshall asked.

"No, not for me. For my parents, though—take that dry dusty homestead, drop the Great Depression in the middle of it, now *there's* some tough times. The amazing thing, both my folks spit in the eye of poverty and got college degrees. Then they went off and whipped Hitler."

"What did your parents do for a living?" Marshall asked.

"My dad worked for the Soil Conservation Service. My mom was a teacher."

Marshall leaned forward and studied the row of photographs. He pointed to a picture of three grade-school-aged boys, arms draped over each other's shoulders, grinning before a background of 60's era automobiles.

"Is this you? You look like you were pretty happy."

"I experienced all the advantages and handicaps of a small-town childhood." Sean stared a little wistfully at the picture. "My folks saddled me with a solid work ethic and enough ambition to be frustrated when my life failed to attain the grand heights for which I imagined myself destined. Not that I have anything to complain about."

"You didn't stay?"

"Shoot, within two weeks of graduating high school, I left for good, though of course I returned to visit. I got my degree from New Mexico State and then chased newspaper jobs into the Pacific Northwest where there's lots of water and mountains on every horizon."

"Are you . . . are you close to your sons?" Marshall asked, sinking back into his chair.

Sean sensed the hesitation in Marshall's question. Again, he considered feeling uncomfortable concerning the personal nature of this line of inquiry from a stranger. The clear sincerity of Marshall's interest, though, convinced Sean to continue.

"Close enough. Like I said, my two oldest, James and Russel, are in the Pacific Northwest. Liam lives here. They visit when they can."

"Did you enjoy being a newspaper reporter?"

"It was a job, like any job. Parts good. Parts bad. I was okay at it, not... great. I wish I'd have worked harder at a few things. You get old enough, you can admit those sorts of things to yourself. I got out before the newspaper industry collapsed. They pushed a lot of us into early retirement. The timing wasn't good. A few months after I left, Wall Street hammered my investments. So, I kept writing—freelance work, some short stories, a couple of abortive attempts at a novel." He pointed to a fat stack of paper next to his computer.

"You were divorced?" Marshall asked.

"Yeah, I visited my kids with that particular affliction, like so many of us Boomers."

Again, Sean considered taking umbrage at the personal nature of these questions, but something about the concern with which Marshall asked them encouraged his cooperation.

"Why didn't you remarry?"

"You're kind of nosey, aren't you?" Sean observed, though he softened the statement with a smile.

Marshall's face wore an apology.

"I came close—three times." Sean added a little wave to indicate he hadn't taken offense. "I met a younger woman who needed children of her own. My kids were still young themselves, though. My conscience wouldn't let me divide my attention that way. Not that I was a great father. Mercifully, I dodged the second bullet, which had misery written all over it. The third one . . . let's just say I would like to have seen how . . ."

His voice trailed off. He studied the pale blue carpeting at his feet. Sean required a moment, even after all these years, to compose himself when thinking of Maggie Stanfield.

He inhaled deeply, then met Marshall's eyes. "Enough memories. Tell me what's on your mind. Why the questions about my hometown? And who recommended me for whatever scheme you've got cooking here?"

"Cecil."

Sean waited for a last name. When Marshall didn't supply one, Sean drifted to the early 1980s, a cramped dark space in what was then a seedy section of downtown Spokane, Washington, across from the old Greyhound Bus Station. The building consisted of an unkempt storefront—a heavy glass door set in an ornate oak frame recessed between two wide plate-glass windows so grimy, light barely escaped a trifling reception area just inside. The shop shared abutting walls with two turn-of-the-century hotels that had become the province of pimps, hookers, Ronald Reagan's displaced mental patients, and a few elderly folks whose residency extended to a time of neighborhood respectability, and whose only economic choice was to remain.

Sean could still smell mingling odors of printers' ink and pipe tobacco welcoming those who ventured through the door of Cecil's Margin Service.

"You don't mean Cecil from Spokane . . . ?"

"Well, he presently lives on a sailboat in the Caribbean."

"Wait a minute. How could you know him? I mean, I don't know how old he was, but certainly several years older than me, and that would make him ..."

"He's 106. I'll leave you a number, but the closest phone is at a marina shack and a kid named Baptiste has to walk all the way down the dock to get him."

"My God." Sean's mind spilled over memories like water over rocks in a stream. "After all these years ... please. Tell me more. How can *I* help you?"

Marshall hesitated. Once again, Sean saw a man struggling with a decision.

"Um ... I was just ... we needed information about the town. And you've been very helpful ..."

"While I may be old, Mr. Grissom, I'm not addled," Sean said. "You didn't track me down to ask questions about weather in Portales. Something I've said here made you change your mind about me."

Again, Marshall paused.

"Well, no ... there are complications I hadn't counted on ... And you're right. I didn't come to talk about the weather. I came because you are one of a very few people left in the world who might be able to ... to help a friend who is ..."

Marshall closed his eyes, taking a deep breath like a man jumping into cold water.

"Please be forewarned, what I'm about to say will sound completely crazy. At the very least, though, I'll promise you it's a good story. More entertaining than anything you'll find on television this afternoon."

2

THE FINAL BATTLE

Limbo Corridor
No Date, No Time

THE HALL MONITOR SOUNDED genuinely regretful. "Oh my, this is disappointing. I am so sorry."

Fear settled over Sheila again. "Why?" she asked. "What's wrong?"

"I've enjoyed our talk. Please believe me, this is not my doing. It's simply inevitable. I've found you delightful." With a heavy sigh, he added, "Goodbye, Sheila Schuler. Your universe is here."

Sheila felt herself departing the limbo, as she had many times before.

This transition to her destination in the past of a parallel universe had always been effortless. Almost sensual. Like a gentle lover slipping inside her. Ooohh, Sheila thought, surprised at the intrusion of such an erotic image during this final instant of her being.

She found nothing smooth about this transition, though. Sheila was dragged across the mysterious barrier as though trying to squeeze through an opening entirely too small. The sensation was not one of pain, merely an impossible resistance as she forced her way into a place she was not meant to be.

Finally, whatever tether binding her to the limbo snapped

and she hurtled into a forbidden destiny with reckless force. Despite her fear, she paid close attention to every nuance of this horror, as she expected each passing second to be her last. Some kind of dark oblivion would swallow her . . . now! Okay, not now but . . . now?

Wait. What's happening?

She felt herself coalesce, felt the familiar comfort of a body surrounding her. She experienced an instant of relief. One brief second to indulge in a hope the physicists were wrong. A host waited for her here, after all.

Then . . . bedlam! All her thoughts, all the experiences tied to the future from which she had come, waged war with the thoughts and emotions of this poor being into which she intruded.

And this fight, Sheila feared, would be to the death.

Her instinct for self-preservation took over. She brought every scintilla of will to the battle. Incrementally, she felt this other awareness succumb, abandon its consciousness to hers. Sheila pressed harder, sensing abject fear and confusion from the withering mentality on which her conquest focused.

She could do this! She could still be Sheila! She didn't have to die!

Then one small thought, one small desperate gasp, pushed its way through Sheila's determination.

"I . . . I am Amanda. And I don't . . . I don't understand. I am Amanda!"

Amanda.

This being had a name. This being—no, this woman— had a life. A life she wanted just as badly as Sheila wanted her own.

Amanda.

Sheila's focus wandered from the battle as she saw herself and where she had come from. The commanding grip of her survival instinct slipped even further. This is wrong, she forced herself to understand. I can't interfere with a past being's right to—

But You'll Die!

Sheila relaxed her grip on the throat of this other consciousness just long enough for one more thought to pass.

Page.

A word changing everything.

Amanda Page? My grandmother? Oh my God!

Sheila cast everything else aside. Her preservation imperative collapsed. Sheila, the real Sheila, returned. If only for an instant. For as she surrendered completely to the mind and will of Amanda Page, she felt all knowledge of her future life and future self being stripped away until only an impossibly blank slate remained.

March 2046
HRI Complex

"Whatever doubts I originally had," Marta Hamilton told the group of conspirators gathered at a sterile little bar called The Time Warp, "Marshall has convinced me we must try. Everyone seated at this table has to understand the oversight subcommittee will *not* approve a projection to the 1960s so we can hunt for Sheila. We've painted ourselves into a corner with our deceptions. They can't know anything about it."

Marta and diplomacy shared only a rhetorical association. A native of Nevis, an obscure Caribbean island, she'd joined the top-secret time travel project displaying the disposition of a rattlesnake. She'd always avoided emotional entanglements that might compromise her role as a British spy and competed with ruthlessness for her place on mankind's first time traveling team.

Her new role as program administrator forced compromise, though, as did her unexpected romantic relationship with Marshall Grissom and genuine friendship with Sheila Schuler. Marta wasn't sure she trusted these changes within herself. Marshall and the others, though, offered intriguing alternatives to what had been a lonely, angry existence.

A neon beer sign over Marta's left shoulder sputtered, dimmed, then glowed bright again as she surveyed her accomplices—traveler Marshall Grissom, genius garage physicist Elvin Detwyler, real physicist Dr. Gretchen Allen, outcast physicist Dr. Leonard Rose, physician Dr. Naomi Hu, and spy Gillis Kerg.

"I think they'll impose these new regulations long before we can put together our Sheila mission, Marta continued, "So, when we do, that's when we'll be breaking their rules. When we all—not just me and Marshall—stand to get in a whole lot of trouble. If there's any chance Sheila's alive back there, Marshall and I intend to retrieve her. Anyone who doesn't want to be involved, tell me now. I'll respect your choice."

"You're both overlooking one very important point," Naomi Hu said, picking at her beer bottle's label. "You and Marshall *can't* do this. Perhaps a person can be sent back to a time beyond their birth if they can find a genetic match close enough to provide a host. Relatives share DNA patterns, and some of those patterns are more closely matched than others. Depending on each individual. Although they are grandmother and granddaughter, the yearbook photo Gillis found shows Amanda Page and Sheila Schuler could be twins, which indicates a strong possibility that their genetic markers are extremely close. Not an exact pairing, of course, but maybe close enough to provide a host for Sheila's consciousness to reside. Genetic matches like the one we're talking about aren't common, though. Odds against any of us finding a compatible host seventy-six years ago are astronomical."

"So," Marshall said, thinking aloud, "I have to find a ninety-something who lived somewhere near Portales, New Mexico, in the late 1960s, then convince them to become a time traveler."

3

A MILDER FORM OF INSANITY

April 1, 2046
Brookhaven Assisted Care, North Phoenix

SEAN WAITED.

"Okay," Marshall said. "Here goes. I guess you could say I'm a historian, of sorts . . ."

"And?"

". . . and if you want to be technical about it, I work for the postal service."

"You're a mailman?"

"Um . . . not exactly. They had to hide us. So, our funding is buried in the U.S. Postal Service budget. It was either that or the Forest Service. Which would have been okay, except we didn't want our physicists fighting fires during the dry season."

"They have physicists at the postal service?"

Marshall stopped again and studied his shoes. "Actually, I'm a time traveler."

He's right. This is *better than television, even if both flippers aren't working on this guy's pinball machine.* Sean swiveled his chair away from Marshall and toward the kitchenette, where the knives were.

"Are you here from the past or future?" Sean asked as casually as he could. *Don't upset him . . .*

25

"Neither. This is my native time. The time we travel from. And we only do the past. The future involves a whole different process and some barriers the smart people haven't figured out yet."

"You say Cecil knows about all this?"

"Yes. He's a member of the secret oversight subcommittee—some senators and congressmen, a couple of members of Parliament—"

"And Cecil?"

"A bureaucratic mix-up. They sent an invitation to some giant Australian firm dealing with exotic alloys or something, but Cecil received it by mistake. And then everyone sort of forgot about it until . . . well, it's a long story."

"Who else knows about . . . about . . . ?"

"Our official name is now the Historical Research Initiative. You won't find that written down anywhere, though. The President might know we exist and what we do, sort of. And the Postmaster General. They pretty much *had* to tell him."

"Wow." Sean mentally measured the distance from an upper drawer under the microwave, just in case. "How did you manage keeping the military out of it?"

"Oh, they were knee-deep back when the program started. Once they were convinced time travel doesn't lend itself to any significant military applications, though, they didn't want their budget drained by a bunch of historians."

"No military applications? I'd think going back in time to screw with your enemy would have all kinds of military applications."

"Yeah, well, that's not the way time travel works . . ."

And so, Marshall's story unfolded.

Sean learned about the early days of the Global Research Consortium, and its cast of players—Marshall, Sheila, Marta, Frank Altman, Elvin, Andrew Gormly, Naomi, Dr. Gretchen Allen, Dr. Yuni Andropov, and Dr. Leonard Rose.

Sean listened patiently, knives never far from his thoughts.

"And you don't do the future?" he asked when Marshall finished.

"Nope. Getting to the future requires travel at velocities approaching the speed of light. Even with enhanced hydrogen as fuel, the future remains beyond our capabilities. Manipulating wormholes using dark matter is what gets us to the past. And, at first, the past was fine with everybody, because they all anticipated a big payoff. Governments and corporations thought manipulating the past could make us more secure, wealthier, more powerful. That didn't work, though, because we don't go to the past of our own universe."

"Well, of course not." Sean felt he needed to humor Marshall.

"No, really," Marshall said, struggling to lean forward on the old recliner's spongy springs. "You can only go to the past of a parallel universe . . . or universes. Turns out there's an infinite number of them . . ."

Sean stood and walked to the kitchenette.

"Just need some water. Please . . . go ahead." Sean twisted the faucet handle with his left hand and hoped his body blocked enough of Marshall's view as his right hand slid open a drawer, then grabbed a carving knife.

"Well, I told you about losing Sheila . . . and when they

sent her back, they projected her to a time long before her birth."

"Before ... when?"

"Before she was born. They sent her to a time before she was born."

"And that's bad?"

"Very bad. See, when a traveler goes into the past, his body doesn't accompany him ..."

"That must be a little ... inconvenient. What happens to the carcass?"

"Um ... well ... Marta and the physicists don't believe me, but there's this parking garage ... in this place we call the limbo where ... boy, this really sounds crazy, doesn't it?"

Sean smiled.

"When you get back, you really smell good because ... well, suffice it to say your corporeal being doesn't make the trip. But your intellect, all your memories and knowledge and emotions, end up occupying your past counterpart's mind. Um ... the 'you' that lives in that other world. Your equivalent being."

"So, if there's no equivalent being ..."

"That's right. Then there's nowhere for the traveler to reside. So, arrive before your birth, you just ... disappear, I guess. That's what Elvin and Gretchen think."

"And that's what happened to your friend, Sheila?"

"Yes. Anyway, we know they sent her to the *Lawrence Welk Show* universe—"

"*Lawrence Welk* has his own universe?" Sean tucked the knife under his shirt before turning back around. He had a vision of millions of people playing accordions in shadows cast by giant bubble machines. "Lord, what a scary thought."

"Um . . . no. It's just how Elvin figured out identifying all the separate universes . . . these universes are named for theme songs from old TV shows. Our universe is *I Love Lucy*, by the way, and these shows . . ."

"Honeeey, I'm hoooome," Sean said, offering his best Ricky Ricardo impression.

"Well . . . okay," Marshall said, adding, "The physics gets pretty complicated."

"I'm sure it must."

"We know roughly the era in which Sheila landed—late 1960s. Because there was no equivalent being to receive her, though, we have no way of knowing where she might have arrived geographically."

"Doesn't that mean your Sheila is gone forever?" Sean said.

"Well . . . maybe. There are a couple of remarkable coincidences at work here, though. First is the connection between you and Cecil. Second, Sheila's maternal grandmother— Amanda Page—is from your hometown, Portales, New Mexico. She was a senior at Portales High School in 1969."

Sean hadn't thought of Amanda Page in ages.

"I remember Amanda," he said. "She was two years ahead of me. A beautiful girl. Had everything going for her. Then she suffered some kind of mental breakdown and . . . kids can be cruel, you know. During her senior year, I think Amanda was very lonely."

"You knew her?" Marshall asked.

"Not well, but yes. I knew her to say 'hi.'" Sean shook his head. "So back to my original question. What do you want from me?"

Marshall hesitated. "We want more information about ... about Portales. About people who lived there. And what was happening when ... There's only so much you can learn from old newspapers. We need to interview people who were there."

"Such a long time ago." Sean raised his hands, a gesture of remembrance. The knife slipped from under his shirt and clattered onto the floor.

"Um ... I can see you're skeptical ..." Marshall stood, staring at the knife as he sidled toward the front door.

Sean did not attempt to retrieve his weapon. "Mr. Grissom," he said, "you were truthful about one thing, at least. This afternoon has been entertaining."

Marshall stopped, and again seemed to debate something within himself.

"Mr. Brody, please, I know how all this must sound. Sheila is ... important ... our friend. May I at least come back and talk with you again? Maybe if you thought about it, you might remember names of some other people we could visit, as well?"

Sean studied Marshall once more. Maybe this guy *wasn't* all there. In Marshall's eyes, though, Sean saw both sincerity and pain. Nothing about this strange young man seemed remotely threatening.

"Come back when you want. I'm always here. And I'll give it some thought. One thing, though. If this is such a big secret, why haven't you warned me not to tell anyone?"

"Well, I *am* committing a felony by telling you all this but ... um ... no offense, Mr. Brody. You're ninety-three years old. If you told anyone a cockamamie story like this one, they'd just think you'd ... you'd ..."

"Gone 'round the bend?"

Marshall nodded.

"Well," Sean said, "I can certainly see how a person might believe *that*."

Only after Marshall had departed did Sean look at the calendar and realized today was April Fools' Day.

4

A NEW MISSION

Washington, D.C.
April 2047

"WE ALL APPRECIATE SCIENCE," Congresswoman Libby Pinch said through a frown, "although some of us do get a little impatient with liberal interpretations of science that seem to characterize so many of our federal programs . . ."

Marta suppressed the urge to leap over the desk and throttle the congresswoman while explaining that science is neither liberal nor conservative. It's just science.

Marta sat at the witness table in the secret basement subcommittee hearing room of the U.S. Capitol building before a microphone. Several rows of empty seats filled a modest space behind her. She faced nine subcommittee members arrayed along a large curving dais, Senator Josiah Mumford positioned at its mid-point.

Mumford, a Delaware Democrat comfortable in his seniority, chaired the secret subcommittee overseeing time travel. Mumford featured a portly bearing, hound dog jowls and a folksy, almost absent-minded manner. But Marta knew not to underestimate his influence, common sense, or political savvy.

Mumford had already dropped the bomb Marta knew was coming. Otherwise engaged, Marta had dispatched

Marshall to Washington, D.C a few weeks earlier for an official announcement that she and her intrepid band of scientists and time travelers should expect closer scrutiny. She'd understood all along that this was inevitable.

Finally, she had been summoned for a more detailed explanation.

Time travel became reality through a secret consortium involving an alliance including some of the world's most powerful governments and corporations called the Global Research Consortium. Hundreds of scientists, technicians and support staff were hidden away at a vast underground Arizona facility. There, the laws of physics were bludgeoned into submission by giving smart people all the money they could imagine.

Hydrogen technology breakthroughs, which ended the earth's fossil fuel era in the 2030s, were also key. A spinoff of the hydrogen age was enriched hydrogen, a costly substance whose energy-per-liter ratio dwarfed any previous fuel source and provided the power necessary to create a worm-hole, maintain it as an open pathway, and operate a mechanism that projected travelers back through time.

Originally, this colossally expensive undertaking was ruled by a complex bureaucracy. Marta knew politicians overseeing the GRC found solace in bureaucratic structure. Oh, sure, elected officials might rant and rail against big government when they were back home huckstering for votes. In reality, though, they welcomed bureaucracy because amid the morass of government busy work, they could always find someone else to blame.

Back when the GRC bureaucracy had been enormous, and its subject matter incomprehensible, supervising politicians let the whole thing drift along its own path. Should disaster occur, bureaucrats could always be stood against a wall and shot. Figuratively, of course. But their careers would be just as dead as if the bullets were real as they were sacrificed to the ongoing well-being of elected officials.

When, however, the inability of time travelers to change the past of their own world became apparent, governments and corporations paying the bills began manning the lifeboats. Hemisphere Investment Group— GRC's largest single investor—bailed first. Most others soon followed. Nobody wanted truckloads of money spent on funding pure research. If the past could not be unambiguously manipulated for profit, big-money guys weren't interested.

Now, Marta sat before a subcommittee comprised of members of the U.S. Congress, Great Britain's Parliament and a representative from the Grand Duchy of Luxembourg. All the others were gone. The only remaining corporate investor was Cecil's Margin Service, and Cecil didn't attend the meetings.

The Global Research Initiative colossus had been reduced to a small, collegial group conducting physics research with the help of a time machine. Their bureaucratic shield had been similarly compressed, so the politicians decided they must pay closer attention.

Marta listened as the subcommittee adopted all of Congresswoman Libby Pinch's recommendations, including establishing a review and approval process for everything except the most routine time travel missions. They would appoint a liaison to reside at the Historical Research

Initiative facility. This person would wield power of approval or denial regarding mission profiles.

"... we want to see applications of time travel research produce more immediate and definitive results," Libby continued. "The subcommittee staff has suggested disputed historical interpretations and unsolved crimes as productive research targets.

"We understand questions have been raised regarding the ethics of time travel," Pinch continued. "The subcommittee directs you to minimize interference in the lives of past individuals and events, while still allowing travelers to effectively observe and research ..."

Marta found herself stuck on ... *disputed historical interpretations? A political quagmire if ever one existed. And...*

"Unsolved crimes?" Marta interrupted, twisting the microphone at the witness table closer to her mouth. A series of thumps and squawks reverberated through the hearing chamber.

"Your travelers can visit known times when crimes occurred and witness those events, then return and tell authorities what happened. Criminals could be held accountable after the fact ..."

"You do understand these observations would not take place in *this* universe?" Marta said.

"Is that a problem?"

"I think it is if you present such evidence to any kind of court. I assume any adequate defense attorney could create some degree of reasonable doubt if his client is accused of a crime witnessed in a different universe."

"Ah, but that's the beauty of it," Libby said. "None of

this ever has to be presented in court. It's like ... like a policeman searching a suspect's home without a warrant. The policeman isn't looking for direct evidence, because he knows such evidence is inadmissible if anyone discovers what he's done. The cop is searching for ... evidence of evidence. He's looking for clues as to how the investigation might proceed."

"Not that anyone is advocating illegal searches," Mumford quickly clarified. "Congresswoman Pinch has a point, though. If a traveler can tell an investigator what he or she observed while visiting the past, that investigator might have a better idea how to obtain evidence of the perpetrator's guilt."

"The fact remains," Marta reminded them, "this observation takes place in another universe."

"I thought we are talking about parallel universes," Malcomb Butterstone, the British representative to the subcommittee, said. "Doesn't this parallel aspect imply identical histories?"

Marta's colleagues would be shocked to know she had to work at not being a little intimidated by Butterstone's theatrical British accent. A native of the Caribbean island of Nevis, Marta had never conquered her Island patois. The contrast reminded her of the beach urchin she'd been as a child.

"With an absence of interference, I would assume a generally duplicate history," Marta said, careful of her enunciation, trying not to harden her 'th's with 'd's or 't's. "As we've clearly seen, though, the details of minor historical events, or even some major ones, can vary. After a traveler or a number of travelers have been sent to a specific universe, the parallelism is skewed. We don't yet know by how much."

Marta voiced another concern.

"And depending on what we're observing, this adds a significant element of danger to an already perilous undertaking. I suspect the people committing these crimes would be less than pleased about being watched."

"Of course, the travelers must be discreet," Libby said. "And we could issue a directive of strict non-interference for their further protection."

"Yes, well, that might be more difficult than you think." Marta's unconscious lapse into island pronunciations increased as did her irritability. "Regardless of guidelines, I know from my own experience and training how difficult standing by and seeing someone assaulted or robbed would be. And I think most of our travelers would react the same way."

"Then why don't we start with something less complicated?" the stubborn Congresswoman insisted. "White collar crimes. Money laundering. Contract disputes. Just to see if it works."

Marta sighed. "Do you have something specific in mind?"

"Well," Libby said, "as a matter of fact . . . Mr. Chairman?"

"Um . . . Madam Administrator . . ." Mumford said. The senator's inflection raised the small hairs on the back of Marta's neck.

Uh, oh, this *can't be good.* She hated being referred to as Madam Administrator. The title made her feel like a woman who scheduled hookers at a Nevada brothel. Mumford only employed such formality when he attempted to tiptoe around something he suspected Marta wouldn't like.

"...would you mind taking a seat in the gallery for a few moments. We have another individual who wishes to address the subcommittee."

Puzzled, Marta pushed a handful of papers into her briefcase and stood.

"I will introduce Mr. Phillip Lucre," Mumford announced. "He is a representative of the Hemisphere Investment Group which, as you all know, was a major financial contributor to the development of time travel through the Global Research Consortium. Mr. Lucre was Hemisphere's liaison for the recent Bush/Gore mission."

Marta watched with a sense of dread as Lucre emerged from shadows at the back of the hearing room. He was scrubbed, polished, coiffed and manicured, wearing a suit undoubtedly costing more than her entire wardrobe. The suit hung on a solid frame. His hair improbably blond, teeth impossibly straight. Marta did not recall Lucre being quite so well-put-together during their encounters late last year as he monitored an attempt to alter the outcome of the 2000 U.S. presidential election involving George W. Bush and Al Gore. Hemisphere had orchestrated that mission as an ultimate test of the future's ability to manipulate the past. Failure of their effort to alter the election's outcome finally drove Hemisphere and the other investors away.

"Thank you, Senator," Lucre said. "I will come right to the point. The Hemisphere Investment Group poured billions into development of time travel. We withdrew our financial support last September when it seemed apparent the past could not be altered. Hemisphere invested in time travel because our company hoped to improve the human condition on our planet while realizing a reasonable expectation of return on that investment. Key members of our board now believe our decision to withdraw may have been premature. Corporate leaders have determined we should consider reinstatement of our financial contribution in return for recovery of our equity."

Marta saw several subcommittee members sit taller and lean forward at the mention of restored funding.

"And what was your equity standing?" Mumford asked.

"Through October 2045, Hemisphere had contributed a little more than twenty-five percent of the program's total budget."

"And you propose to resume that level of funding?"

"Conditionally," Lucre said carefully, "we would—for a larger piece of ownership."

"Conditionally?"

"Yes. Our board members would require another mission testing the program's viability in terms of—"

Marta could contain herself no longer.

Seated immediately behind Lucre, she stood. "Senator, please. Hemisphere left the program because its board members determined—"

The sound of Mumford's gavel rang through the hearing room. "Ms. Hamilton, please don't interrupt. You'll have your turn. If you wish to address the subcommittee, you must be seated at the witness table."

Lucre waived for Marta to join him. He even pulled out a chair for her.

Marta regarded Lucre with disdain as she sat.

"Please, Senator," Lucre said, "allow Ms. Hamilton to continue."

Marta leaned toward her microphone.

"Hemisphere left the program because its board members concluded the past of our world cannot be manipulated in such a way to produce a profit for their shareholders. You have just put into place a policy prohibiting our travelers from unnecessarily interfering in the lives of past beings or attempting to manipulate events. I don't see how you can now embrace a corporate entity whose entire agenda involved interference with the past."

Mumford's gaze shifted to Lucre.

"One of several things our board has concluded," Lucre said, "is that our original expectations were not realistic. Everyone—the United States government included—stepped into this unknown arena harboring unrealistic expectations. Nobody understood the physics. Ms. Hamilton is correct. We—along with every other investor, both public and private—sought profit or strategic advantage through alteration of past events. Given the reality of the situation, though, we now believe historical observation may be quite valuable. We want one more test to determine—"

"You had your test," Marta said. "Hemisphere and other private investors were chief architects of the Bush/Gore mission. A mission which demonstrated conclusively limitations of the future's ability to affect historically significant past events."

"Again, Ms. Hamilton is correct. And please, reluctant as I am to air internal disputes outside our company, let me be completely frank. A situation has arisen in which we feel observation by one of your travelers of a meeting three years ago might resolve a dispute threatening to cost Hemisphere millions of dollars."

"How so?" Mumford asked.

"I ask that subcommittee members hold what I am about to say in the strictest of confidence as our dilemma involves internal personnel matters."

"The security standards set for the entire travelers' program apply to anything discussed in our hearings," Mumford assured him.

Lucre nodded and continued. "This dispute has resulted in a lawsuit scheduled for trial later this year. Before we take that last step into a courtroom, we propose using a traveler to determine who is telling the truth."

"As we've already discussed," Marta said, "nothing you'd learn through such a mission could be presented to a court. Besides the issue of events occurring in a different world, you'd have to violate every security restriction in order to tell a judge and jury about the time travel program."

"Senator," Lucre said, "Ms. Hamilton misinterprets our intentions. We have no desire to use anything we might learn in any public manner. We simply want to know the truth. We will be defending one of our corporate officers—company President Warren Pitts—at this trial. If he is not telling us the absolute truth about what happened, then we have the option of cutting our losses and making the best settlement we can. Not to mention severing ties with an employee who has lied.

"On the other hand, evidence of Mr. Pitts' innocence allows us to defend our company and our president more vigorously. This lawsuit was filed over two years ago and has reached the point where a decision to settle or go to trial must be made. If time travel can help us make such a decision, our board will see marketability through its development as an observation tool. We see revenue potential. We would be willing—even eager—to restore our financial support."

Marta struggled to maintain a sense of decorum. She did not now nor would she ever trust anyone associated with Hemisphere Investment Group. She would rather eat tree bark than let Hemisphere and their thugs anywhere near her program again. She wanted to testify that a representative of Hemisphere had conspired to murder two time travelers and had come very close to killing both her and Marshall Grissom. Raising those concerns, though, demanded explanations concerning secrets Marta dared not disclose.

Instead, she said, "I think . . . I think we should be very careful about reintroducing into the program influences that go hand in hand with outside funding—"

"Even if such funding allows opportunities for accelerating your research projects?" Libby Pinch demanded.

"We're getting along fine," Marta said. "Speaking from experience, when they were involved in the program, Hemisphere and other private sector investors applied pressures compromising both safety and the science."

"We won't be pushing anyone to do anything," Lucre countered. "We like to think we, too, learned some important lessons during our previous involvement. Existing technology is completely capable of accomplishing this single, simple mission."

"Ms. Hamilton," Libby said, "this is the practical application of time travel our subcommittee sees as the future of this program. Many unrecorded crucial moments occur during both government and corporate histories. An ability to sort out exactly what happened could be something for which the private sector might pay a significant fee. Those fees will help fund your research."

Mumford looked at Marta then Lucre. "Mr. Lucre, please submit specifics of Hemisphere's new mission proposal. In accordance with Congresswoman Pinch's suggestion, I am appointing a mission profile approval group to consider Hemisphere's request. I want your Arizona staff to do the same, Ms. Hamilton. We will give Mr. Lucre his answer by next week."

Marta waited until almost everyone else had cleared the hearing room. She sorted through documents in her briefcase, made sure she had everything packed away. With a sigh of resignation, she plodded along a lengthy, curving basement corridor of the U.S. Capitol building in search of an elevator.

Gradually, the curve revealed a bench where Josiah Mumford waited near closed elevator doors.

"Ah, Ms. Hamilton." He stood to meet her, groaning a little as he did so.

Mumford was a big man, gone overweight with age. His suit coat draped across one arm, tie loose and askew at the collar of a white shirt. Although Marta found the basement corridor temperature comfortably cool, Mumford's ruddy complexion offered the impression of a man perpetually suffering from heat and humidity. He had a thick white mane demanding a comb as one long shock of hair draped onto his forehead. His most expressive feature was a set of improbably thick eyebrows which shifted constantly, telegraphing his emotions.

He seemed weary.

"Senator," Marta nodded.

She smiled at the contrast the two of them posed. An observer would see Mutt and Jeff. Marta stood a little over five feet tall. She had unblemished mahogany skin. She wore her coarse black hair short, requiring practically no attention. She was slender, her body hard from hours spent in gyms.

She wore a white blouse, a navy-blue skirt, and a rather severe matching jacket. Following Mumford's example, she removed her jacket, hanging it in the crook of her arm.

"I hope you're not too upset with Libby," Mumford said. "She is very . . . enthusiastic."

Marta was spared from her search for a diplomatic response when the elevator dinged its arrival. Mumford allowed her to enter first and said, "Join me in my office for a drink if you have a moment."

Mumford leaned heavily against the elevator's back wall as he fumbled in his jacket pocket and withdrew a huge cigar. He closed his eyes and ran the cigar under his nose, inhaling deeply, then caressing it between thumb and index finger.

"You realized all along, didn't you," he said, "we would establish more formal controls?"

"Of course, Senator. I only hope the process doesn't get too . . . complicated."

Mumford smiled at her careful statement.

The elevator dinged again. Mumford pointed Marta toward a tunneled walkway where a security guard waited to guide them to the building housing Mumford's office. Another guard nodded, then held the door for them.

"I'm sorry these guys have to stand here all day like this," Mumford said as he crossed the empty outer office and headed for another door behind a vacant receptionist's desk. "But Mr. Wishcamper insists." He held the next door for Marta, asking as she stepped through, "Do you think I'm still in danger?"

Marta walked into a chamber from another age. Mumford's office was gilded and plush, featuring deep rugs and antique furniture—likely beyond price given the histories of its previous owners. Historical paintings and a marble fireplace dominated one wall. Mumford directed her to a high-backed chair, likely a relic of the 1700s. The senator occupied its twin facing her.

A few weeks earlier, a Capitol employee named Victor Franz had threatened to stab Mumford with a letter opener in this very office. Franz, they learned, was being manipulated by a future counterpart from the *Gunsmoke* universe.

"I don't know, Senator," Marta said. "We're still sorting things out."

"Fortunately, Marshall Grissom happened along and handled the situation quite adroitly," Mumford said. "Knew almost immediately what was happening. A lucky coincidence."

"Elvin Detwyler would argue it wasn't coincidence at all." Marta smiled. "He'd say Marshall acted as a tool of . . . history, for want of a better word . . . thwarting the future's attempts to change a significant historical figure's past."

Mumford gave a little snort, furrowing his eyebrows into bushy vees. "History, I fear, overestimates my significance." He shook his head. "I wonder more and more what we've gotten ourselves into. Whether Ms. Schuler was right. We should've left time travel alone. By the way, did you hear that poor Mr. Franz was killed? A car accident."

"I did not." Marta's heart beat a little faster.

"Yes. Mr. Wishcamper investigated and found no sign of foul play. Just Franz's time, I suppose."

"The *Gunsmoke* version of Victor Franz died in an automobile explosion," Marta told Mumford, "but I doubt his death in that world was an accident."

Now, Mumford's eyebrows transformed themselves into snowy peaks.

Protocol called for submission of a detailed report by Marta to the subcommittee concerning what happened when unscrupulous individuals from the anomalous *Gunsmoke* universe made unauthorized use of their time machine in an attempt to murder Mumford. But Mumford's investigator, Sheldon Wishcamper, ordered the incident be kept secret as he explored whether anyone from the present was—or likely would be—complicit in the attempted assassination.

"So, you've heard the details through your counterpart from this *Gunsmoke* world?" Mumford asked.

"Yes. The man who directed the plot was Jason Pratt—"

"Wait, isn't he the janitor who disappeared from the complex last year? Sheldon can't find any sign of him. Sheldon thinks the Pratt from our world is long dead."

"Well, he's certainly dead in the *Gunsmoke* universe, along with two men who helped him operate the time projector."

"And you know that, how?" Mumford asked.

Marta weighed her response, then spoke bluntly. "I killed them, or should I say, the *Gunsmoke*-Marta killed them."

"Were you, um . . . was she able to question Mr. Pratt before—?"

"I'm afraid not, Senator. Mr. Pratt didn't give her that option."

"So, we have no idea who was directing him?"

Marta shook her head no.

Once again, she considered the web of lies she'd spun to hide the truth of Sheila's disappearance. She couldn't tell Mumford that the Jason Pratt native to this universe had died almost a year earlier, killed because he'd sent Sheila Schuler to the oblivion of a distant past. Or that Pratt had worked for Hemisphere under the direction of a ruthless henchman named Andrew Gormly. Worst of all, Marta couldn't shout that Mumford and his subcommittee had just offered this same corrupt corporation keys to a time machine.

5

THE SEVEN

"THAT'S IT?" GRETCHEN ASKED as she scanned the faces of her fellow conspirators. "That's all Hemisphere wants? And they'll restore their funding?"

Marshall felt dismay that HRI's science staff—Gretchen, Naomi and Elvin included—seemed so focused on the money.

Marta returned to Arizona bearing news of the latest Hemisphere intrusion. Now, tucked into a storage closet at the farthest unoccupied outpost of their underground complex, the small clan knowing the truth about Hemisphere's deceit gathered.

We seven. Marshall counted those crowded into the room. Marta, Elvin, Gretchen, Leonard, Naomi and Gillis.

Marshall killed the thug Jason Pratt on the evening Sheila Schuler had been murdered. Or, Marshall hoped, banished to the distant past of the *Lawrence Welk Show* universe. Marta ordered Hemisphere's Andrew Gormly exiled to a world where he'd never be found. The others abetted or helped hide these crimes. And here they were, sharing the gloom of a poorly lit room, occupying folding chairs that had to be dusted and checked for black widow or brown recluse spiders.

Marshall told the others he wanted to turn himself in, confess his crimes and trust the authorities would understand he had acted in defense of themselves and Sheila. Marta and Gillis pointed out, though, they'd all indentured themselves to a clandestine program where the regular justice system would not come into play. The very people who had hired Gormly and Pratt might have influence over those who decided the conspirators' fates should their sins be discovered.

This group, Marta and Gillis convinced Marshall, must protect its secrets.

"We did tell you, didn't we," Marshall said to Gretchen, "that Andrew Gormly offered each of us who were there that night millions of dollars if we'd ignore what they'd done to Sheila and let him continue his manipulations? This offer of restored funding is just another bribe."

"And it's not all they want," Marta agreed. "The mission they describe is all too simple. Something more is involved here. We don't know what we're really getting into. Gillis, I'm putting you in charge of finding out."

Gillis Kerg offered a nod of agreement.

"They want to eavesdrop on a conversation," Gretchen said. "What's sinister about that? It's what the subcommittee wants us to do, anyway. Certainly, you realize how many unanswered questions we have concerning what we thought we knew about discrepancies we now know exist. We're crawling along given our current staffing levels. If funding is restored—"

"Just look at how intrusive they were at the end, even dictating the details of the missions," Marshall said. "We'd be under their thumbs forever."

"Maybe Gormly acted on his own initiative concerning his spying and . . . and what they did to Sheila," Naomi said. "Maybe the Hemisphere people didn't know the extent of what was happening . . ."

"After all, none of us knew a thing about Gormly until you and Gillis figured out who he was," Gretchen said to Marta. "Lucre was up front from the start about who he represented during the Gore/Bush planning."

"Fat chance," Elvin said, swatting at something crawling along his pant leg.

Marshall didn't hide his surprise at Elvin's response.

"Hey, I want the money, too," Elvin said. "But let's not kid ourselves here."

"Lucre's apparent openness doesn't mean anything," Gillis agreed. "Gormly could take a surreptitious approach as only one rather innocuous person among a cast of a thousand back when this program ran full bore. He could bribe and blackmail on the fringe. There are too few of us here for that to work now. The *only* option Lucre has is to announce his presence. I don't take that as a sign anyone connected to Hemisphere can be trusted."

In the silence following Gillis's observation, Marshall's gaze found the man who hadn't said anything yet.

"What about you, Leonard?" Marshall asked. "What do you think they're after?"

Much as he despised what Leonard had contributed to Sheila's disappearance, Marshall could not bring himself to share the utter contempt the others felt for Leonard Rose.

As the Global Research Consortium took shape, Leonard felt intense jealousy toward Dr. Gretchen Allen's command of the physics group. Contrition over Sheila's fate produced a confession that he'd considered himself every bit Gretchen's intellectual equal when it came to theoretical physics. He didn't want to be just a bit player when the history of time travel was written.

Marshall recalled Elvin Detwyler's elevation from computer technician to Gretchen's chief assistant. A closet genius, Elvin understood many of the nuances of this new technology and had developed a process of targeting specific universes as destinations for time travelers, rather than flinging them back into histories of random universes.

Elvin's promotion pushed Leonard over the edge. He couldn't tolerate a promotion elevating a lowly computer tech and "garage physicist" to such a prestigious status. So, Leonard found himself susceptible to Andrew Gormly's overtures, recruiting him as a spy in assistance of Hemisphere's grab for control.

Marshall realized Leonard had helped lure Sheila into Gormly's trap the night Gormly and his henchman, Jason Pratt, used a taser to cripple her and spirit her off to an impossibly distant past. When Leonard tearfully claimed he didn't realize Gormly had intended to kill Sheila, Marshall believed his remorse was genuine.

On that bloody night, Marshall feared Marta would add Rose to the list of fatalities. Expedience, though, rather than mercy had saved Leonard's life.

"You could send me to prison, Leonard," Marta said, *pistol in hand. "I don't want to go to prison. I want to continue to work here, and I want us to be more careful in how we go about our research. I need an advocate for that point of view."*

"Of course," Rose said.

"You're crazy," Elvin said to Marta. *"How can you*

possibly consider trusting this guy? Your ass isn't the only one hanging out here, remember?"

"Security is already investigating too many mysterious disappearances," she'd responded. "I'm afraid one more might be too much for the authorities to digest. What I figure we have here is a stalemate. Sure, he could cause difficulty. But he's an accessory to Sheila's murder. I have Sheila's voice message to prove it. If we go down, he does, too."

"That's right," Rose nodded. "I'd be crazy to say anything."

"And you do understand what I'll do if I even suspect you are passing any kind of information to anyone?"

Rose nodded. "Thank you, Ms. Hamilton."

"Get out of here before I change my mind."

So, Leonard and Marta declared an uncomfortable truce. Marta couldn't implicate Leonard in the assault on Sheila, because Rose could reveal the role she and Marshall played in Jason Pratt's demise and the disappearance of Andrew Gormly. If those facts came to light, Marta's criminal violations of her contract while acting as a British agent would be revealed.

Now, Marshall felt sorry for Leonard given the lonely, frightened existence he endured here.

Leonard answered Marshall's question while staring at his hands, still folded before him.

"Mr. Lucre did not attempt to contact me during the Bush-Gore mission. And while Andrew Gormly certainly didn't confide any details regarding his relationship with other Hemisphere executives, I'm sure Gormly didn't act on his own. I'm sure Hemisphere's corporate leaders insulated themselves from any detailed knowledge of Gormly's crimes. But I believe Gomly represented their interests and did so with at least their tacit authorization."

No one spoke until Elvin bent over and squinted at a tiny carcass beside his chair.

"The little gray spiders aren't the mean ones, are they?" he asked anxiously. The others offered no response.

"Then we must assume Lucre's mission involves more than meets the eye," Marta said. "Hemisphere is attempting some sort of manipulation. Mr. Lucre can pull strings, but he can't act directly. He'll need help. We are too small a group for him to introduce someone new. A newcomer will be too obvious a suspect. He'll recruit someone already working here. Gillis, you do your thing and learn what's going on."

Gillis stood and offered a semi-bow. "At your command, m'lady."

"Yeah," Marta said, a little taken aback. "Don't let's make a habit of that, Gillis. Now, for the second item on our agenda. We need updates regarding the Sheila project. Elvin?"

"We know the universe in which she landed." Elvin glanced again at the dead spider. "And now, I think, we have a pretty good handle on the time frame."

"And we know that how?"

"Amanda Page," Naomi said.

"You think Sheila's host seventy-eight years ago is her grandmother?" Marshall asked.

"That one little glimmer of a lifeline tells us she found a host, at least momentarily," Elvin said. "So, yes. We think her initial survival was at least possible."

"We know when travelers go to the past of another universe," Naomi continued her explanation, "they share the consciousness of their equivalent being in that universe.

While equivalent beings are not always biologically identical, they certainly must share fundamental DNA patterns. Relatives share DNA patterns. Some of those patterns are more closely matched than others, depending on the individuals. The yearbook photo Gillis provided shows Amanda Page and Sheila Schuler as identical in appearance. That indicates a strong possibility their genetic markers are close. Not an exact match, of course. Maybe close enough, though, for Amanda to act as Sheila's host."

Gretchen Allen shifted cautiously. Now, she, too, studied Elvin's spider.

"The chance any aspect of Miss Schuler's intellect might remain viable seems a practical impossibility," Rose said. "We know only a matter of days are required for a past being to absorb and block the consciousness of its future counterpart."

"But we also know," Marshall insisted, "the lifeline can be restored when a past being is made aware of its future counterpart."

"If the disruption is brief. But after all this time?"

"There's only one way we can know for sure," Marshall said. "We have to send a traveler who will try and resurrect Sheila from Amanda Page's consciousness."

"And what about Sean Brody?" Marta asked.

Marshall had been dreading the question. He'd already summarized his meeting with Sean for Marta.

"He doesn't believe me, of course," Marshall said. "He is intrigued, though . . . or maybe entertained is a better word. I'm seeing him again tomorrow."

"But there's a problem," Marta informed the others.

Marshall sighed. "Yes. He has implants. An artificial

knee. The standard embedded visual hardware. And a heart regulation system."

"That *is* a problem," Naomi said, shaking her head. "I'll need his medical records. It's unlikely a man of his age could survive without a supplemental heart system for more than a few days."

Still, a few days is long enough to send him back... Marshall reprimanded himself for even thinking such a thing.

"I'm sure he'll help us search for someone else," Marshall said. "He attended high school with Amanda. Surely he'll know someone."

The gloomy lighting of the compact storage area matched fallen expressions on the faces Marshall confronted. They, too, realized how long the odds were of finding another candidate fitting this narrow profile.

Gillis broke the silence. "If we do find someone, how accurately can we target a projection so far into the past?" he asked Elvin. "Getting our elderly traveler there within a few days of Sheila's arrival, then handling the issue immediately is the cleanest, simplest approach."

"No chance of hitting our arrival that precisely," Elvin said. "I can get us to the *Lawrence Welk Show* universe. What I can't do with a target so distant is pinpoint Sheila's arrival any closer than the range of a few months. The only safe approach is projecting our traveler to a point well after Sheila got there. Months. A year maybe. If our guy arrives even a couple of weeks before Sheila does, his consciousness would be absorbed before Sheila even shows up. He'd be useless."

"None of this matters if we can't find the right person

and if he or she isn't willing to help us," Marta said. "So, let's focus on that issue first."

6

THE DASTARDLY TOTAL DICK

May 21, 2046

"THERE'S A GUY HERE," Betty the receptionist told Marta.

Marta glanced from a report she read at her cluttered office desk. Betty stood in Marta's doorway, banks of computers and monitors beeping and humming behind her.

"What do you mean, a guy?"

"A male person."

Betty had never distinguished herself as a receptionist, and since her brief journey into the past a few months ago, her attitude had deteriorated further. She didn't want to be a receptionist anymore, she'd told Marta. She wanted to join the traveler corps because the pay was so much better. Marta didn't need any more travelers. She needed a receptionist.

"One of *our* male persons?" Marta asked.

"No."

"Well, how did he get down here? This place is secret. You can't let just anybody—"

"*I* didn't," Betty said. "Security guys at the front gate let him in. They said he had credentials . . ."

The phone on Marta's desk rang. Betty reached across

and lifted the receiver. "Ms. Hamilton's office. I'll see if she's available." She reached to punch the hold button. "It's Senator Mumford. Are you here?"

"Of course I am." Marta restored the connection. "Good morning, Senator. How can I help you today?"

"Sorry I didn't reach you sooner," Mumford said. "This has sort of happened all at once. We've informally okayed Hemisphere's proposal. Mr. Lucre has been authorized to join you at the site."

Marta closed her eyes and silently shook her head as a show of exasperation. "I must ask, Senator," she said slowly, "just what sort of influence will Mr. Lucre and Hemisphere have as we go ahead with this . . . plan?"

"He's an observer, a resource. Listen, I understand your concerns. Quite frankly, I think several subcommittee members are much more comfortable with the way things are now. The private investors *were* getting pretty heavy-handed before they withdrew. Excluding an entity having so much invested is difficult, though."

"An entity wielding so much political influence," Marta added.

"Yes, there's that, too."

"So, we'll begin planning for your mission within the next couple of days," Marta told Lucre.

She looked at him and thought of a cartoon weasel, albeit an elegant one. Though he did not present himself as stylishly as at the subcommittee hearing, his suit was still expensive, hair still perfect. He spoke with an affectation of Northeastern society. Attempting charm, joviality, and a benign good nature. His expression, though, defaulted to a superior and smug look of distaste during unguarded moments.

"Anything we can do to help," he said. "That's why I'm here."

"I'm not sure if you're aware, the subcommittee sent a security expert here last year—a Mr. Wishcamper—he found faults with the system. He made it a point to resolve those issues before he left."

"I'm sorry, Ms. Hamilton," Lucre said offering a puzzled expression. "I'm not sure what you're suggesting."

"I'm suggesting nothing, Mr. Lucre. I impress upon anyone who comes here that, although our staffing is much smaller than a year ago, we still take security very seriously."

"As you should. Big brother is watching. I understand. Well, it's been a long day for me, and the drive back to Superior is daunting so—"

"Since we are undertaking planning for a major mission— your mission—I've reimposed a restriction of all personnel to the campus," Marta said. "I think you'll find our accommodations comfortable."

"I wish I would have known," Lucre said. "I've left everything at my motel room. I have a couple of loose ends I've got to tie up . . ."

. . . *before*, Marta extended the thought, *all your communications with the outside world are monitored.*

"I apologize, but it can't be helped," Lucre continued. "The most pressing issue is some medication I left there. I have a serious allergy."

"We have a complete store of medical supplies here."

"I'm sorry," Lucre said. "I can't take the chance."

"Very well. We'll see you early tomorrow. Plan on being here for the duration."

Phillip Lucre felt pleased with himself.

He'd met new administrator Marta Hamilton and judged her a nonentity in terms of future interference. She was a novice bureaucrat. Lucre doubted she had the political skills to counter any pressure Hemisphere could bring to bear through its hold over a couple of oversight subcommittee members.

He'd reacquainted himself with the other key players and found them distant, even bordering on hostile. Well, that made sense. He was an outsider. They would see him as a threat to their independence.

The one who perplexed him, though, was Marshall Grissom.

Among the skills that had elevated Lucre to his position as Hemisphere's Dastardly Total Dick was an ability to read people. And Lucre's intuition told him Marshall was behaving very much out of character.

Lucre had shared Marshall's company only a few minutes when he had Marshall pegged. Here was a man easily intimidated, a peacemaker who, given any opportunity, wanted only to apologize and get along. Like any Dastardly Total Dick worth his salt, Lucre had long ago mastered an intimidating stare, which should have brought Marshall right into line.

It didn't.

Marshall met Lucre with a cold rigid stare of his own. Lucre found it particularly discomforting to be despised by a man who likely had almost no experience at despising.

By the time Lucre reached his hotel room, though, all thoughts of Marshall were put aside. Things were starting to move, and he had details to which he must attend.

He unpacked a tiny encrypted satellite phone and placed a call.

"So, what do you think?" Warren Pitts said by way of greeting.

Lucre dispensed with formalities, as well.

"The administrator and a few key people are openly hostile. While Mumford remains as subcommittee chair, we can't afford being too heavy-handed. Mumford will always be an obstacle, but he won't be around forever. If we're patient, we can reclaim our position."

"Not too patient, though," Pitts said. "Remember, patience is what cost us all those millions in the first place."

"I understand."

"Have you found anyone there who can help us?" Pitts asked.

At this point, Lucre balked.

"Mr. Pitts," he said carefully, "when Andrew was running things, elaborate steps were taken to ensure you . . . and others . . . were insulated from—"

"Maybe that's one of the problems. We're beyond hiding our involvement. Especially while Andrew is out there somewhere, operating as a lone wolf. This time, we could be his targets."

"Mr. Gormly's been gone a long while," Lucre said. "He may not be a factor anymore."

"That old asshole is too tough to die. But back to my question. Is there someone—?"

"I recruited our collaborator months ago during the Gore/Bush project. A cover-our-bases sort of thing. Someone in need of funds. A number of folks counted on getting a big payoff at the end of their contracts, but when the program downsized so abruptly those payoffs did not occur, leaving some employees . . . overextended. Getting a commitment is largely a matter of choosing the right people and making offers. I made arrangements within the security staff at the same time."

"But how did you know who would stay?" Pitts asked, his voice betraying admiration.

"I spread the money around. We were a bit lucky."

"Can you trust the person you've chosen?"

"I would never assume so," Lucre said. "But I followed up with a forensic financial expert and my recruit used our initial payment to chip away at a large bill owed to some unsavory characters of the Russian persuasion. If this individual has a change of heart, our evidence of these indiscretions will give him no choice but to continue his cooperation."

Two Days Later

"Sir . . . there's nothing down there. The whole wing has been closed."

Lucre turned and peered along the concrete corridor at the silhouette of a back-lit figure, unmistakably female.

"What? Oh, I'm sorry. I wanted some exercise and there are all these miles of hallways . . ."

"Well, just don't get yourself lost. If you have any trouble knowing where you are, wave at one of the security cameras . . ." The figure pointed at the dark bulge of a camera shield embedded in the ceiling above her. ". . . and we'll send someone to get you. We've got them set on motion-activated mode throughout the areas we aren't using anymore."

Lucre gave the silhouette a nod of thanks and wandered farther down the same corridor until he found a tiny red chalk mark near a light switch—a sign from his security staff contact. He swiped the wall clean using his sleeve. The chalk mark confirmed for him that cameras would remain dormant along this stretch of hallway.

He opened a door marked Men's Locker Room and found himself among a half-dozen rows of lockers. The red glow of low-voltage emergency lights provided the only illumination. A film of dust on benches and counters told Lucre no one had used this space for weeks.

Near the end of a middle row, he found locker number 103 and quickly affixed a data wafer the size of a postage stamp inside. Even if someone managed to find the wafer, the encryption levels were so complex no one without the thirty-character pass code could even attempt to read it without destroying the chip.

He returned to the hallway.

As he had every evening since Phillip Lucre took up residence at the HRI campus, Gillis Kerg booted a computer he used to hack into the complex's video security system and followed Lucre's herky-jerky progress as he passed through the range of one motion-activated camera after another.

Gillis, a veteran traveler, had entered the time travel program as a spy for his government, the Grand Duchy of Luxembourg. Like Marta, who entered the program as a spy for Great Britain, Gillis's field was industrial espionage. He had the added advantage, though, of being among the world's leading security technology experts. He knew how to defeat all these brand-new gadgets.

Since her appointment as administrator, Gillis had become Marta's right hand when she had need of spy craft. Like Marta, Gillis knew the security staff at HRI couldn't be trusted. These civil servants at the lower echelons of the facility's pay scale were completely susceptible to bribes players such as Hemisphere's scoundrels were willing to offer.

Gillis watched Lucre with a bored disinterest as the man strolled.

Lucre didn't appear furtive. He sauntered as someone who belonged, hands in pockets, reading signs, occasionally testing whether doors were unlocked, glancing inside if they were.

At one point, a woman stepped into camera range from an adjoining corridor. She called out. Lucre turned. She spoke, then pointed at the camera. Lucre nodded, continuing on his way.

After passing through the range of two more cameras, Lucre's image jerked slightly. He emerged into the next frame walking the opposite direction. Now Gillis leaned toward the computer image with a good deal more curiosity.

"That was a little sloppy, Mr. Lucre," Gillis said aloud. "Let's see what you really did back there."

With the stroke of a few keys, Gillis switched to another video recording of the same hallway. Gillis had installed a marvelously useful bit of software when he'd breached the complex's security system many months ago. Any time a camera or series of cameras were shut down, Gillis's program reactivated those cameras, then diverted their feed exclusively to a server kept hidden in an unoccupied part of this underground labyrinth.

Gillis watched Lucre enter a men's locker room, where another camera recorded his progress. Lucre proceeded to the end of a row, opened a locker, reached inside, then closed the locker and departed.

"Our Mr. Lucre was up and about last night," Gillis told Marta. "So, he's already gotten to the security staff. The cameras were off, but my software worm captured him."

Marta rolled her chair from her office desk, leaned back, and put her hand over her eyes. "What do we do?"

Gillis occupied the chair opposite her desk. Marta's ongoing contact with her counterpart from the *Gunsmoke* universe—named for the ancient television theme song which entangled itself in the incredibly complex bundle of information emitting from each universe's peripheral data— left Marta puzzled concerning Gillis. In the *Gunsmoke* universe, which had dramatically diverged from the historical paths characterizing most worlds they'd visited, Marshall had been presumed dead for many months. *Gunsmoke*-Marta never initiated an intimate relationship with Marshall. *Gunsmoke*-Marta unquestionably liked Marshall. Upon his safe recovery, though, she still avoided an emotional entanglement she feared he would represent. Instead, mostly as a distraction from any uncomfortable feelings she sensed regarding Marshall, she initiated a limited relationship with Gillis.

The *I Love Lucy* version of Marta considered Gillis, and simply didn't see the attraction. His slight stature—Gillis stood only an inch taller than Marta—didn't put her off. He was handsome in his way. Dark thick hair, darker eyes. He clearly maintained an excellent physical condition. A little cold. Again, though, not an issue. The profession they shared required emotional distance. Gillis projected an air of fastidiousness, though, she found unsettling. She saw borderline obsessive/compulsive tendencies.

"He set up a dead drop," Gillis said. "Left a data wafer in one of the lockers at the other side of the complex. I snagged the wafer early this morning. Elvin and I examined it."

"And?"

"Unreadable. The encryption is very good. Elvin says he could run the problem through the mainframe computers and get a solution in a week. The messages won't last long enough, though. This is organic-based encryption. After a few days, the coded information essentially rots."

"Can we refrigerate it? Even freeze it?"

"We thought of that. Turns out the data is only accessible at room temperature. Even then, you can't copy it in a nonorganic form. I had to put it back in the locker. I've got my own camera set to catch whoever else shows up."

"So, we go to the subcommittee right now," Marta said. "Call Wishcamper. Prove that Hemisphere, or at least Lucre, is corrupt and manipulative. Have this stupid mission canceled before it even gets started."

"Well," Gillis said as he leaned toward Marta's desk and adjusted three pens so they were parallel, "the only real proof we have exists on a system illegally hacking security computers. If my equipment is discovered, I will face serious charges. All we have on the official record is a few minutes of missing video. Suspicious, but not enough to bring down anyone backed by the political clout of Hemisphere."

Marta leaned back and covered her eyes again. "Bugger!"

"Let's let this thing play out a bit longer," Gillis said. "We need to know who among us Mr. Lucre has compromised."

7

THE GOOD LUCK PIECE

May 23, 2046

"SO, WHERE ARE THEY?" Gretchen Allen asked with a roll of her eyes. "Still in the locker rooms, I suppose?"

"You should have sent me this time," Marshall whispered to Marta. "This thing between Gillis and Macy is—"

Marta's elbow gave Marshall's ribs a poke. She simultaneously fixed a withering stare at Gretchen. "Hey, at least you're not the only one providing entertainment at the start of a mission anymore. Be thankful for that."

Gretchen and Marshall followed Marta's cryptic gaze to a mousy man wearing a bow tie. Upton Groose had positioned himself near the projection platform. Gretchen's dismay had clearly drawn Groose's interest.

On one hand, Marta thought she should have briefed Groose concerning the bawdy realities of time travel. He had not, however, extended her the courtesy of announcing an estimated time of arrival. He'd just shown up. So, Mr. Groose could piss off.

From the moment Marshall had disrobed as a participant in the first human passage through time, he had been notorious throughout the Global Research Consortium complex. When a newcomer's presence required a word of warning, Marta never knew exactly what to say. Simply describing Marshall as large was an understatement of the phenomenon. If, in fact, Marshall was merely large, the novelty might have run its course.

The discovery through animal testing that nonorganic matter could not be projected through a wormhole had lent an entirely unanticipated carnal aspect to time travel. Because travelers must be naked, program directors had attempted to create projection protocols as businesslike and nonsexual as possible.

Marta smiled as she recalled the futility of their efforts. *Best laid plans . . .*

Sheila Schuler radiated sensuality. She hid her anxieties behind a touch of exhibitionism and a sense of sexual mischief. Her foil was usually Marshall. Marshall, a terribly self-conscious and insecure man, couldn't control himself in the naked presence of Sheila. Had he been able to maintain a flaccid state, Marshall might have gotten away with "large." At full mast, though, Marshall almost defied comprehension.

Elvin Detwyler only complicated matters by organizing Marshall Grissom betting pools. During the early days of the program, GRC personnel were confined underground for the five-year periods of their contracts, so they took their entertainment wherever they found it. Soon, nearly everyone with access to the projection lab was placing wagers on *how hard and how fast.* As the size of the wagers grew, so did a program-wide interest in Marshall. The effect had been a desensitization of program participants to a sexually charged atmosphere and inured them to events uninitiated observers found shocking.

"Yes, Marta," Marshall replied, "I'm relieved someone else is at least helping pander to the collective prurient interest..."

"You're right, though," Marta whispered. "I wouldn't have assigned Gillis and Macy to this one if I'd known."

"Marta, these delays are exasperating," Gretchen said. "Can't you do something about..." Her annoyance melted into a more conciliatory tone as she absorbed another of Marta's glares and the fastidious man wearing a bow tie seemed focused on Gretchen's concern.

"...about...about that problem with the shower... water pressure... which is low... which is why our travelers have been delayed," stammered Gretchen, who lacked creativity in instances of spontaneous disinformation.

Marta stole a quick glance as Groose made a notation in an old-fashioned paper tablet he'd drawn from his jacket's inside pocket and stepped forward. "A plumbing problem is causing this delay?"

"Yep," Marta darted a glance at Gretchen. "Water pressure. Comes and goes. The travelers, you see, must take a shower, a nice strong shower. We must be sure any inorganic particles are removed from their bodies. Even a tiny bit of dust will cause a painful burn."

Groose made another notation.

He'd appeared on the scene unexpectedly just an hour ago. Marta cautioned everyone that the subcommittee liaison would show up at some point, although she thought she'd have a little more warning. This morning, Groose, who for the past decade had kept an eye on the U.S. Postal Service as an accountant with the General Services Administration, would observe his first projection. Marta hoped everyone would behave so she could ease Groose into the earthy time travel culture.

Marta's preoccupation with Phillip Lucre, though, made her space out the composition of today's traveling team. Macy and Gillis enjoyed a preprojection ritual Macy relied on to ease her anxiety through the limbo's eternity and make integration with her past self less traumatic.

Marta remembered finding Macy at the facility's makeshift bar—The Time Warp—nursing a beer, trying to hide tears.

"I don't think I can do this, Marta," Macy had told her. "Other people say they can relax in the limbo, but I'm almost, I don't know, claustrophobic. And the integration . . . when my past self panics, instead of trying to calm her, I lose it, too."

Marta confided that she also struggled with integration. "Except for one time," Marta said offering a grin. She related her experience during an early mission. As she arrived, her past self was experiencing the throes of orgasm. "Sheila had a theory," Marta said. "She suggested strong emotion or intense physical sensation at the moment of integration blocked a lot of the *background noise* and made the integration less difficult."

"And you think that might work?" Macy's expression brightened.

"Well, that one time it sure worked for me."

This was also at a point when Gillis was moping around after realizing—given Marta and Marshall's budding relationship—his infatuation with Marta would probably never be consummated. Consequently, Marta told Gillis about Macy's problem. Gillis and Macy found solace in each other.

By reaching orgasm as near to the moment of projection as possible, Macy said, she found she handled the process better. And their ritual—Gillis called it his *good luck piece*—was not much of a distraction when Gillis and Macy confined themselves to one of their apartments or even the janitors' closet down the hall.

As Macy tried timing the peak of her pleasure ever nearer to the moment of departure, though, they recently had moved their preprojection performance venue to a women's locker room immediately across the hall from the projection lab.

"If we hit the limbo when I'm still *going*," Macy confided to Marta with a sort of dreamy expression, "it just sort of lasts on and on and on . . ."

In retrospect, Marta realized she should have imposed some restrictions. But over the months, everyone had pretty much surrendered concerning the whole nonsexual protocol thing. Given a workplace where nudity was a requirement, a certain frankness concerning sexuality had evolved. Marta didn't want to seem prudish.

When Upton Groose appeared, Macy and Gillis were already well into their ritual. So, Marta had to wing it.

Marta smiled at Groose. "I'm sure they won't be much longer . . ."

He made another notebook notation.

Then, from the corridor outside—the one leading back to the locker rooms and showers—came a scream.

"Oh God. Ooooooohhhh God! Aaaaaaahhh!"

Macy was a yeller.

Groose's eyes grew wide with concern. "Is someone injured?"

"Um . . . no," Marta said. "That's Macy. Water's back on. Must have been cold."

Groose turned to face the commotion as Macy sprinted for the platform, followed by Gillis. Macy ripped off her robe in full stride, shoving it into the hands of the person nearest her. Upton Groose.

Before Marta's eyes, Groose withered into a helpless lump of incredulity as the wonderfully endowed Macy Gardner bounced onto the platform. Groose staggered, as if he'd been shot, when a nude Gillis Kerg leapt into place beside her.

"Come on . . . come on . . . let's go," Macy shouted between quick spurts of breath as she waved at Gretchen.

The projector hummed, a sheen of protoplasm crawled across the huge silver globes, and the travelers disappeared.

Still holding Macy's robe, Groose stared open-mouthed at the empty platform for a moment before turning imploring eyes to Marta. His lips made several attempts to form words before he finally managed, "Those people were naked . . ."

"Yeah, well, welcome to time travel," Marta said offering a matter-of-fact shrug.

"God, I love this job," said Elvin.

Upton Groose required only a week to establish himself as a total pain in the ass.

He hovered. Nitpicked. Counted pencils and batteries and rubber bands. He criticized lack of procedure. He questioned the Time Warp's existence and asked if the facility had followed correct procedure in obtaining an Arizona State Liquor License.

"I don't know," Marta told him.

"How can you not know? You're the administrator."

"I was not the administrator when the facility was planned and built," Marta told him. "Facility planners apparently felt people confined here needed some distractions, like a bar."

"Planners are not always mindful of adherence to state and local regulations," Groose said. "As administrator, it's incumbent upon you to research the regulatory status of—"

"Mr. Groose, I can't begin to tell you, given all the subjects demanding my attention, how low on my list of priorities this particular issue ranks."

"Then I shall take it upon myself to inquire of the appropriate authorities," Groose said.

"Knock yourself out," Marta said. "I suspect Senator Mumford is more lenient than I am. He'll probably just have you jailed. If it's left to me, though, I'll call security and have you shot."

"I beg your pardon!" Groose said, mustering his most officious tone.

"This is a top-secret facility. You can't make any inquiries of anyone in Arizona State Government about anything we do here."

"Well," Groose said, "I'll be addressing the subcommittee concerning your attitude."

"Don't hold your breath waiting for a response," Marta said.

Among many unintended consequences of time travel, the concept of verb tense is rendered hopelessly naïve.

Only a few days after her Time Warp dispute with
Upton Groose, Marta delivered this truth with smugness
that, in retrospect, she considered unbecoming an effective
administrator. As much as she wanted to tell Groose to fuck
off, Marta understood that the bothersome little man could
not be ignored. She could not dismiss him out of hand
without incurring the politicians' wrath.

Offering to have him shot had probably been a mistake.
So, she determined to do better.

Her resolve lasted two days.

"Ms. Hamilton," Groose said, his words drifting
through her office doorway, "I'm wondering if you could
help me concerning a technical issue regarding time travel
nomenclature."

Sitting at her desk, head bowed, Marta hoped that, from
Groose's perspective, this posture appeared to be one of
intense concentration on the report open before her. In
truth, she'd nodded off as she tried to plow through a
pointless tome. Groose presented her with at least one of
these a day—the man must spend all night at a keyboard—
and copied them to the subcommittee.

Marta hoped she hadn't given a start when his high-
pitched voice, always bordering on a whine, snapped her from
a sleepy haze putting a scowl on her face and malice in her
heart. Only discipline borne of training kept her from snarling
at him. Instead, she held up one finger—not the finger she
preferred—indicating she needed a moment further to
complete a paragraph. Marta used this silence to gather herself,
stifle her irritation, then reply with some modicum of civility.

"A technical issue?" *Perhaps she could dump Groose on
the physicists.*

"A technicality in the grammatical sense. Concerning your reports to the subcommittee."

"You're questioning my grammar?" Marta said.

"No, not exactly. Mostly a matter of consistency. I submit my own reports, as you know, and I think we should establish some sort of protocol concerning verb tense."

"Verb tense."

"Yes. I note in your recent mission proposal you say, for example, *travelers will be attempting to observe . . .* as if this event is a future occurrence. In reality, travelers will perform this task in the past, so I think proper grammatical form is *travelers were attempting to observe . . .* of course, that could be confusing, because subcommittee members might mistakenly infer the mission has already taken place, when in fact it has not. So perhaps we can just agree that all communications to the sub-committee will be stated in present tense. *Travelers are attempting to observe . . .*"

He tucked his chin and peered over his glasses offering a helpful smile.

Marta regarded him in silence for a long moment. "Does it matter?"

Groose's smile collapsed. "Ms. Hamilton, I am by training an accountant. To an accountant, everything matters. Communication should be precise and unambiguous and consistent. Through precision and consistency, we communicate clearly therefore eliminating potential errors of misunderstanding."

"Okay, Mr. Groose, then let us be precise. You have, of course, carefully studied the summaries Dr. Allen put together explaining the nature and physics of time?"

"Well, I'm getting to those as my duties allow—"

"To summarize, space and time, in terms of physics, are inextricably linked. And just as every point in space exists at once, so does every point in time. Past, present, and future are concurrent. So, if you wish our reports to be precise, the only correct tense to use is all of them: *travelers were, are, will be attempting to observe* . . .

"You see," Marta continued, "the rules of grammar were established long before Mr. Einstein articulated his theory of special relativity."

"Well," Groose said, clearly taken aback, "I can see how that would be a little cumbersome—"

"Don't forget was, will be and has been cumbersome."

"All right, I see your point." He turned to leave.

"And I hope, am hoping, and will have hoped, that you had, are having, and have had, a lovely day," Marta called after him.

Groose did not look back.

8

THE ABDUCTION

MARSHALL KNOCKED ON SEAN'S DOOR at Brookhaven a couple of times a week during the months of April and May. Sean looked forward to Marshall's visits.

When he returned the first time, Marshall brought a Portales High School Yearbook from 1968.

"My God, where did you find that?" Sean asked as he leafed through the pages. "I haven't seen one of these in seventy years."

"Can you go through the book with me? Tell me what you know about the people, who might still be alive, and where they might be?"

"You've got all those computers and search engines and you can't track down a bunch of old folks?" Sean asked, all the while relishing the prospect of digging through old memories.

"That gets a little tricky," Marshall said. "With the new privacy laws, we'd have to submit warrant requests, and we can't do that. We have to keep our search for Sheila a secret."

Sean laughed and shook his head. He wished Marshall would just say what he was *really* after. Why time travel?

Why such an elaborate, improbable cover story? Sean constantly sought to expose the flaws in Marshall's deception.

"So, what do time travelers do? When they get there, I mean."

"Well . . . different things. We observe . . ."

"What about the last trip?"

"The last . . ."

"The person who traveled through time most recently. Was that you?"

"No. Gillis and Macy were who—"

"So, what did they do when they were . . . there?"

"Um, they investigated a case of copyright infringement—"

"Copyright infringement?" Sean laughed. "Copyright infringement? You folks use time travel to check on copyright infringement?"

"Um . . . well . . . not only . . . there are patent disputes and—"

"Why aren't you assassinating future evil doers or alerting whole populations to impending natural disaster? Why aren't you saving the world?"

"Our charter limits us to observation. See, we can't really change things."

"So, you observe copyright infringement?"

"Just this once. After all, we're not the FBI. We're not the CIA. We're the Postal Service."

And why was Amanda Page at the center of this? Sean truthfully didn't know if Amanda Page was dead or alive. Or most of these other people from his high school yearbook, for that matter. He'd kept track of few former classmates.

He couldn't shake a nagging sense that during his first

meeting with Marshall he'd somehow failed a test. And while he had been Marshall's initial target for whatever this scam was, now Marshall sought someone else. The whole thing would seem sinister if Marshall wasn't such a damned likeable guy.

Sean was particularly pleased to discover Marshall's love of baseball. As Sean expected, Marshall followed the Arizona Diamondbacks. "My heart is with the Nashville Athletics, though," Marshall told him. "They were in Oakland back then. I don't know why, but I just sort of gravitated to the American League. My mom and I came to Phoenix every year for a couple of Spring Training games. The A's were who I always wanted to see."

"For me it's the Seattle Mariners," Sean said. "I moved to the Pacific Northwest in 1978, the year after the franchise was established. I've followed them ever since."

"Jeez," Marshall said, "talk about a glutton for punishment..."

And if the invitation hadn't involved baseball, Sean thought later, he probably would never have gotten into Marshall's car.

June 3, 2046

Sean answered Marshall's knock on the first Saturday of June and invited him inside. Sean detected a difference, though. Marshall's smile seemed a bit forced and his gaze nervous, eyes shifting here and there rather than looking directly at Sean for more than an instant.

"Are you all right, Marshall?"

"Um . . . sure. I wondered if I could talk you into a baseball game . . . an Arizona Rookie League game over at Mesa. The A's are playing the Mariners team, and that kid who was the M's first round draft pick is on the roster . . ."

"Today?"

"Yes. We'd have to leave right away. I hate missing the first pitch."

Sean tried but couldn't think of a reason not to go. What else did he have to do?

The route south along Highway 51, and then the jump onto 202 East, seemed correct to Sean, although Marshall's uncharacteristic nervousness continued to pick at him. Sean didn't know for sure something was amiss until the sign heralding the last Mesa exit disappeared behind them.

"I guess we're not going to the ballgame?"

"No, Sean," Marshall said. "I'm sorry about the deception. I just had to get you into the car. Technically, I guess, I'm abducting you."

Sean considered being concerned. Countering his fight or flight instinct, though, he found Marshall about the most nonthreatening person he could imagine. And even under these circumstances, Sean couldn't bring himself to believe Marshall wished to hurt him.

"So, where are we going?"

"The desert, past Superior. I want you to meet Marta and the others."

"Look here, Marshall, over these weeks I've come to like you. I enjoy your company. While I haven't decided what you really want with a geezer like me, as you promised, the whole experience has at least been entertaining. I might even concede there are times when I believe *you* believe . . .

well ... I know you think there's not much an old man could do, but if you plan to cause me harm, I won't make it easy for you."

Marshall kept his eyes on the road ahead. His voice wavered when he said, "Sean, I don't know if this is right or not. The thing I'm most afraid of is that we will, indeed, cause you grave harm. I promise you, though, these are good people you'll be meeting. And not one of us will put you in harm's way without your permission."

Marshall coasted to a stop at a gate that interrupted a chain link fence. The fence stood a good ten feet high—slanted outward at the top, edged with coils of razor wire—and disappeared to both horizons. A dozen yards behind that fence was another, just as formidable, running parallel to the first.

"Jesus!" Sean asked, "Who are you trying to keep out?"

Marshall used a remote-control unit to activate the first gate. It slid on rollers, closing behind them as the car edged toward a guard's station. When Sean searched for soldiers or policemen, he saw the station was unmanned. Marshall merely waved at a small camera mounted on the side of the security hut. A second gate rolled open.

Beyond, a paved road ended at a parking lot adjacent to an outsized two-story rectangular building standing alone.

"I guess the government didn't want to spend much on an architect," Sean said.

Marshall guided Sean into a reception lobby where another security station confronted them. Again, no guards. This time, Marshall swiped a card and stared into the lens of a scanning device. With a flourish of beeps and lights, they passed through and headed toward a bank of three elevators.

"Over here," Marshall said, adding as they waited for a car to arrive, "Marta gave everyone the weekend off so there's only a few of us on site."

The elevator doors slid closed behind them. Sean saw a control panel featuring an up button, a down button and a red button labeled "emergency." Marshall pushed the down button and they plummeted. The door finally opened onto a bright halogen-illuminated corridor fading into a distant darkness on both the left and right.

"The guy who drives the golf cart is off this weekend," Marshall said. "Wait here for just a second. I think the carts are parked around the corner."

Marshall returned driving an open electric car featuring two sets of seats and a small platform on the back for golf clubs. They rode a quiet whirr through a maze of hallways, past doors with labels such as *Physics Lab* and *Mathematics Division* and *Biomechanics Conference Room*. Some doors bore the names of individuals. Sean endured the journey in wide-eyed silence, thinking that, whatever the truth of this hoax, Marshall's cohorts had certainly taken elaborate steps to further this deception.

Marshall stopped at a door marked *Projection Lab,* offering his arm to Sean as they disembarked.

"Watch out down here." Marshall pointed to a lip at the threshold of the entry. "There's a little step here because it's an airlock. Lots of people trip."

An inner door swung open. Sean confronted a smiling Chinese woman clad in a white lab coat.

"Sean, this is Naomi. She supervises the medical and psychological aspects of our program."

"You're a psychiatrist?" Sean asked.

"I am."

Sean patted Marshall on the arm. "Well, it's good to know you're getting help."

Marshall's response didn't register, though, because Sean looked beyond Naomi and saw two huge gleaming globes flanking a white, brightly lit platform tinged by a throbbing green glow beneath its surface. Banks of computers, monitors and cameras edged the platform on three sides.

The globes pulsed with a bluish electronic sort of ooze that seemed to creep along their surfaces in random patterns. Where Sean could have sworn an instant before had been empty space between the globes, he saw a lovely, petite, and very nude black woman standing before him. He wondered if she had been there all along, and he'd somehow missed her among the computers and cameras and other shiny things. But . . . no. Old as he might be, Sean was pretty sure he could still tell the difference between a computer and a naked lady.

He felt frozen. He could not bring himself to speak or move. Like a needle stuck on an old phonograph record, his mind simply could not jump beyond this particular groove.

A comforting arm slipped through his and Sean found Naomi beside him.

"I'm sure you're finding this a bit overwhelming. Do you need to sit? Can I bring you a bottle of water?"

Sean stared silently into the small Chinese woman's black eyes for a moment before turning back toward the nudist.

"Hello, Mr. Brody," said the woman, who now wore a white robe. "I know my entrance was a little theatrical. And I apologize for that, but we wanted to impress you. I'm Marta Hamilton. I think Marshall has mentioned me? You've just witnessed my return from a brief conference with my counterpart from another universe a few days past. And I do have to admit the timing wasn't coincidental. We needed to get your attention."

Sean continued to stare. He found this reality too much to process.

"I know Marshall hasn't given you all the details yet. I sincerely hope you will agree to help us, though. We will be asking—"

"My God," Sean croaked through a sandpaper dry throat, believing all this for the first time. "You people want me to be fifteen years old again."

9

HISTORY'S CHOICE

MARSHALL KNEW HE SHOULD do something, say something, at least smile reassuringly. As he viewed Sean seated opposite him, though, Marshall's conscience flogged him.

"I'm right, aren't I?" Sean said eagerly. "You want to send me back in time to a place none of you can go because you're too young."

"Um . . . well . . . yes," Marshall said. "Can we wait for Marta? She'll be right back."

Marshall looked at the others. They waited in the projection lab. They could have retreated to Marta's office, but with all seven conspirators gathered here a larger space was required. Elvin and Gretchen had pulled chairs from behind computer desks and arranged a small circle near the projection platform.

"I don't need to wait," Sean said. "I'll do it. I'm ninety-three years old and my life . . . you know what my life is like, Marshall. I'm bored. Truth is most people my age are bored."

"There are implications you don't know about that you must consider," Naomi said. "A journey into the past, particularly for a person of your age and condition, is not a simple undertaking. And we must be sure you understand exactly what you'd be consenting to—"

"Naomi," Marshall said, "he's not senile. I've spent a lot of time with Sean. He understands what's going on around him as well as any of us."

"That's right ... uh ... uh ... say, what was your name again?"

Marshall turned wearing a startled expression.

Sean cackled. "I was just pulling your chain there, Fred ... I mean, Marshall."

"I see the discussion has already begun," Marta said as she joined the group. She wore a form fitting white T-shirt and jeans.

"What about Upton Groose?" Gretchen Allen asked Marta.

"He's still out."

Marshall was relieved. When Marta announced the weekend off, Groose had insisted on staying, which certainly would have complicated Sean's visit.

"So, how'd you finally get Groose to leave?" Marshall asked.

"No, I meant *out* like unconscious. Naomi doped his coffee."

"And we can't do that again," Naomi said. "As a doctor, I can't be indiscriminately drugging people."

"I promise it's just this once," Marta said.

"I was just starting to inform Mr. Brody concerning some of the issues ..." Naomi began.

"Mr. Brody," Marta interrupted, "here's the problem. There's a very good chance you won't survive."

"So much for breaking it to him gently," Marshall said.

Silhouetted in the greenish-blue glow pulsating behind him, Sean's gaze shifted from face to face.

"So, I might die," he said finally. "I might die tomorrow just sitting in my living room. How old does a person need to be, anyway?"

"Mr. Brody," Marta said, "if we project you into the past, you must understand you will be arriving in a different universe. You will be gone from this world . . . forever. We have no way of bringing you back."

Marta's blunt assessment seemed to set the old man on his heels. Marshall thought they'd lost him.

Marshall stared beyond Sean at the green glow and shook his head. "I . . . I'm sorry, Sean. We looked. There isn't anyone else."

Sean frowned. "So, I'd just, what, disappear from here?"

"Yes . . . we'll make arrangements to—"

"What will happen to me in this other world?"

"We don't know," Naomi answered. "We suspect your consciousness will occupy the body of your fifteen-year-old self in that universe. Because, to our knowledge, only one other time traveler has been sent there, we think the world you find will be essentially identical to the past you remember here. You will bring all knowledge of our world's future. You'll know, at least for a short while, the details of your own future. And this knowledge will burst into the brain of your fifteen-year-old self all at once. This flood of information will overwhelm him, and a very real danger is involved. He might suffer some mental impairment. And if that occurs, he—and you, we think—would be stuck in a pretty miserable existence."

Sean twisted in his chair, indulging himself with

another look at the silver globes. "Marshall says several of you have traveled through time a lot. All of you folks seem to have survived okay."

"Problem is, you'll be going much further into the past than any of us ever have," Naomi explained. "Meaning your past counterpart will have more information to process than anyone ever before. Except, we hope, Sheila, of course. We have some techniques we think will help mitigate the impact on your past self," Naomi continued. "Things that will help regulate the flow of information. Let me emphasize, though, we've never gone this far. We can't guarantee a successful result."

"All right. Suppose I get back there, and the kid handles everything okay. What happens then?"

"We think you will remain aware of your future for four, maybe five days. During that time, we have an assignment for you."

"And after three or four days?"

"If you react the way most travelers do, you will lose awareness you ever had a different life. In all likelihood, you will relive the life that history has already mapped for you there—and here."

"Marshall says you think your friend Sheila is stuck inside the girl I knew as Amanda Page."

"Yes. Perhaps."

"And maybe I can revive Sheila so you can bring her home."

Marshall touched Sean's shoulder. "That's right."

"Okay, once she's here, why can't I come back, too?"

"Because," Naomi said gently, "to send you on this journey, we essentially have to kill you."

Sean stood and spread his arms as emphasis for his question. "Why? You all seem pretty healthy to me."

"Only organic matter can pass through the wormhole," Naomi said.

Marshall couldn't stand the knife thrusts to his conscience any longer. He wrapped an arm around Sean's shoulders and guided him to the projection platform where they stood together, bathed in the eerie sheen of pulsating green and blue light. "Sean, I desperately want to know if my friend Sheila is alive. And if she is, I must do everything possible to bring her home. Honestly, though, I never would have approached you if I had known about—well about the complications your physical condition represents."

Naomi joined them at the platform. She clasped both of Sean's hands in her own.

"Mr. Brody, none of our travelers have an internal heart regulation system. They don't have prosthetic knees. They don't have artificial optics to assist vision. You do. And if we are to return you to your youth, we must surgically remove those items. The heart regulation system is the most significant issue. I've examined your medical records. I don't think you can survive much more than a couple of days without that system. So, you see, if you go, you *can't* come back."

Sean returned Naomi's gaze and seemed lost for a few moments. Finally, he asked, "What happens here? Will my past . . . change?"

Marshall felt the tick of *his* heart beating more rapidly. *Clearly, Sean's still considering doing this!* Once again, Marshall's conscience berated him for such hope.

"We don't know," Marta said. "We've had very little

success changing the past in any significant way."

"Sean, the first day we met," Marshall said, "you asked if you knew me from somewhere. I said the correct answer would be that I knew you from some *time*. In researching this mission, I traveled to several universes and briefly observed your life as it contrasted with this one. And even in universes we'd never visited before, where even the nuances of histories should be the same, I found a number of variations—more pronounced than the subtle differences we've found dealing with our own pasts. And we simply don't understand what that means."

"Different . . . how?"

"In most cases, I looked at records. I examined your professional life—your newspaper career and the things you wrote about," Marshall said. "Internet research, essentially, because I didn't have the time to travel around in most of those worlds and see you personally . . . but in a few cases, I was able to meet you, talk with you and—"

Naomi interrupted. "Offering you details of different lives wouldn't be fair to you, Mr. Brody. We'd be influencing your decision one way or another by implying changes we can't guarantee and don't understand."

Sean appealed to Marshall, his expression painful to see, but Marshall could only offer a helpless shrug by way of response.

"We can't promise anything," Gretchen said.

"And you need to know something else," Marshall added. "Sheila would be completely opposed to this plan. She was a remarkable person. Among many other things, she was our conscience. She thought time travel is wrong, because she knew we could never see or calculate the cost in terms of the lives we are affecting. We have no way of knowing how we are disrupting lives of innocent people when we intrude in their universes. And she wouldn't for a moment have agreed to a manipulation of your past, even if she thought it would save her."

"Then why—?"

"Because," Marta said, "something's going on here. Some *thing*—history for want of a better term—has directed us to you. One person might call it fate. A religious person might see it as divine intervention. An agnostic grounded in science might call it the vast grinding mechanism of the universe. One thing we all reject, though, is coincidence."

"Unlike everyone else we've come across, Sean Brody might not have to repeat his past," Marshall said. "History may want something different for you. And if Sheila returns to us, I will justify our actions by saying that history *invited* us to make your life different."

"Different," Naomi added quickly. "But remember, different doesn't necessarily mean better."

"Why me?" Sean sounded overwhelmed. "I am utterly inconsequential."

The question was met with a round of incongruous expressions and shrugs.

"That may be the very reason your past might be more flexible," said Elvin. "But then your guess is as good as ours."

PIVOTAL MOMENTS

"MAYBE THE FIRST THING we should be asking," Naomi said to Sean, "is whether you even want a different life. You told Marshall about your regret that you didn't take different paths. It's one thing to wish for something different. Confronting the *reality* of something different is quite another. The life you described to Marshall seems to have been a good one."

The room fell silent, except for the creak of artificial leather as Marshall settled into one of the rolling chairs he'd commandeered from a computer station. He watched the old man's face crumble a bit.

"A certain . . . honesty, I guess, comes with age," Sean said presently. "You spend so much of life acting out a performance you hope will impress others, but you just end up confusing *yourself* about who you really are. Then, you get to the point where most of those other people are gone. No reason trying to fool anyone, anymore."

Sean's shoulders sagged. Marshall felt the connection between the two of them draw tighter.

"I have lived a thoroughly innocuous life. I have many acquaintances and few friends. I've made precious little difference to anyone. I have three great kids—James, Russel, Liam's the youngest—don't get me wrong there. I wouldn't want to change their presence in my life. And the fact they've turned out well must be due, at least in some small part, to my influence. I've never done anything extraordinary, though. Not that a spectacular contribution like curing cancer or something is necessary to live a fulfilled life. Still . . . I guess, the thing is, I've always played it safe. If the road forked, I took the safer, familiar path. And had I, at any of those points, gone the other way . . . well, I think my life might have been very different. The thing I'm most ashamed of? I've let fear of failure limit my choices."

"For instance." Naomi leaned forward, her eyes a gleaming reflection of intense interest.

"Okay," Sean said. "I was a newspaper reporter. Not a bad one. Not a spectacular one, either. I wanted to be a novelist, though. Of course, I expect every newspaper reporter aspires to write a novel. But I'd come home from a day of writing news stories and use that as an excuse not to do any writing for myself. A guy who worked at the desk next to mine talked about writing books. I dismissed him out of hand. I was arrogant enough to think he wasn't as good a writer as me. While I was making my excuses, though, he went home and wrote every night. He put in the time to learn his craft and became a best-selling novelist."

"Why didn't you take his example as encouragement of what *could* happen?" Naomi asked.

"His success intimidated me, I suppose. What if I tried and failed where someone I knew had succeeded? What if I wasn't the writer I imagined myself to be? What if I simply wasn't capable of anything more than forty inches of news copy? What if I wrote something and people thought it was just . . . stupid or trivial? So, I chose not to write at all. I should have made the time. I should have exercised more discipline, more courage."

Naomi reached across and patted the old man's arm. "Tell us about your pivotal moments," she encouraged.

"Pivotal?"

"Yes. Most of us can look back at a few instances of our lives that stand out vividly. While we forget most of the fine details of our pasts, these few instances—"

"I was almost killed riding a motorcycle when I was sixteen. A guy driving a Volkswagen tried to pass me from behind as I was turning across an oncoming lane of traffic. I turned right into his path. He was going about sixty. Hit the front fork of the bike and took it right out from under me. Missed hitting me by a couple of inches. I was just lying on the pavement staring at the sky, completely uninjured and wondering why I wasn't dead. The motorcycle was a tangled mess about a hundred yards down the road."

"Yes," Naomi said. "Obviously, though, that's a result you probably don't want to change. What else? A life-changing event doesn't have to be so dramatic."

Sean cast a blank gaze back to the projection platform.

Marshall worried for a moment they were being too intrusive.

Sean's attention came back into focus, though, and he said, "Does a baseball game seem too trivial?"

"Nothing is trivial if it's an experience you think altered the course of your life."

"Okay. I've always loved baseball. I went out for the team when I was a high school sophomore. The coach didn't know much about the game and didn't have the background or skill to teach it. He was also the football coach. That's all that really mattered to him. He ordered the best football players to go out for baseball so he could keep an eye on them. I spent the season attending practice, doing nothing to distinguish myself, and sitting on the bench. Which, for the most part, was okay with me. I just wanted to be part of a team, be closer to the game than just a seat in the stands, you know?"

Marshall knew exactly what Sean meant.

"Finally, half-way through our season, we took a school bus twenty miles down the road to Clovis, New Mexico. Their population, and their high school, was twice as large as ours. We played Clovis every year. Football, basketball, baseball. We never expected to win." Sean closed his eyes and smiled. "I can still see and smell the day. Mid-April, seventy-five degrees. Normally, the wind howled across the high plains in the spring. Not that day, though. So, the smells were all there. The pine tar, the leather, the sweat and liniment. Everywhere I've ever been, that's how baseball smells. Anyhow, I sat there, cheering and ignoring the looks from football guys, who thought me and my friends had no business wearing a uniform of any kind."

"Yes," Naomi said. "The psychology of sports can be quite exclusive."

"A half-dozen of us bench-sitters were our own little enclave. As expected, by the fifth inning, the starters were getting creamed. Removed from any direct contact with the slaughter, though, our group sat spitting sunflower seeds, trying to appear appropriately grieved in light of the circumstances. But then someone would make a comment, or someone would fart, and a round of laughter rippled through us. Finally, the coach wheeled on us and yelled, 'Hogan! Get a bat and hit for Terry.'

"Well," Sean continued as he chuckled at the memory, "all the color drained from Arty Hogan's face just like somebody had opened a vein. Arty looked at us and said, 'Me?' as if we could do something about it. We all kind of slid away from him and did our best to look somewhere else."

Now Sean stood, stepped to the middle of the circle of chairs and began acting the scene—sliding along an imaginary bench, looking away, mimicking the fear scrawled across his friend's face. Marshall found himself hanging on every word. He glanced around the room at the others. They, too, leaned forward with interest. Even Elvin smiled.

Sean Brody knew how to tell a story.

"First, he had to find a batting helmet, and he went through a half dozen before he got one to fit. And then, while he stared at the bats, the umpire screamed at him to get in the box. So Arty grabs this club that's way too big for him—one of the linebackers from the football team was the only one who could swing it—and practically runs to the plate.

"We heard him tell the umpire he was sorry. The umpire growled and told him he'd better swing the bat. And that's what Arty did. First pitch, a fastball on his hands. He dragged that heavy bat through the zone and caught the ball just above the label. The bat broke into two pieces—and the linebacker was really pissed off, I'll tell you. The ball blooped into fair territory, though, just a couple of yards beyond the third baseman's reach. Arty gave a couple of little leaps . . ." Sean did his best, despite his artificial knees, to mimic jumping for joy ". . . and practically danced to first base where he raised his arms and us bench guys went crazy."

"So how did you get involved?" Elvin asked. Perched on the edge of his chair, the computers whirred softly behind him.

"I'm what happened next," Sean said. "*Now*, our coach was royally pissed."

Marshall laughed aloud as Sean pulled at his own shirt and pantomimed being dragged along.

"He grabbed me by the front of my jersey, hauled me off the bench, and said, 'You go run for Baryshnikov over there. Steal, first pitch. And don't get picked off!'

"So, I trotted across the diamond to where Arty stood on the base and I told him the coach told me to run for him. 'But I got a hit,' Arty says, as if he wasn't going to leave. Then, I think Arty realized he was off the hook. He didn't have to risk doing something stupid running the bases. Doing something stupid would be left up to me."

Sean offered a smile of pure pride.

"Now, you have to understand, when I was young, I had one and only one athletic gift. I could run. And not just a little bit. I wasn't fast for a kid in a small town. I was fast for a kid anywhere. The problem is, though, being fast doesn't have much to do with being a good base runner. You don't run bases well on the strength of pure speed. Stealing bases is all about an efficiency of steps and movement and getting a jump."

He mimicked dancing off first base.

"Getting a jump is all about reading the pitcher, watching

his moves to first, knowing when he's throwing to the base or going to the plate. Good pitchers lull you with sloppy moves that are like old threadbare suits. They build your confidence while you easily get back to the bag before the ball gets there. Their mediocrity encourages you to get just a little longer lead the next time. Then they break out the tuxedo. A malicious move smooth and cold as granite. Even before that ball leaves the pitcher's hand, you know you are a dead man."

Sean punctuated his story with a dismissive wave.

"Well, back then I was completely ignorant of all that. I took a timid lead. I watched the pitcher go into his stretch. I waited way too long before I broke. I was going to be out by a mile."

Sean closed his eyes.

"I can still see and hear every detail as if it was a slow-motion replay. The hitter made contact. The second baseman stepped toward the baseline, fielded the ground ball, tagged me effortlessly as I ran by. Then, he threw to first base and completed a double play. I should have stopped in the baseline. Forced him to decide—either me or the guy running to first base. But I didn't possess those instincts back then."

Sean's eyes opened. He spread his arms wide, as if to apologize.

"And the coach was angry at your failure?" Naomi asked.

"No. I think he was glad about it. See, Arty got a hit, so the coach pretty much had to let him stay. Not me. He called me into his office after the game. I remember his speech word for word: *You can continue coming to practice, but you won't play anymore. And you WON'T sit on the bench during games and tell wise-ass jokes with your buddies. You won't suit up for any more games. My suggestion? Hand in your uniform and find a better way to invest your time."*

"It may be foolish," Sean told his audience, "but I've always felt that if I'd stolen that base, my high school life would have been different. At the very least, I should have kept going to practice. Who knows what that might have led to? I let my coach intimidate me into quitting. What's worse is, for the longest time, I blamed him. But the fault was mine. I *allowed* him to take something important from me. I should have stuck with it. Even though that might seem a silly or innocuous thing from an adult perspective, I think it set a pattern for my life that I'm not sure I ever really overcame."

Marshall considered Sean with new eyes, feeling he understood this man as well as anyone he'd ever known.

"Yes, Mr. Brody," Naomi said. "That's the sort of thing I'm talking about. You might want to pick a crossroads later in life, though. If you were able to change something when you were so young, many things you appreciated and valued later might be changed, too. Family, children, professional relationships, all might turn out differently."

Sean smiled as the face of Maggie Stanfield stole into his consciousness. And, as usual, the smile was swallowed by a wave of melancholy that continued to insinuate itself even after passage of more than fifty years.

"Oh, that's easy," he said. "I made a poor choice when I was forty-one years old. But you folks don't want to hear another old man's memory."

"Understanding these things is important if we are to . . . go ahead with this," Naomi said.

Would he? Sean wondered to himself. *Go ahead with this? The smart thing . . . at least the safe thing . . . just go home. And I always do what's safe . . .*

Sean paused for a moment, a courtesy giving the others a chance to make their excuses and leave. They probably had work to do. He remained standing in the middle of their circle. Nobody moved. Nobody spoke.

"This gets pretty personal," he warned. "Probably a bit maudlin."

"Would you be more comfortable if fewer people were—" Naomi asked.

"No, I don't suppose it makes any difference. As I said, I'm too old now to care much about what folks might think."

Everyone remained.

Sean sighed.

"Okay, where can I start . . . April of 1993. Beth Ramsey and I were supposed to go out. This was six or seven years after my divorce. Beth and I had been involved for a few years. Some nights I stayed at her house. She occasionally stayed at mine. She had a son at home and couldn't leave him alone. I had my kids most weekends. And on this night Beth and I hadn't seen each other since . . . I guess it was my birthday, a couple of weeks earlier.

"For my birthday we'd gone to one of those Japanese places where everyone sits around the same big table with a grill built into the middle, and the chef puts on a show of chopping and cooking. Well, seated across from us was a woman about Beth's age, and she was, like Beth, a genuine beauty. The man she accompanied was at least twenty years older. Beth struck up a conversation and this other woman talked about trips to Las Vegas and Mediterranean cruises, a Florida condominium. I guess I chose not to see the extent of envy in Beth's eyes."

Sean glanced again around the circle of his audience. The smiles were gone, but their attention remained evident.

"Beth had been pulling back for a couple of months. The whole thing should have been obvious to me—her moodiness, her evening obligations with friends who were 'going through a bad time' ..."

"How long had you been together?" Naomi asked.

"Almost three years. We had a past, though. We first met during my sophomore year of college. She was from Clovis, and we discovered we knew some of the same people. She was beautiful, and I was just some guy. I was amazed when she seemed to be interested in me. We dated for a couple of months. I really fell for her. Then the other guy showed up. What can I say? He had a Pontiac GTO convertible. She liked him better."

"So, she reappeared how many years later?" Naomi asked.

"Twenty." Sean eased himself back onto his chair, elbows on knees, leaning into the circle.

"Hmmm. Some powerful psychology at work there," Naomi said.

"Tell me about it," Sean said. "When we ran into each other again all those years later, she apologized. Said she wished we'd stayed together. Suddenly, my whole past felt validated. And I welcomed another post-divorce fling. Our relationship pretty quickly evolved into a lot more than that, though. Anyway, back to the night in April. I was thrilled she'd called. Until I got inside the door. Beth met me with a quivering chin and a confession. She'd been seeing someone. She was confused. She just had to be honest with me. She needed time.

"The reality was she'd been seeing several someones. She really wasn't all *that* confused, and I'd just as soon she'd been honest with me about six months earlier. She didn't need time so much as she didn't need me around anymore."

"Hah," said Elvin, shaping the fingers of his hand like a pistol and pointing at his head. "That's women for you."

Sean saw Gretchen, Marta and Naomi blast Elvin with lethal glares. Elvin withered.

"I wallowed in an emotional swamp for a little more than a year."

While telling his baseball story, Sean had engaged each listener employing eye contact and animation. Now, he retreated to his chair and stared absently at the floor.

"Every few months Beth called, usually late at night when something had gone temporarily wrong with her life, or when she'd been drinking, or when she needed money. She encouraged me to *hang in there* a little longer while she sorted through things.

"Finally, after one of the most emotionally miserable years I ever endured—and some therapy to understand depression—friends convinced me to let them arrange introductions to other women. I got back to a place where I could see a future without Beth, and things didn't seem so bleak. I was determined to meet some people, have a good time, make no promises I couldn't keep, and form no life-changing attachments. That's when I met Maggie. Someone we both knew arranged a blind date. Maggie had been widowed two years earlier, and she was making a reentry of her own." Sean closed his eyes and savored the memory.

"Maggie was tall and blonde and pretty. She confronted the world with a perpetual smile. She found a way to laugh in almost any circumstance. If someone angered her, or if something went wrong during her day, she didn't allow those conditions to take control. She simply set them aside, dealt with them at an appropriate time and lived with grace and hope in the very moment she occupied. She lit up my world." He peered cautiously around the room, then said, "She was an enthusiastic and uninhibited lover."

Sean saw Marshall blush and Marta grin. Naomi offered a rather clinical nod of approval. Elvin dug an elbow into Gillis's ribs.

"She gave me the sense that with her, I could be myself, without guile or apology. And yes," he said, turning to Naomi, "it's been many, many years since I knew Maggie. And I'm sure I'm idealizing her."

Naomi encouraged him with another nod and smile.

"Maggie worked harder than anyone I'd ever been around. She raised her children as a single mother. She found work as a receptionist for a small company. By the time I met her, she managed that company. Her kids were unselfish and caring, all headed to successful careers and families of their own. We saw each other a lot over the next few months. At the same time, I was seeing other women. I told Maggie the truth about it. I warned her I wasn't ready to make any commitments. I even prepared a little speech. *Always before,* I told her, *I've entered into relationships as a response to people who chose me. If they expressed an interest, I felt a guilty obligation to return the favor. Well, this next time, I'm going to choose. I'm sorry if I sound harsh or unfeeling, Maggie, but I want you to know the truth.* And you know what she said?"

Elvin shook his head. The others waited.

"She said, 'Well, when the time comes, I hope you choose me.'" Sean's voice cracked. He took a deep breath.

Naomi produced a small bottle of water. "Sean, this is getting quite personal. I think you might feel better if we asked the others to go."

"Whoa," Elvin said, rising from his chair. "You can't just leave us hanging."

"Why, Elvin," Marta said. "You're just a romantic slob."

Sean waved a hand. "No, it's all right. They might as well hear the rest." He continued with a sigh. "Then one day, Beth called me completely out of the blue. She needed to see me. She knew she didn't deserve it after the way she'd treated me, but could we talk? Please? Maggie had to work that evening, and I had no plans. I agreed to meet Beth at a downtown bar. She'd had her fling, she said. She'd gotten it out of her system. She knew what she wanted. She convinced me to go home with her, and once again, I let someone else choose.

"I saw Maggie the next day. She took one look at me and that beautiful smile fell away. I told her Beth wanted to try again. *And I think I have to,* I said. *I think I've got to know for sure whether . . .* Maggie was angry when she said, '*Please pay attention to the words you're using. Beth* wants. *You* have *to. Remember, you get to choose this time.*' I told her I was sorry, but I thought for now, I had to choose this. She gathered herself and said it was okay. She said she wanted me to be sure. '*I don't want to be anybody's second choice,*' she said. '*If we were ever together, I wouldn't want you to have any regrets.'* Then she kissed me goodbye.

"Well, to cut through the details and tell you what you've already guessed, Beth stayed for a little less than a year this time. We had a good couple of months before the old patterns emerged. I never made this connection before, but this is another pivotal moment involving baseball. The thing that finally ended our relationship was a dispute over a vacation. Beth made plans for us to go skiing in British Columbia that coming January. She made sure I adjusted my vacation time. Late that summer, though, I started hearing advertisements during Seattle Mariners baseball games for the Mariners Fantasy Camp here in Arizona. A thing where old guys like me went to the Mariners spring training facility. The coaches—retired Mariners players—chose up teams and we'd play baseball for a week. I'd started playing baseball again, a Spokane thirty-five-and-over league, and I thought a baseball fantasy camp sounded like fun. It would cost $3,000—$4,000 if Beth wanted to come and watch. And it coincided exactly with the dates of the skiing trip.

"I tried my best to talk her into a baseball vacation. She grew angrier every time I brought it up. I asked her what if I went to Phoenix for baseball, and she took a girlfriend skiing? That wouldn't work, she said. If I pulled my money from the skiing trip, she couldn't afford to go. So, we took the ski trip. I felt resentful. She was angry and two weeks later we were finished. She made no excuses or apologies. She simply wasn't interested anymore. I think she eventually married some older guy who had a lot of money." Sean looked away, a little embarrassed he'd served up this stew of nostalgia to an audience of strangers.

"Wait a minute," Elvin said. "Why didn't you go find Maggie?"

"Elvin, please . . ." Naomi said.

But Marshall, also captivated by Sean's story, asked, "Yeah. Why didn't you?"

"Oh, I thought about calling her pretty much all the time. I didn't want to be a . . . I don't know . . . a pitiful figure in her eyes. Someone running to her on the rebound from one more failure. So, I waited. One evening, I was at a restaurant downtown, and I heard the sound of her laughter from across the room. She was seated with a group of friends. Next to her was a man I didn't know. She was listening to him talk, alternately smiling and laughing. At one point she reached over and touched his cheek. The intimacy conveyed by that small gesture made me realize what a horrible mistake I'd made.

"I hoped she hadn't seen me, and I left as quickly as I could. As I stood outside and grieved over my loss, I felt a presence beside me. One of the women sitting with Maggie's group. The mutual acquaintance who'd arranged our blind date. She said she wanted to ask a favor. I nodded. '*Please, leave her alone,*' the woman said. '*She was shattered when you stopped seeing her. She's found a good man. Her life doesn't need any more complications.*'"

Sean looked around the room and shrugged.

Naomi stood and offered Sean a hug and more water.

Elvin gave a short snuffle, dabbing under his glasses with a tissue.

"The most ironic thing," Sean said added, "is that when Maggie granted me my leave to go be with Beth, she did so, she said, because she wanted to be sure I wouldn't suffer any regrets. Well, I'm ninety-three years old. I've regretted it every day of my life since." He peered around the room once more, this time settling his gaze on Marta. "So, where do we go from here?"

Marta started to speak, but Naomi intervened.

"I don't want you making any decisions right now, Sean. You need to spend some time considering everything we've told you."

"And I wish we had more time," Marta countered. "Things are beginning to move pretty quickly, though. We'll need an answer within a couple of days. A lot of details will have to be attended to."

"I don't think I need any more time," Sean said, but Naomi held her hand up like a traffic cop.

"You have many things to consider," she said. You must understand you won't be able to choose differently because of any knowledge of the future. By the time you ride your motorcycle or play in that baseball game or make your choice about Maggie, in all likelihood you won't remember anything about us or time machines or parallel universes. All of your memories of time travel, any knowledge you gain from us about the future world, will have long since been lost."

"I could write a note to myself, or make a recording or—"

"You can certainly try," Naomi said. "We've found, though, that history doesn't care for that very much, either. If you do this, we think you'll simply be at the mercy of whatever history wants for you."

"The other thing you need to understand," said Marta, "is that we—all of us—have committed a number of felonies by bringing you here and showing you a time machine. So, we'd appreciate it if you didn't discuss this with anyone."

"Don't worry—" Sean said with a dismissive wave, but Marta continued.

"And if you return here of your own free will, you will be complicit in those crimes and equally guilty."

11

CONFLICTING DATES

June 5, 2046

MARSHALL WAS A LITTLE ALARMED that he found the prospect of strangling Phillip Lucre so appealing. Maybe he was just tired after the long drive, getting Sean back to Phoenix the evening before.

During the drive, Sean prodded Marshall for details of Sean's varied pasts. And Marshall was tempted. Naomi made Marshall promise not to offer any hints, though. And ultimately, Marshall knew she was right. Sean might interpret the vague, differing scenarios Marshall provided as either improving or diminishing his life experiences. And without a broader context, offers of hope could be false. Marshall had lived long enough to know that apparent disasters were sometimes pathways to growth and unimagined rewards.

In order to forestall Sean's persistent probing, Marshall fell back on his standard confession.

"I'm allergic to anchovies," Marshall told Sean.

"Really?" Sean said. "So am I."

So, Marshall remained conflicted on this morning-after, concerning his recruitment of Sean Brody. And he had no patience for the arrogant condescension of Phillip Lucre, who at this moment sat with his smug expression opposite

Marshall in the conference room adjacent to Marta's office. Marta, Groose, Elvin, Gretchen, Naomi and Gillis were present as well.

Marshall did not consider himself a violent person. Quite the contrary. Mostly he just wanted to get along, and almost invariably throughout his life had found a way to do so. Okay, there was that time he shot the janitor. But nobody's perfect, right? Marshall regarded the incident as a mistaken lapse of reason and courtesy that just sort of . . . happened.

Still, Marshall found he could not look at Phillip Lucre without envisioning his hands clutched around Lucre's windpipe as the man turned a satisfying shade of purple and was saying "Gaaaack, gaaack, gaaack," with that superior tone of his.

Like now.

"What could be simpler?" Lucre asked through his greasy smile as the projection team heard details of the mission Lucre and Hemisphere had cooked up.

Here, Mr. Lucre. Don't mind me. You've got something there on your collar . . . gaaack, gaaack, gaaack!

"Indeed," said Upton Groose, busily taking notes, "your proposal sounds as if it can be handled with a minimum of interference in the . . . what is it? . . . the *Gomer Pyle USMC* universe? I feel foolish just saying it. Couldn't you people come up with a numbering system? After all, I must submit written reports—"

"We'd be dealing with some pretty big numbers," Gretchen Allen said, "since we have an infinite number of universes from which to choose."

"We have a more formal system," Elvin lied. "If you

prefer, this is the Series 4.59-dimensional plane XAB532Mq spatial azimuth 4.6 billion to the 23rd power third universe on the left. But we find it more expedient to just say *Gomer Pyle*."

"Well, whatever," Groose said. "The proposal easily meets the subcommittee's standards. I think we can expedite approval."

And on its surface, Marshall conceded, the mission sounded simple enough.

During late spring of 2043, Hemisphere Investment Group held a meeting of select board members at their Phoenix office tower. "During a break," Lucre said, "one of our corporate officers—our president, Warren Pitts—allegedly had a hallway conversation with a representative of Comco Dynamics, a small independent company which had been awarded a contract to manufacture a key component for our newest generation of communication satellites.

"Comco's representative claims he and Warren discussed a proprietary aspect of the component in question. Subsequent delays forced Hemisphere to assign development of the component to one of our own subsidiaries and cancel Comco's contract due to nonperformance. Comco claims this hallway conversation provided Hemisphere the proprietary information necessary to produce the component on its own."

"Why would the Comco guy reveal proprietary information?" Marta asked. "And in a hallway? With people walking back and forth?"

Lucre reached for a bottle of water and took a swig.

"We've asked ourselves the same question. It seems illogical and, we believe, evidence that Warren is telling the truth—the conversation never took place. The Comco representative says he didn't think Warren had the technical background or raw brainpower to make sense of the details they discussed. Comco also says their man thought he could trust our company's top executive.

"In any case, Comco is suing Hemisphere for millions, claiming theft of intellectual property and breach of contract. Our attorneys are confident we can win at trial. We see a larger issue, though. Warren Pitts is a controversial figure among our board and shareholders. He is a brilliant but aggressive man, who has been accused of ... drawing outside the lines a number of times before.

"Warren says he talked with dozens of subcontractors during the Phoenix meetings. He concedes some of those conversations might have taken place during breaks outside the meeting rooms. He adamantly denies that any conversation with a Comco representative went into detail concerning the satellite component. He says Comco officials invented their story because they couldn't produce the component on time, and the lawsuit is retaliation for loss of the contract. If we can determine that Warren is telling the truth, we will vigorously defend him. If, however, Warren is lying, the board will likely cut our losses, fire our president and reach an out-of-court settlement."

"And finding out whether Pitts is lying or not would merit a billion-dollar reinvestment in the time travel project?" Marta asked conveying more than a hint of skepticism.

Lucre steepled his fingers and rested his elbows atop the oak table.

"Yes. Consider potential future liabilities we have as a company if our president is guilty and continues to act recklessly. By dismissing him, we may be saving millions in future costs. And if we can sort through our own problems, we think we've found another source of potential revenue. Many legal issues might be dealt with in this fashion. Sort of an historical arbitration process. We think many companies would pay a significant fee to reconstruct a disputed event and, perhaps, save time and expense of taking a case to court."

"Do I have to keep reminding you, this will all take place in another universe?" Marta said.

"We understand that." Lucre's voice conveyed a note of impatience. "But Mr. Detwyler tells me the, um ... *Gomer Pyle* universe was chosen because you have not yet sent travelers there, so the histories should be running along identical tracks."

"And your meeting took place when?"

"May 18, 2043."

Something about the date nagged at Marshall, disrupting his murderous fantasies. He checked his pocket computer, then displayed a 3D image of a calendar above the table.

"May 18 ... this won't work," Marshall said.

"And why not?" Lucre asked.

In Marshall's mind, the words just came out, *gaaack, gaaack, gaaack.*

"On the day you want us to spy on your Phoenix meeting," Marshall said, pointing to the calendar, "we were all here. May 18, 2043 was the day after the travelers' candidates arrived at the Global Research Consortium campus. The day we signed our contracts and were officially confined to this facility for the next five years. We can't witness your meeting because our past counterparts won't be able to leave the complex."

"Actually," Lucre said, "it's not entirely true that everyone was here. At least one travelers' candidate of whom we are aware didn't arrive until two days later. There may have been others—"

"How do you have that fact at your fingertips?" Marta asked.

Lucre appeared flustered, but only for a moment. He fumbled to uncap his water bottle and drink again before answering.

"My predecessor as liaison here was a man named Andrew Gormly," Lucre said. "He became acquainted with a few traveler candidates and recalled a gentleman who said he became ill on his way here and was delayed."

"Andrew Gormly told you this?" Marta asked.

"He made a note in his files. Mr. Gormly kept meticulous files."

"And he was your predecessor? Where is this Gormly now?"

"Mr. Gormly resigned. The point is, we are aware of at least one candidate who was not here. There may be others."

"There aren't," Marta said. "Only one of the candidates was late. And we can't run a mission like this with a single traveler."

"You've occasionally recruited others beyond the original candidate pool," Lucre countered. "Some of the scientists and staff people. Perhaps one of them?"

"Why don't we just cut through the crap and *you* tell *me* who else was off campus on May 18?" Marta said.

Marshall was both surprised and comforted by the

undisguised hostility in Marta's manner. He glanced from her to Lucre and saw the man's eyes go cold.

"Why are you surprised we'd investigate this? We've had past issues concerning the objectivity of travelers chosen for critical missions. Some of you have political agendas tainting your judgment. We have a huge investment here."

"Who gave you access to personnel records?" Marta asked.

"We requested them from the subcommittee, and they complied." A sneer settled over Lucre's face, matching his tone.

"How about telling the rest of us what's going on here?" Marshall asked.

Marta placed her palms flat on the tabletop and leaned forward, her eyes locked on Lucre. "He's talking about Frank. I remember Sheila telling me the story. Remember she and Frank hung out together a little bit at the start? Frank arrived in Superior the night before we were supposed to be bussed here. He met some bimbo at a bar. They shacked up for a couple of days. Frank told the HR people he was late because he got sick, then overslept due to his medication. He had some bogus note from a doctor."

"I don't know the details," Lucre said. "I do know Frank Altman is a qualified traveler who was not confined to the GRC campus on the day of our Phoenix meeting."

"Frank Altman also left the program," Marshall said. "He took his money and ran."

"Mr. Altman is not a very good steward of his money," Lucre said. "Mr. Altman finds himself short of funds. He welcomes the opportunity to report for work."

"You've already talked to him?" Naomi asked.

Lucre leaned back in his chair and didn't disguise his smugness. "And to the subcommittee," he said. "We've formally requested that he be reinstated."

"Even so," Naomi said, "you don't have a viable mission. Have you ever met Frank Altman? With millions of dollars at stake, do you really want to rely on Frank? And who can you find to accompany him? A mission of this nature should involve a team of five, or even six."

"I'll remind you," Lucre said with a nod toward Groose, "the subcommittee has placed a high priority on this mission because of its funding implications. You people have solved the physics of time travel. Are you telling me you can't resolve something as simple as a conflict in dates?"

12

SEAN'S CHOICE

AS THE MEETING DISPERSED, Marshall felt Marta's hand on his arm, signaling him to wait. Gillis, too, hung back.

"Their plan is really pretty clever," Marta said. "They've constructed a situation allowing them to hand-pick their travelers unless we can get some other people off campus that first week."

"But why?" Marshall said. "And what if there isn't someone else who was gone on—"

"Oh, there was *someone*. Bet on it. As for why, I don't know yet. We can't let them get away with whatever they have planned, though. There's more involved here than just a conversation."

Marshall didn't understand. "If he's got his own travelers already, why does he need to sneak around this way?"

"Don't assume Frank is his guy," Gillis warned. "It could be someone from the scientific or technical teams. Gormly recruited Rose, remember, and relied on him to manage Frank. Of course, Frank wasn't bright enough to know he was being managed."

"Certainly, though," Marshall said, "Frank must be a prime suspect."

"To do what?" Marta's voice held a note of frustration. "That's what has me worried. This is the most innocuous mission anyone could contrive. We're sending travelers to eavesdrop on a conversation. They don't need a spy or an informant or a saboteur for a mission like that."

"I don't understand it either," Gillis said. "After our experience with Jason Pratt and Andrew Gormly, I'm not allowing Lucre benefit of any doubt, though. They will try and manipulate something. We *do* have some things going for us, though. Lucre has no idea we know the truth about Gormly. Lucre and the Hemisphere hierarchy think Gormly is a ticking bomb hiding somewhere, just waiting to extort them."

"We can go to the subcommittee, I suppose," Marta said. "We can explain our concerns without telling them the *whole* story."

"No, we can't," Marshall said. "And not just because we all might get in trouble for the Gormly-Pratt thing. We need the confusion of a big, complicated projection so we can hide our Sheila rescue mission. With Groose looking over our shoulders, that's our only chance to send Sean on his way."

"Which brings us back," Marta said, "to the question of travelers. Gillis, is there *any* way you can get two or three of us under the fence just a day after we've all arrived?"

"No. I can probably get myself out, so at least we'd have someone watching Frank and whoever else Lucre has found."

Marshall's heart sank. "So, we're stuck?"

"No," Marta said, snapping her fingers. "Why didn't I see this before? We have a much simpler solution. None of us comes onto campus to begin with. We *all* show up late."

"But if we're not on time to sign the contracts—" Marshall said.

"Nothing will happen," Marta said. "Frank showed up late and nothing happened to him. The rest of us, of course, are more responsible than Frank Altman. We cringe at the thought of being late for anything, much less a new job. Think about it, though. Think about Elvin's intractability of history. *We* are the travelers. *We've* made history in a spectacular way. We won't get washed out because we're a couple of days late."

"I don't know, Marta," Marshall said. "Not all of us believe Elvin's—"

Marta cut him off.

"None of it matters without Sean," Marta said. "Marshall, go. See if Sean still is willing to start his life over again."

June 8, 2046

Marshall did not arrive at Sean's apartment until late evening. After the long drive to Phoenix, several details needed attending to, just in case. So, Marshall could not enter Brookhaven through the front doors where a receptionist would record him as a visitor. Rather, he and Gillis chose an emergency exit just a couple of apartments along the corridor from Sean's place. Neither the entry lock nor its alarm was any match for Gillis's technological prowess.

Sean met Marshall's knock and said, "The answer is still yes. I want to do this, except . . ."

"Except..." Marshall experienced a sinking feeling in the pit of his stomach as he stepped inside.

"I understand I can't call my kids and grandkids to say goodbye. I understand that, as far as this world is concerned, this is the day Sean Brody dies. And that's okay. My sons have been attentive the last few years. We've said all the important things to each other. And this is how it would be if I was lucky and died of a heart attack or something else quick. One moment I'd be here, and the next I wouldn't. Just disappearing, though... with them never to know what happened? No resolution? That seems too cruel to me."

Marshall put his arm around Sean's shoulders and guided him to his chair.

"Gillis is waiting for us in the parking lot," Marshall said. "If you decide to come with us, here's what will happen. A car belonging to one of the other residents is way at the back of the lot. The owner no longer drives, and his car just sits there. Tragically, authorities will decide, when it was refueled, months ago, the hydrogen became contaminated."

"Um... okay."

"Now, I don't understand how all this works, but Gillis says he can induce the correct chemical reaction. While regular hydrogen is relatively safe, investigators will conclude from Gillis's constructed evidence that during all this time sitting there in the heat, a chemical reaction has occurred, enriching the hydrogen so it's like the really volatile gas we use to power the time projector. Anyway, this stuff is dangerous. Investigators will recognize it for what it is when they dissect the accident.

"Their conclusion will be that you suffered some

confusion—perhaps a small stroke resulting in a bout of dementia—and found your way to the parking lot, located a hidden spare key, and drove off into the desert east of town where an explosion will take place. When they follow the evidence, police will decide the car was a bomb waiting to go off, and in your confusion, you inadvertently saved the lives of many innocent people by taking it away."

"What about a body? You're not going to have to . . . kill someone else?"

"With an enriched hydrogen explosion," Marshall said, "there won't be enough left to find. As we leave tonight, you'll go to the parking lot and go through the motions of getting in the car and driving away. When police check the video from security cameras, they'll conclude what happened."

"Can I . . . can I take anything with me?" Marshall followed his gaze to a photo of Sean and his grandchildren. At that moment, Marshall knew he should warn Sean away. This whole scheme could unravel at any one of a hundred seams, and Sean's sacrifice would count for nothing.

Instead, he said, "No, Sean, you can't. And if you're doing this, we have to go."

13

FRANK ALTMAN RIDES AGAIN

June 15, 2046

"HEY, EVERYBODY," Frank smiled as he walked through the projection lab airlock for the first time in months. "It's great to be back!"

Marta glanced from Elvin's monitor where she, Gretchen and Marshall had been leaning over Elvin's shoulder, studying his latest data from the limbo.

"Yeah, right." She returned her gaze to the monitor.

"Come on," Frank said, striding across the room. "What's the deal here? I thought you guys wanted me back."

"No, Frank," Marta said. "Those guys—the suits at Hemisphere—wanted you back. We were getting along just fine."

Even though Marta generally despised Frank, she still felt the same initial reaction most women experienced with Frank. He was the male version of Sheila Schuler—drop-dead gorgeous. While Sheila's intellect had been every bit the equal to her looks, though, Frank was vacuous. Marta considered him a preening, egotistical buffoon capable of conquering new frontiers of narcissism, except he didn't know what the word meant, nor could he get the spelling close enough to look it up.

Seeing Frank, Marta again cursed the flawed traveler candidate selection process, a legacy of the original Global Research Consortium program. The GRC, a worldwide conglomeration of governments and corporations—all more comfortable with competing rather than cooperating— debated and micro analyzed and compromised over every undertaking. When they finally set the selection standards for choosing those who would travel through time, everyone was too tired to argue any longer. Hence, each government and corporate entity picked someone they wanted to have confined to an underground complex hidden in the Arizona desert for the length of their contracts.

"Just look around the office and see who you might want to be rid of for five years," Marta had told her old boss back at the British Secret Service, "and you'll understand the caliber of people we have here."

Marta had since learned that Frank, a Phoenix landscaper during his pre-time-travel days, was chosen by a corporate contributor whose wife enjoyed Frank's landscaping entirely too much. The corporate honcho offered Frank the opportunity to see what this remote secret project was all about. The mogul, who had relatives in the garbage business in New Jersey, made it clear this was an offer Frank could not refuse.

Marta glanced at Frank again. She mentally kicked herself because he saw her do it. He responded with the hint of a wink.

Frank possessed the body of a Greek statue. When he stood nude on the projection platform, he set hearts aflutter. Marta clearly recalled that many women seemed more than willing to set aside his inability to carry on a conversation. Frank suffered by comparison only when standing next to Marshall. Marshall's sheer size was one of the few things that seemed to damper Frank's ego.

"Hello, Frank," said Marshall as he cast a scolding glance at Marta. "Good to see you."

Marta watched Marshall step forward and offer Frank his hand. *Even under these circumstances,* she marveled, *when the man was someone who had often made fun of him, Marshall is incapable of being openly rude.*

"Gee, thanks, Marshall," Frank said. "At least someone hasn't forgotten their manners."

"I'm the boss now," Marta said. "Manners aren't in my job description."

"Hey, I don't know what your problem is. I didn't come to you, or whoever. They came to me. They asked if I would come back and after a lot of careful thought I—"

"Tell me, Frank, how does a person burn through two and a half million dollars in a matter of months? I don't think I could do that even if I tried."

"It wasn't two and a half. It was two point three. And . . . and . . . I'm not exactly sure. But it really wasn't all that hard. Anyway, here I am. So, do I have a job or not?"

"Yes." Marta said with a reluctant sigh. "You have a job."

"Great, well, I'm going to get something to eat."

"Ah, just like old times," Gretchen said as Frank walked away.

"We should at least be nice to him," Marshall said. "Even if—"

"Nice is overrated," Elvin said. "Now, can we please get back to the data? I think we've got this *Joey Bishop* thing nailed. We thought it happened when two versions of the same traveler met in the limbo. That wasn't it, though. After all these months of studying the data, Gretchen and I believe Carla O'Neill met herself at the interface between the limbo and the *Joey Bishop Show* universe. Since she did not survive, we can conclude that event set off the phase shift that killed the universe."

"Why would that trigger a phase shift?" asked Galen Postelwait, who had joined the conversation. Galen was the program's top theoretical mathematician.

"Any number of reasons," Elvin said. "My guess is this interaction disrupted the quantum shield."

Galen offered a puzzled expression.

"Quantum particles are constantly popping into and out of existence throughout space," Elvin said. "This creates quantum waves that spread over the entire vastness of space. And, we think, that's what causes the universe to keep expanding faster and faster, rather than—as the laws of regular physics would suggest—slowing down with the passage of time. The dark energy driving these waves *should* destroy everything they encounter. But something, some sort of quantum shield, keeps that energy contained. If we disrupted that *something . . .*"

"What are the probabilities of that happening again?" Marta asked. "The chance of a traveler meeting himself in the limbo is pretty remote. The odds against the two meeting at the interface of the limbo would seem to be astronomical. I mean, consider how many universes you guys think exist parallel to ours. And think how many projections all of us in all those universes have conducted since the time travel project began. And we've only fried one universe."

"That's one way of looking at it," Postelwait said. "If you

are assuming a statistical sample that is a finite number, you are correct. If your statistical sample is infinite, though, you come to an entirely different conclusion."

"Which is . . ." Marshall asked.

"The likelihood that every day, every hour, every minute, perhaps this event is occurring somewhere out there amid that infinity of possibilities, and universes are constantly being destroyed." He shrugged. "Who knows?"

14

THAT'LL BE THE DAY

SEAN WOKE TO THE CLATTER of equipment being moved through the gray corridor outside his hiding place. Last night's journey through the underground concrete labyrinth had left him disoriented.

Marshall and Gillis spirited him through the entry gates during dark early hours when the complex's aboveground building was deserted. Marta had the security staff's attention focused on a prearranged problem with power feeds to the projection lab cameras when, at Gillis's command, Elvin tripped a main breaker, and the entire facility went dark.

"Okay, we've got to move now," Gillis said.

A slight glow of ambient light filtered through the building's lobby. Sean shuffled carefully through the gloom, Gillis leading and Marshall trailing after them. The red glimmer of a battery back-up system lit the elevator as they plunged downward. When they came to a stop and the red light was swallowed as the elevator door shut behind them, Sean found himself immersed in total darkness.

"The only way to get across the complex without cameras catching us is doing it this way," Gillis told him. "I have only a single set of night vision equipment. I'll guide you and Marshall to the golf cart—each of you take my hand—and we'll be on our way."

The ride became a vertigo-inducing ordeal as the cart's electric whirr was the only sound and darkness so complete Sean felt as if his body continued to rotate and tumble as they completed each turn.

Finally, after guiding him to a bed and then helping him feel his way along a wall to a doorway where the bathroom was, they'd left him.

"I'll have the lights working as soon as I can," Gillis said, "but I need to get Marshall back to where he belongs and return the cart. The timing will depend on whether we have to hide from anyone along the way."

A clattering noise woke Sean to semidarkness offset by a glow seeping under what he remembered being the front door, and a bathroom light, which had been left on. Sean was uncertain whether he should investigate the noise outside or try to hide. The issue was resolved when a quick knock preceded a flood of light.

"I'm sorry if we woke you," Naomi said as he sat up. "Just checking to see that you're okay."

"Fine." He wouldn't admit to feeling a little confused.

"Sorry about the furnishings. We had to move stuff down from some of the other apartments. We're at the lowest and most outlying level of the complex. Even when we were fully staffed, this wing was pretty much deserted."

More clatter echoed from the hall. Marshall leaned through Sean's doorway.

"Okay, I think we've got it all." Marshall gave Sean a quick wave, which Sean returned. Gillis and Elvin stepped inside behind Marshall.

"We're moving things down a piece at a time," Naomi explained. "We don't want to draw Groose's attention. He counts everything. I'm installing a surgical suite next door so I can perform the necessary procedures to remove... well, you know. We're commandeering things from other medical labs throughout the complex."

"Okay," Sean said. "If you'll give me a few minutes, I'll get cleaned up and dressed."

"Of course." Naomi smiled.

A half-hour later Sean walked from the corridor's harsh lighting into a room containing a gurney, light stands and other medical equipment.

"So, you can do everything here?" he asked Naomi.

"Don't worry. By the time we get it all in place, this will be a completely functioning surgical suite, absolutely state-of-the-art. When they built this place, the government got the best of everything."

"We'll be down to see you as much as we can," Marshall assured Sean. "There's food and water and some beer in your refrigerator. Do you need any help with—"

Sean dismissed the suggestion with a wave. "I've been taking care of myself for a long time, Marshall. Go do what you need to do."

Elvin and Gillis took their leave. Marshall hung back for a moment, because he didn't want to interrupt Naomi just to tell Sean he would return as soon as he could.

"I'll be spending quite a bit of time with you here over the next few days," he heard Naomi tell Sean. "We must prepare you for the physical and psychological rigors of the journey ahead. I'll demonstrate some mental exercises to help you cope with the trauma of integration into your past self's consciousness. The first few hours will be the most dangerous, because of the massive information flow your past self will confront. We'll use hypnosis and another trick or two to help you regulate the flow of that mental exchange."

Sensing a break in the discussion, Marshall said, "Sorry for the interruption . . . I'm going to head back . . ."

"Would you stay a moment, Marshall?" Naomi asked.

"Um . . . okay."

"I have something to go over with Sean. I haven't discussed it with Marta or any of the others. But you need to understand this, Marshall, because this is your mission. I know we all want to find Sheila if we can. Without your persistence, though, your focus, I'm not sure we would have ever gotten here. And I know you . . . psychologically, I mean. I know you feel a heavy responsibility—guilt, for want of a better word—for recruiting Sean into the role he will play."

Marshall felt a flutter at the pit of his stomach. He looked at the jumble of chrome instruments, electrical monitors and IV stands and understood Sean would, essentially, die here in a few days.

Sean stepped to the gurney and with some effort, boosted himself carefully onto its taut white sheets. He wobbled slightly in the process. Marshall moved forward to catch him should he fall. With Sean safely settled, Marshall hoped he hadn't embarrassed the old man by implying that Sean couldn't perform the maneuver by himself.

Sean only smiled at Marshall. Naomi hopped up beside him and took his hand. Marshall found a chair and pulled it closer to the bed.

"In this journey, Sean," she said, "I think you will deal with a set of issues that none of our other travelers has encountered."

A slight quaver in her voice betrayed her concern.

"If this was a typical projection—as if there is such a thing—I would say you should have three or four days before you lose memory of your future life . . . awareness of your future self. I want to be completely honest with both of you, though. We can't depend on that this time. I think everything will come down to whether that fifteen-year-old boy who is your past self wants you there at all."

"I don't understand," Marshall said. "We've never had problems with—"

"Yes, we have. Think back to Elvin's first experience, when he was visited by his future self during the *Joey Bishop Show* crisis. Elvin did not want to share himself. He fought the integration. Sheila had to tackle him and practically throttle him before he settled down."

"He did finally calm down and cooperate, though," Marshall said. "He didn't refuse—"

"That interface was between two beings of essentially the same age. The future-Elvin was only a few days older. They were both rational adults . . . well, okay, this is Elvin we're talking about. Semirational adults."

"I guess I don't see what you're getting at," Sean said.

"You are ninety-three years old, Sean. You will be integrating with the mind of a fifteen-year-old boy. In our other projections, one thing that's mitigated the trauma, I think, is that both entities have a shared-life experience . . . shared values. Even though the future entity may be a few years older, they *are* the same person. While the past entity may not understand fully what's going on, there is a level of . . . eventual trust . . . of recognition that smooths the way.

"However, fifteen is probably the most irrational, hormone-driven age in the life of a male Homo sapien. Your experiences over ninety-three years have shaped your values, your feelings, your intellect far beyond the person you were as a teenager, so common ground will be difficult to find. Almost certainly, your values will be at odds with his. The last thing a fifteen-year-old wants to listen to is a mature voice of reason. And many of his instincts will seem to you reckless and irresponsible."

"When I went back ten years to my hometown," Marshall protested, "we got along fine."

"Did you? Can you honestly say the young Marshall willingly did everything you directed him to? Remember, you and he both were in love with Samantha. You had that shared investment in common, and still, you told me during your debriefing that past-Marshall expressed anger a couple of times at the realization he would be left to live with the consequences of what you were asking him to do, while you got to return to your future and not worry about it."

Marshall realized Naomi's assessment was accurate.

"Amanda Page is someone the fifteen-year-old Sean Brody doesn't know well. So, he doesn't have a compelling reason to go along with our plan. And we haven't really considered that our past selves might not have been willing participants in the tasks we've required of them during some of our previous missions.

"I've thought a lot about my own projection experience and the reaction of my past counterpart. I've extensively interviewed all the travelers. The experience of being joined—especially for the first time—is overwhelming. Not only does it create an initial state of total confusion for a host entity, that experience can be terrifying."

Naomi smoothed the sheet on the gurney beside her, allowing both Sean and Marshall a moment to digest her words.

"Psychologically," she continued, "I believe this initial experience temporarily renders a past being incapable of making an independent decision about his or her participation in whatever that mission requires. I think the past being is so intimidated, he or she will do whatever the future being tells them, whether they might want to or not."

And Marshall saw it. "But the hosts eventually begin to question, don't they?" he said.

"Right. And, in due course, they begin to squeeze that future being out of their consciousness altogether. After all, they are the stronger of the two. They are flesh and blood beings who live physically in that space . . . the ones who own that body."

"We've always assumed that fading awareness of our future selves is just a natural occurrence, a matter of time," Marshall said. "Are you saying the past being is actually making a decision not to let us stay?"

"Once the past being is over the panic stage, I think that past being, either consciously or unconsciously, is completely capable of pushing his or her future counterpart into some primitive and unused portion of the brain where that future being either perishes or—we hope—lies dormant."

"So, this kid might not want me there?" Sean asked.

Sean sensed the burden weighing on Marshall as the younger man left the cluttered surgical suite.

"He needs to understand," Sean said to Naomi, "I *want* to do this."

"Yes, he does. But I'm not sure he will. Marshall is not a man who is casual in his friendships. Once he grants that gift to someone, he sees it as a binding trust."

"He sees me as that kind of friend?"

"Very much so."

Sean offered a solemn nod and looked carefully at the woman seated on the gurney beside him. He wondered if she was even five feet tall. Her oriental mystique was punctured when she spoke. Not a trace of accent. She had the gift of . . . empathy? More than that, though. Sean felt as comfortable—and comforted—with her as he'd ever been with anyone.

"So, what are my odds? Not of survival. I don't worry about that. If I'm dead, I'm dead. What are my chances of living a different life . . . if I get that far?"

"None," Naomi said with a shake of her head and an ironic laugh. "I'm sorry. I told you I would be honest. I mean, I believe we have to do this. And, like Marshall, I'm grateful for your . . . sacrifice. Based on all the hard evidence we've seen, though, I think the answer has to be no. You've heard of the butterfly effect?" she asked him.

Sean's uncertainty was evident in his facial expression.

"The idea that, somewhere in the distant past, if a butterfly fluttered its wings at a different instant of time, that barely perceptible breath of a breeze would set in motion a chain of events changing everything. All of history would be different. Well, I think that's a crock. You could fly a jumbo jet through the corridors of the past and history wouldn't budge."

Her voice trailed off for a moment before she added, "We've been completely unsuccessful at changing anything except a few incidental details of the past . . ."

Sean heard the upturned lilt of a question at the end of that sentence, however. And although his journalism career had been a long time ago, he was still a perceptive interviewer. "There's a 'but' in there, though?"

"I must admit," she continued, "this whole thing about coincidence bothers me. The coincidence of you being native to the same town and going to high school with Sheila's grandmother. Your past relationship to Cecil and *his* very unlikely connection to this program. The hope that we're all being manipulated by something we can't account for through our scientific or medical experience is tempting. That's just too . . . mystical for me to accept, though."

Sean nodded. They sat quietly for a while.

"If you *could* change just one thing about the past," Sean asked, breaking the silence, "what would it be?"

"How would *you* answer that question?"

"Typical psychiatrist." He laughed.

"Really. I want to know."

"I know you're hoping for something profound," Sean said, "something sweeping. Like Miss America wishing for world peace." He shook his head and smiled. "I'm afraid I'm a lot shallower than that."

"You want to be rich?"

"No." Sean ran his hands over the crisp white sheets pulled taught under the gurney's mattress. "Portales, my hometown, is sixty miles from a place called Lubbock, Texas. Now, you're a young woman from China, so you probably won't understand this. Back when I was young, there was a kid from Lubbock named Charles Hardin Holly. He was a singer and a songwriter who died in a plane crash when he was only twenty-three years old.

"He died when I was too young to be aware of the emerging era of rock and roll. But I heard his music a few years later and learned that he recorded a lot of his stuff at Norman Petty's studio just twenty miles away in Clovis. So, I was a big fan.

"His formal career lasted a total of one and a half years. But during his brief life, he wrote some of the most amazing music you can imagine and was a profound influence on many of the most successful performers to emerge during the sixties and seventies. Just before he died, he created this wonderful song—for my money, the best love song anybody ever wrote—called *True Love Ways.*"

Sean smiled and closed his eyes, recreating in his mind the first haunting acapella notes of that ballad with Buddy's tenor voice reaching down to hit a lower register: *Just you know why . . .*

"You listen to a song like that, and you can't imagine how anyone with such little life experience could have produced something so beautiful, so haunting, so understanding of that elusive emotion we call love. And I've always wondered, when a creative genius dies young, just how much does that cost all the rest of us?"

Sean sighed and peered back at a time so far and so simple that, even in memory, he could hardly glimpse it in the distance.

Naomi waited.

"If I had the chance to change anything," Sean finally said, "I guess I'd tell Buddy to stay on the bus."

"Well," Naomi smiled and punched him lightly on the arm, "that'll be the day."

Sean grinned back, only a little surprised. "Yep," he said. "That'll be the day."

15

MURDEROUS INTENT?

"WHO IS IT, AND WHY?" Marta asked, her voice a little slurry.

She, Gillis and Marshall sat at a darkened table in a far corner of the Time Warp. Since Marta had restricted everyone to the campus during preparation for the Hemisphere mission, activity at the saloon had perked up again.

Tending bar became a voluntary thing, but the jukebox still worked as did the old disco ball glittering above the dance floor. About a dozen others were here, a rotating cast of characters coming and going, the music loud.

Marta suffered a sour taste in her mouth when she walked through the door with Marshall and found Phillip Lucre sharing a table with Galen Postelwait and a couple of female technicians.

Gillis stood behind the bar.

"And what'll it be for the two of you?"

"How about a mojito, Marshall?" Marta suggested.

"Never again," Marshall replied, recalling the misery of a rum-induced hangover during a recent trip to the Caribbean. "I'll have cranberry juice, please."

Marta glanced again at Lucre and said to Gillis, "Make

mine a boilermaker. Get something for yourself and join us."

"A boilermaker?" Marshall wondered as he followed Marta to a three-stool high top located as far as they could get from Lucre's group.

"Been a long week" Marta said. "I need some help this evening."

Gillis set a glass of juice before Marshall and put a mug of beer and a shot glass of bourbon at Marta's elbow.

"Depth Charge," Marta said.

She smiled at the men, dropped the shot glass into her beer mug and drank the whole thing with one long chug.

She slammed the mug down and smiled at two sets of arched eyebrows. The tension she felt walking this tightrope of politics, secrecy and betrayal was taking its toll. She craved relief.

Gillis wore a bemused smile.

Marshall seemed worried.

"What?" she said. "I was thirsty."

She directed Gillis to bring her another. Marta had to come up for air three times before she finished this one, then motioned for Gillis to slide his chair close. She posed her question. "So, who is it and why?"

Gillis shook his head. "I don't know, Marta. Believe me, I've been working on it. I've seen no more evidence of Lucre communicating with anyone. Which probably means he recruited his cohort before we started tracking him. If they don't communicate again, I'm not sure we'll know until it's too late."

"What about Frank?"

"Lucre, or someone from Hemisphere, was obviously in

contact with Frank before he came back. So, the whole computer disk thing could have been a sham just to steer us away from Frank. Think about it, though. Would you choose Frank?"

"Okay, how about Leonard?"

"Too obvious," Gillis said. "I don't think so. Besides, he's scared to death of you."

"Have you looked at the money?"

"Money?" Marshall asked.

"Yes. Lucre will likely pick someone who's either in financial trouble or just plain greedy," Marta said as she enjoyed a warm glow flushing through her body. "So, we're back to Frank."

"Again, that's pretty obvious," Gillis said. "Everyone knows Frank blew his money. To the extent that I can, I've checked the others. Nothing else jumps out. Elvin would be my first choice along those lines. I think he plays some pretty high stakes blackjack in Las Vegas every chance he gets. He could have dug himself a hole there."

"Elvin wins at blackjack," Marshall said. "He wins so much, they ban him from playing. He's always complaining about—"

"They've black-balled him because he's a good player," Gillis said. "That doesn't mean he always wins. And how do you know he wins?"

"Well, he says he wins."

"If every gambler won who says he won," Gillis said, "Las Vegas would have gone tits up years ago."

"So, we can't eliminate him." Marta's glow morphed into a buzz that began to soothe the back of her brain. She heard herself slurring her words. "And he's someone who could really do something to manipulate a mission."

Gillis shook his head. "I'm leaning toward a traveler. The best way to disrupt a mission is if you're on the ground."

"Before we head in that direction, what about Gretchen or Naomi?" Marta asked.

"Wait a minute," Marshall interrupted. "They're our friends. Surely, you can't suspect them."

"First rule—suspect everyone." Marta poked Marshall in the chest with her index finger as the effects of the alcohol continued to multiply. "And don't call me Shirley."

Marshall looked confused. Marta giggled.

"Marshall," Gillis said as he shook his head and smiled, "you have done wonders for this woman."

"Um ... okay."

"Let's shift to the why part," Marta enunciated carefully. "Why recruit anyone to do anything evil or handed-under, um ... dander-hundred ... shitty to begin with? What is it about this meeting ..."

"Of course, this wasn't a meeting they publicized, so few public records are available to check," Gillis said. "I did, though, find a news release including an interesting name."

Gillis glanced quickly around the room. He withdrew his pocket computer and pushed a couple of buttons, screening its three-dimensional image from the vision of anyone beyond their table. The virtual keyboard popped into view. He accessed a brief news story and photo dated May 18, 2043.

Marta and Marshall slid around to see the screen and read silently.

"Former Ohio Governor and rumored Presidential candidate

Benjamin Franklin Dobler made an unannounced stop in Denver today. Several reporters covering Mayor John Williams's daily press briefing at City Hall recognized Dobler. The former governor and Williams were college roommates at Ohio State University. Dobler refused comment regarding his future political plans and said his visit with Williams was 'purely social.' "I serve on the board of the Hemisphere Investment Group," Dobler said, "and I'm here to attend a meeting. I just wanted to stop by and say hello to the mayor while I'm in town."

The story continued with a brief background of Dobler's political career and speculation about his role as an unannounced aspirant to the Republican presidential nomination.

"Wow," Marshall said. "President Dobler was at this meeting?"

"Of course, he wasn't president then," Gillis said.

"So maybe he's what this mission is about?" Marta said, poking Marshall's chest again.

"Probably just a coincidence," Marshall said. "If he's not one of the guys in the hallway, he doesn't have anything to do with what we're looking for."

"You don't think they could be that stupid, do you, Gillis?" Marta slurred.

Gillis stared at her for a long moment.

"What would be the point?" Gillis said. "He's their guy. Their board member. What could be better for the Hemisphere Investment Group than Benjamin Dobler as President?"

"And how would they possibly think they could get away with it?" Marta wondered, looking again across the room at Lucre, whose arm now rested along the shoulder of the woman next to him as he laughed. "How could a traveler possibly think he or she could get away with it?"

"Ah, that's the beauty of time travel," Gillis said. "A traveler *could* get away with it. He wouldn't be risking himself. He'd be risking his past counterpart from another universe."

"The past counterpart would never go along, knowing what jeopardy he'd be putting himself in," Marta said. "Remember, he's the one who has to physically do the deed. And he's the one who has to live with the consequences."

"Yes," Gillis agreed. "Not to mention all the evidence that you just can't change the past life of a major historical figure."

"Get away with what?" Marshall asked. "What are you guys talking about?"

Gillis and Marta said simultaneously, "Assassination."

Marta and Marshall left Gillis at the Time Warp. Marshall helped guide Marta—who was wobbly and bumping into walls—back to their apartment. They had removed interior walls from several apartments in one of the housing corridors and were turning the place into an urban warehouse-style living space.

The biggest problem with combining apartments was they now had three Happy Home Companions to deal with instead of one. A corporate contributor to the early time travel project funding specialized in artificial intelligence and had equipped the underground apartments with their Happy Home Companion software. The company's representative described the installation as corporate generosity. Marta figured the whole thing was really some kind of beta testing.

The software bestowed each apartment with a voice and personality that was supposed to adapt to its resident and be a helpful, encouraging and entertaining entity. Their specialty was "bucking up" their human during his or her five-year term in the underground labyrinth making up the Global Research Consortium campus.

Marta hated her companion and, try as she might, could find no way to turn it off. So, she intimidated it into silence through psychological warfare. Although her association with Marshall had softened this aspect of Marta's personality, she still couldn't bring herself to be civil to a bunch of microchips.

The combined apartments were terrified.

"Where is she?" they asked Marshall each time he came home alone.

"Um . . . she'll be here in a minute. Is there anything I—"

"She hates us, Marshall Grissom. Why does she hate us?"

This put Marshall on the spot. Marta did hate them. But it was not in Marshall's nature to be blunt or cruel even with a virtual being.

"Um . . . no. No, she doesn't hate you. She's just having a bad . . . decade. Your program includes patience, doesn't it?"

"Our program does, Marshall Grissom, but she threatened to fill our orifices with epoxy if we speak to her again."

"You don't have orifices," Marshall said.

"Yes, well, we're not sure we want to take the chance."

"Back to patience," Marshall said. "Hang in there for

another decade or so. I'm sure she'll come around and you can fulfill your programming."

As Marta and Marshall entered the apartment, Marta offered a preemptive caution. "I'm warning you! Not one word!"

Silence.

Marta smiled a triumphant smile.

"You can't be serious about this assassination and conspiracy stuff," Marshall said as he sat on their bed and watched Marta undress. "It's got to be a coincidence."

"Could be. Remember, though, you can never trust coincidence."

With a big yawn and stretch, she stood nude before him.

"The thing is," Marta continued, "if you wanted to kill a major political figure, this would be the ideal time— before Secret Service protection. Before crowds and entourages. While he's still just an ex-governor."

"But how can you think anyone here could do such a thing?" Marshall asked, doing his best to remain focused on the issue at hand. "Even Elvin. As much of a jerk as he can be at times, he's still a decent guy. And Frank? Frank's a full-blown narcissist with the attention span of a turnip, but he's not a killer."

"Anyone is capable of anything," Marta said, running her hands over her body and doing a slow 360-degree turn. "Personally, I suspect it's the work of the diabolical Dr. Dingus Doonaughty."

"Um ... do you want to keep talking about this?" Marshall asked. "Or do you want to do something else?"

16

THE SEARCH CONTINUES

June 18, 2046

"HERE'S THE TEAM THAT WILL conduct the Hemisphere mission," Marta announced.

"Marshall and Gillis, of course—"

"I don't understand," Phillip Lucre interrupted. "As you told us a few days ago, Mr. Grissom and Mr. Kerg were already confined to the GRC campus by the time this meeting took place."

"And your response," Marta said, "was, if we could figure out how to travel through time, we should certainly be able resolve a conflict of dates. Well, we did. We also made it clear to you that we would not conduct a mission with a single traveler."

"Mr. Altman was not the only experienced traveler to have been absent from the GRC campus on that date," Lucre protested. "Talking over drinks last night, I learned Galen Postelwait had been in Phoenix that weekend. So, he will already be near the site of the—"

Marta had wondered how Lucre would finesse Galen into the picture. She'd suspected Lucre had someone else up his sleeve all along. She had tasked Gillis with tracking down who among those remaining program participants had been

147

off campus May 18, 2043. Gillis had required only a matter of hours hacking into personnel records to pinpoint Postelwait.

"The rest of the team," she said, cutting Lucre off, "will be Frank, Macy and Dr. Leonard Rose."

"I wasn't aware Dr. Rose was a qualified traveler." Lucre stood and spread his arms wide in a gesture of frustration.

Several others mumbled agreement.

"I believe," Galen said, "if a member of the scientific team will participate, I should have priority over Dr. Rose. And I thought he was excluded from the mandatory mission because of a pacemaker."

"That's what he claimed," Marta said, guiding a suspicious gaze from Lucre to Galen and back to Lucre again. "We've learned he doesn't have a pacemaker after all. Naomi and her team didn't check Leonard's medical records. They just took his word for it. By chance, Naomi recently came across some of those records. Leonard made it all up to keep from participating."

Marta glanced to the far end of the table where Leonard sat. She was beginning to think this man she'd despised for so long might have some redeeming qualities after all. During the early days of the project, Leonard had suffered a burning jealousy of Gretchen Allen and Elvin Detwyler, considering neither his intellectual equal. That envy had led him to an arrangement with Andrew Gormly. Rose acted as Gormly's internal spy, and Gormly used his political influence to have Rose named second-in-command of the physics group.

Although Rose did not know Gormly planned to kill Sheila Schuler, he helped lure her to the projection lab on the night of her disappearance. Since that time, at every juncture, Rose had demonstrated his remorse by working hard and doing what he could to assist in the search for Sheila. The only time he balked was when Marta dictated that all members of the scientific team would undergo a projection.

"I've done my best to work hard here and contribute to the effort," he had said privately to Marta. "I think this program is important, and I wish to continue. I am genuinely sorry for what happened to Ms. Schuler. If I get on that platform, though, orchestrating an accident would be easy for you and then you'd be rid of me. Which would solve a problem, wouldn't it, Ms. Hamilton?"

Marshall had convinced Marta to let Leonard claim to have a pacemaker, which would make it impossible for Leonard to survive a projection.

"Dr. Rose," said Groose, "is this true? You lied about having a pacemaker?"

Leonard nodded, and bowed his head as a show of contrition.

"So why," Groose said to Marta, "are you assigning him to this mission? I don't see why you simply don't remove him from the program."

"The only condition under which I will *not* remove him Marta said, "is if he accompanies this mission. I required all the key members of the science and technology staff to undertake a projection, because as a traveler, I consider it essential for the scientists and engineers to know what travelers experience.

"I think both Gretchen and Elvin will tell you that Leonard has made valuable contributions to the physics group. He wants to continue his research here, and frankly, he would be difficult to replace. So, I'm overlooking his lie, and giving him this opportunity to—"

"Why this of all missions?" Lucre demanded. "We can't afford any slip ups. And clearly Dr. Postelwait is more qualified. Can't you project Dr. Rose at some other time?"

He appealed to Groose with a shrug and a glare.

"Mr. Groose does not make the personnel decisions around here," Marta said. "Mr. Groose's role is to see that we adhere to the subcommittee's mission profile guidelines. And as you have said to us several times, Mr. Lucre, this is a completely innocuous mission. Go back, listen to a conversation. We are sending five people. More than enough to handle the task and help Dr. Rose through the trauma of integration as well. Dr. Rose need not even go to the meeting. He will pose no distraction. I think the subcommittee would much prefer we piggyback Dr. Rose on a simple mission such as this one, rather than create an entire projection just to get him the experience I believe is critical."

"Then why not send Dr. Postelwait, too?" Lucre asked. "The more, the merrier."

Again, Marta glanced from Lucre to Postelwait.

"No problem," she said. "Galen, you're in."

"So," said Marshall as he followed Marta and Gillis into Marta's office and pulled the door closed behind him, "now that we know who Lucre's guy is, why did you agree to let him participate?"

"I wouldn't be so quick to draw the obvious conclusion," said Gillis.

Marshall frowned. Every time he thought he had things figured, Gillis or Marta would point out that he was allowing himself to be victimized by the obvious.

"Why else would Lucre insist on Galen?"

"Cover," said Marta. "He could be trying to steer us away from someone else."

"I've looked carefully at Dr. Postelwait, along with all the rest of you," Gillis said. "There's nothing about his background or current financial circumstance that appears to make him vulnerable to any coercion from Lucre."

"Wait. You checked my financial circumstances, too?" Marshall asked. "Just what else did you look at?"

"Oh, we investigate very thoroughly," Marta said. "The age of digital information is a wonderful thing."

"How closely?" Marshall asked.

"Well, I know all about that notebook computer you kept under your bed when you were a teenager, and those 'frequently visited' web sites," Gillis said. "I can give you a list if you like."

"Marshall!" Marta said with a tone of shock and disgust. "You didn't . . . you don't mean to tell me that you . . . you touched yourself?"

Marshall shook his head. Gillis and Marta laughed.

"Okay, okay," Marshall said. "I'm glad I can be of some amusement to the two of you. But we were talking about Galen."

"Yes, we were," Marta said.

"Maybe he's like what you said before. Maybe he's just greedy."

"Maybe. He will certainly bear continued investigation. And we'll keep watching everyone else, as well."

She peered at Marshall with a mischievous smile. "And now that I know about your youthful indiscretions, I think we may have to look a little harder at you as a security risk."

"Security risk? Me?"

"Yes . . ." Marta said. "If you have a sordid sexual past, you're vulnerable to blackmail."

"Who would want to blackmail me?"

"You never know." Marta added a lascivious wink. "What'll you give me to keep quiet?"

17

A CRISIS OF CONSCIENCE

June 20, 2046

THE PRICE OF MARTA'S SILENCE offered Marshall a suitable distraction over the next week as the calendar marched toward projection day. The Hemisphere mission, which would provide cover for Sean's journey to his youth, was scheduled for the twenty-first of June. The point of no return was the surgical removal of Sean's implants twenty-four hours prior to the projection.

And with each passing day, Marshall's conscience was tugged like a wishbone at Thanksgiving dinner.

He knew the issue of coincidence made Marta, Gillis and the scientists wary, as if they were missing something. As if they weren't seeing the clues, or obvious scientific truth, and that their oversights would lead to some disastrous event they *should* have anticipated.

To him, though, the coincidences only offered assurance. Some mysterious something *was* at work here, and this mission would succeed . . .

Maybe.

Then doubt and insecurity gnawed at him again. The others were smart, experienced, expert, and he was . . . Marshall.

Finally, only hours before Sean's surgery, Marshall walked down the long corridor to Sean's quarters to see the old man for a final time. Before Marshall could knock at the door, though, Naomi beckoned him to the mini operating suite. She wore her surgical scrubs.

"What are you planning to say to him?" Naomi asked, her dark eyes imploring.

"I . . . I'm going to say thank you."

Naomi paused, as if calculating the weight of her next statement. "I guess I'm a little disappointed."

Marshall didn't understand. "Why?"

"You need to let him off the hook, Marshall. I thought you'd come to that conclusion by yourself. He needs to know he doesn't have to do this, and I think you're the only one who can give him that permission. At first, he saw this mission as a big adventure. Now, when for all he knows he'll be dead tomorrow, he might have second thoughts. But Sean is very concerned about . . . well . . . not letting you down."

Marshall glanced around the suite, his gaze passing a tray containing gleaming medical tools. He quickly looked away. "We've come so far. This is the only chance . . ."

"I think I understand you pretty well," Naomi said. "You've done all this for Sheila, not because of some crush you have, or because of some lustful obsession, or because you want to manipulate her somehow. She was your friend, and friendship is a very powerful obligation to you. Please think about this, though. Sean is your friend, too. I've watched the two of you. I've talked to him. There's a very real connection there. And I'm afraid for you. You've burdened yourself with the guilt of Samantha's death and the loss of Sheila. Now, you're setting yourself up for the same obsessive grief where Sean is concerned."

With Naomi's diagnosis swirling through his mind, Marshall attempted a protest. "Sheila is . . ." He found he couldn't complete the thought.

"Sheila is young," Naomi said for him. "And Sean is old. Society values youth over age. You need to be careful, though. I'm not sure you, in your heart, can live with having made that distinction."

Marshall had no answer. He felt torn by an impossible dilemma. So, he said nothing, wheeled abruptly, then knocked at Sean's door.

The old man smiled at his friend.

Marshall felt his eyes glisten with tears.

Sean pulled him inside. "Hey, don't worry. For the first time, maybe ever, I feel as if I'm embarking on a genuine adventure. I'm not taking the safe road this time."

"No," Marshall said. "No, you're not . . . listen, Sean, I just want to say . . . you don't . . . you don't . . . I just want to say . . . thank you."

He clasped Sean's brittle frame in a fierce embrace.

"And I told them," he whispered, "that you're allergic to anchovies. So, they won't . . . well . . . anyway . . ."

Then he turned to see Naomi standing behind them.

She gave Marshall one last imploring look, sighed deeply, then said, "Sean, it's time."

Marshall set off through the maze of corridors, brooding

over his failure. Naomi was right. He should have . . . and now it was too late. A wave of helplessness overtook him, and he realized how bone-weary he was of that feeling. So, he became angry. Anger was an emotion Marshall revealed to almost no one. Acting or speaking out of anger, his mom had drilled into him, only compounded problems. Not that he didn't get angry. His anger was just a private thing he kept in check. At this moment, though, it offered an alternative to his guilty sense of helplessness, and he let that animal's venom simmer, then boil.

He paid scant attention to where his hike took him until he saw the figure of a man emerge far down a long gray corridor. Marshall began to compose himself. He looked at signs on the doors and numbers stamped into walls at his current location. As the man drew nearer, the task of taming his anger became more difficult.

"Mr. Grissom," said Phillip Lucre, "you seem to be wandering far afield today."

Marshall took a deep breath and answered carefully. "Yes, well, I like to walk before a mission. Helps with the tension."

Marshall's inclination was to keep going. Instead, he stopped. "I don't think your status as a corporate liaison allows you to be . . . What are *you* doing here, Mr. Lucre?"

"I confess that, at times, I get lost in this maze of tunnels," Lucre said with his unctuous smile. He made a show of studying his surroundings. "I'm oriented now, though. So, good day."

Lucre continued toward an adjoining corridor.

Again, Marshall's instinct was to just leave it alone. Something, though, about Lucre being all the way out here, roving the uninhabited reaches of the sprawling complex raised Marshall's hackles. And Marshall hated the helplessness.

"Mr. Lucre!" he called sharply.

The man stopped, turned, then peered back at Marshall, surprise and question on his face.

"Those people who will be on that projection platform tomorrow are my friends," Marshall said.

Lucre cocked one eyebrow. "I'm glad you get along with your coworkers."

"Sheila Schuler was my friend, too. I don't want any more of my friends to get hurt."

Marshall felt he could hold the stare they exchanged forever. In the end, Lucre simply turned and walked away.

Marta regarded the somber gathering before her.

"Someone," she said, "has been paid off by Phillip Lucre to somehow manipulate this mission. Gillis has been working hard to discover who. So far, we've had no success. And because of that, we can't rule out any one of you."

This final gathering of conspirators took place in an empty administration building office. The late hour precluded anyone, other than a skeleton security crew, from being anywhere nearby. Marta told security the gathering was a last-minute planning session of key personnel. Gillis brought along his magical device, which soaked up electronic emissions and protected them from snooping cameras or microphones.

The group processed Marta's statement with an uncomfortable silence. She watched them struggle with the concept. None of them, she knew, wanted to believe the worst about people with whom they had endured so much.

Marshall. Gillis. Elvin. Gretchen. Naomi and Leonard.

Along with her, they formed the conspiracy to find Sheila and thwart the Hemisphere Investment Group. Discovery of their plans and actions would certainly cause their dismissal from the project. More likely, though, Marta considered as she scanned from face to face, was criminal prosecution by the oversight subcommittee via a trial that would not be held before a jury of their peers. They inhabited a realm that did not exist—and could not exist without several of the world's most significant governments making some painful and embarrassing public revelations. Any punishment dealt to them would be just as clandestine as the program to which they had devoted their lives for these past several years. They would simply disappear. Whether they ever emerged from their incarceration would be left to the conscience and whim of politicians and bureaucrats who presided over these secrets.

And now the conspirators learned that one among them might have already chosen a path of betrayal.

They were beginning to sweat, but Marta attributed that to the warmth of the small room as the building absorbed desert heat. All these people were accustomed to cool air circulating through underground rooms and corridors.

Elvin challenged Marta's assertion. "How do you know that?" he said. "What proof do you have?"

Marta deferred to Gillis.

"Everything is circumstantial, Gillis said. "We can't prove a case against anyone. However, I've no question that something is amiss."

"Then who do you suspect?" Naomi asked.

"It could be anyone," Marta said.

"You must have some ideas," Gretchen prodded.

"Based on observation and investigation," Gillis said, "my top four candidates are Elvin, Leonard, Frank Altman and Galen Postelwait."

"I understand why you'd be suspicious of Leonard," Elvin said, wiping his forehead with his sleeve. "Why me?"

"You gamble. You could need a big payday to compensate for losses."

Elvin nodded. The air conditioner whined as it tried to keep up with heat generated by seven bodies occupying such a small space.

"That makes sense," Elvin conceded. "With all your digging, though, you didn't find any evidence of big financial losses on my part, did you?"

"While my investigations are thorough," Gillis said, "I would not fall into the trap of assuming they are infallible."

"May I say once again it's not me," Leonard Rose said. "I would hope that by now I've—"

"I'm sorry, Leonard," Marta said. "You'll always be at the top of the list. Your history makes you impossible to ignore. Nothing personal, though."

"Well, Frank is a pretty obvious candidate," said Gretchen. "Everybody knows he blew all his money. Why Galen?"

"Lucre is anxious to have Galen included," Marta said.

"I thought Galen's family had money," Elvin said.

"Yes," Gillis said, "they do. And that's the frustrating thing. I can make a case against all four of you, while at the same time, offer valid arguments to the contrary."

"So, we're just going to go ahead?" asked Gretchen.

"We have no choice," Marta said. "The subcommittee

has dictated we undertake this mission. We can't tell them anything about our concerns without getting ourselves in trouble. And our plans to find Sheila rest on this mission, as well. Naomi performed Sean's surgeries earlier today. Without his cardiac implants, we must get him safely to the past no later than tomorrow morning. So, as far as the Hemisphere projection, all I can ask is for everyone to be vigilant. Expect someone to try something. And Elvin, I hope it's not you, because you're facing a very challenging day tomorrow. I'll hate having to be suspicious if anything goes wrong."

"I can't help what you might suspect," Elvin said. "Even with all of us making our very best efforts, there will be plenty of opportunity for things to go wrong. A simultaneous projection with two widely different time and dimensional destinations will be really tricky."

Again, Marta held Gillis and Marshall back until the others had gone.

Marta told Gillis she was vetoing his suggestion that the travelers be sent back two days prior to the Hemisphere meeting.

"Too much time to screw around," she said. "If Lucre's recruit is one of the travelers, two or three days give him or her too much time to prepare an ambush. I think we're better off if we get everyone there twenty-four hours prior to the meeting. May 17. For that time period, Gillis, we'll need to monitor everyone closely to be sure they don't communicate with some unknown confederate. I think everyone on our crew arrived in Superior that day and boarded the buses running to the site the next morning. Elvin will target an early morning arrival, and we'll gather everyone at one place so we can keep an eye on them that night. We'll limit any opportunities for someone to obtain a weapon or meet with anyone else."

"That's a good point," Gillis said. "Do you think Elvin can be that precise with the transfers? Especially with the distraction of getting Sean back to the 1960s at the same time?"

Marta knew she expected Elvin and Gretchen to do something that might not be possible. While the physicists had made great strides honing the accuracy of their projections, they still didn't understand time distortions caused while passing through the limbo. Projecting multiple travelers simultaneously did not by any means guarantee a simultaneous arrival.

"Elvin says we should expect variations up to a few hours. That's the best he can do."

Marshall appealed to Gillis. "Who is it? This is our last chance to . . ."

Gillis could only shrug.

"Your best guess," Marta said.

"I'd eliminate Elvin or Leonard first," Gillis said carefully. "Lucre couldn't have known you'd assign Leonard to the projection team. So, if it was Leonard, he'd have to do something on this end of the projection. And unless they are all working together, I don't see how Elvin or Leonard or Gretchen, for that matter, could do anything. Everybody is looking over everyone else's shoulders. And you've got all the recording devices. Pretty tough to cover your tracks."

"So, it's either Frank or Galen?"

"If I had to place a bet," Gillis said, "that's where my money would land."

18

WHERE THERE'S SMOKE . . .

June 21, 2046

"DOES ANYONE KNOW what's causing our delay?" demanded Lucre. "Does Ms. Hamilton need to be reminded of the importance of this mission? Don't we have a schedule to keep?"

"Actually, no," Elvin said, stabbing Lucre with a black look. "We have a time machine. We can make adjustments."

Lucre harrumphed and muttered something about *no way to run a railroad*, then slinked to his chair on the observation deck. Next, the second-most annoying intruder into Elvin's domain made himself heard.

"So where *is* Ms. Hamilton?" Upton Groose said with a huff. "The subcommittee has made the gravity of this mission clear. How can she be so cavalier as to be late?"

"With all due respect," Elvin said to the irritating little twit hovering over his shoulder, "if you don't shut up, I'll strangle you with that bow tie you're wearing. Some of us have to concentrate here."

"Well, I . . . I . . ." Groose made such a furious tablet notation, he broke the point of his pencil.

During his brief tenure at the HRI, Groose had managed to annoy nearly everyone. Wearing his tired business suit and bow ties, he wondered aloud at the informality of dress in the workplace. Although he had grudgingly accepted the reality that some people didn't dress at all.

He hovered. Like a stealth drone with his ever-present notepad and pencil. Although his job was to review mission profiles and monitor missions to assure compliance with oversight subcommittee guidelines, he could not tame the federal accountant within him. He was constantly complaining to Marta about laxity regarding work schedules, or the inefficiency of the maintenance staff, or the nonproductivity of physicists who were wont to sit for long periods staring at blackboards, or people who left lights on.

As irritated as he was with Groose, though, Elvin was pissed off by Marta's tardiness as well. Everyone stood ready to go. Some critical timing issues needed to be met if they were to pull this off.

Macy and Gillis had already made their last dash from the shower, expecting everything to pop as soon as they got to the lab. But not today. Today, the program administrator hadn't yet arrived.

"Um... I'm sure she's on her way," Marshall said, though he did not seem sure at all. Macy stood next to the platform, her face a mask of concentration and she tried to cling to the last vestiges of her orgasm. Frank and Galen sat at the edge of the platform with folded arms. Leonard Rose clutched his robe closed with such ferocity, his knuckles turned white.

Marta's voice flowed into the room. "Galen, you can stand down. You're not going anywhere today."

Elvin turned to see Marta, her dark skin and hair glistening, clearly the result of a careful pre-projection shower.

"What's going on?" Marshall asked with alarm.

"Galen's staying behind. I'm traveling instead."

Lucre jumped to his feet.

"Why are—" Galen began.

"Don't worry, Galen," Marta said. "You'll get mission pay for this one. I've made my decision, though. We're configured to project six people and one of them will be me. Now, let's get started."

"Marta," called Elvin, "hang on just a second. I need to recalibrate for your lifeline . . . Marshall and Gillis, I need to check yours, too."

Elvin moved from behind his computer monitors, pushing past a pouting Galen Postelwait. Frank and Macy stepped onto the platform and waited. Elvin carried a small electronic wand and waived it over Marta to a series of beeps.

"We're really cutting it close with the fireworks," he whispered.

"You'll have to adjust."

"Why'd you choose Galen and not Frank?"

"If it's Frank," she whispered, "he'll find a way to screw up whatever Lucre has planned. I've dealt with Frank during missions before."

"Are you sure about this?" Marshall asked.

"If I have any trouble, I know you'll help me. I have to do this, though. If something's going down, I need to be there."

"Okay, we're good," Elvin announced, returning to his station.

The six travelers shed their robes.

Groose averted his eyes.

Four of the travelers stood comfortable in their nudity.

On one end of the row, Marshall squeezed his eyes closed. Elvin guessed he was conjuring some horrific scene to substitute for the erotic image of his naked female companions—baby seals, perhaps, with large innocent eyes, being consumed by walruses. His effort, however, was failing.

At the opposite end of the row, Leonard Rose scrunched as low as he could, covering himself with both hands.

Elvin nodded to the technician next to him, who flipped a switch and pushed a throttle forward. A silent wave of glowing, pulsating plasma shimmered across two giant silver globes that bracketed the platform. Five travelers winked away. The sixth was lost behind an intense flash of light and a curtain of hot heavy mist that created a dense cloud when it hit the projection lab's cold air.

Elvin shielded his eyes as a mind-numbing light flashed with a crackle. He glanced quickly to Naomi and Gretchen, seeing that they, too, had taken precautions to protect themselves from the blinding jolt.

"What ... what happened?" Galen asked, blinking against the lab's spotlights reflecting off the fog, his eyes dilated to huge black dots.

"I don't know," Elvin said. "I think what I'm seeing here is some kind of feedback through the wormhole! We've got to evacuate while I check for radiation!"

"What about the travelers?" Groose asked, his voice pitched an octave higher than normal.

"Everything's gone off-line," Elvin said, "so I can't say what's happened to them. I just know they aren't here."

The fog's density increased and continued to swirl.

"Go on," Elvin said. "Leave here until I tell you it's safe."

"You'll need help getting things back online," said Gretchen. "I'm staying."

"And you'll need me to monitor the radiation levels," Naomi said.

"All right. Everyone else out! Now!"

Groose led the charge to the hallway, followed by Galen Postelwait and a half-dozen technicians.

"And close the airlock," Naomi called after them. "If we're getting radiation back through the wormhole, we've got to contain it!"

Elvin waited a couple of beats before he whispered, "Is everyone gone?"

"I think so," Naomi said. "Maybe we overdid the fog a bit. Leonard, are you there?"

"Yes," a disembodied voice called through the mist. "Somebody, hand me a robe. I'm not coming out without a robe."

Gretchen chose one of the garments and flung it into the haze. A moment later, Leonard emerged like the Creature from the Black Lagoon rising from the mist.

"Okay," Naomi said to him. "Help me with the floor panels."

Naomi hurried to a corner behind the projection platform wielding an electronic screwdriver. She quickly removed four screws anchoring one floor panel. Leonard pulled it away to reveal a narrow, corridor where pipes and cables ran.

Secreted in the crawl space, Sean Brody lay on a small stretcher, covered by a blanket, where Marshall and the others had carefully placed him before the projection crew arrived. Dropping to his knees, Leonard grabbed handles at one end of the stretcher. Naomi and Gretchen held the opposite end, and carefully raised Sean to floor level, then gently transferred him to the projection platform surface.

From his vantage point at the computer station, Elvin barely discerned Sean's huddled form under the blanket. But when the blanket was removed and they placed him onto the bare platform while the lab's air exchange system cleared away fog, gruesome details emerged.

Sean was no longer the spry old man whose eyes glowed with an interested sense of amusement at the world around him. His skin had acquired a papery, almost translucent thinness. A network of intravenous drip lines trailed into his arms. He wore a gray pallor courtesy of his rapidly failing heart. His head had been shaved to facilitate removal of the optical system that had been placed behind his eyes and right ear. He wore a pair of temporary glasses to facilitate failing vision. Naomi gently pulled the glasses away along with bandages covering wounds stitched loosely closed with organic thread. She carefully extracted needles attached to each IV line. His chest had a deep gouge where the heart assisting hardware had been. His lower legs were attached only tenuously due to removal of his artificial knees.

A bulky set of headphones providing a noninvasive anesthetic was clamped over his ears. Elvin understood that electronic signals transmitted through the headphones targeted and confused pain centers of the brain, disrupting their neural messages. Still . . .

"I'm so sorry," Naomi said to Sean as she beheld his broken body, only a towel draped across his waist.

Leonard appeared pale and queasy as he turned to Elvin. "All the video feeds are off, right? We don't want anyone to see—"

"It's taken care of, Leonard. Every computer data tracking device is shut down."

"Okay, Leonard," Naomi said, "your turn."

Rose squeezed his bulk into the space vacated by Sean.

"It's a tight fit, I know," she said. "But hang in there. You've got water and a bag for . . . you know. Take the pills when things get too uncomfortable. They'll help. We'll get you out as soon as we can." Naomi and Gretchen replaced the floor panel.

"What pills?" asked Gretchen.

"Um . . . don't worry," Naomi said. "They're only slightly hallucinogenic. Leonard will enjoy his time in confinement."

Naomi bent to kiss Sean's forehead.

"Tell me when you're set," she called to Elvin, "so I can remove the pain blockers."

"Any time."

"Sean," she said. "This will really hurt. Hopefully, not for long."

Hopefully, thought Elvin. *Who knows, though, what will happen in the limbo. Isn't it just as likely the pain will persist for an unrelenting eternity?*

"Are you ready?" Naomi asked Sean.

Elvin barely heard his whispered response. "Yes. And

thank you. Tell Marshall this is what I want."

Naomi pulled away the headphones and leapt from the platform.

They waited ten more minutes before opening the outer door.

"Well?" demanded a frantic Upton Groose.

"I don't know what happened yet," Elvin answered, sounding as annoyed and anxious as he could. "Like I said before, I think we had some feedback through the wormhole somehow."

"I don't see any sign of a fire," Groose said.

"Because there wasn't one," Elvin said. "Just a cloud. Water vapor. Something about the cold temperature of the lab and warmer wet air that somehow siphoned in from . . . from out there somewhere. It'll take time to determine exactly what—"

"So, they're all okay?" Galen asked.

Elvin pointed to the array of monitors.

"At least five of them are," he said. "I've got good lifelines for everyone who got to *Gomer Pyle*."

"Who didn't make it?" demanded Galen.

"Leonard," Elvin said. "I've got a lifeline, but he ended up somewhere else. It's not that big a deal. We used to have this problem a lot."

"Not anymore, though," Galen protested. "We've been much more consistent in hitting our targets."

"Well, we didn't this time. Something happened here, and it will take a while to understand exactly what. Now, either be quiet and let me work, or go someplace else."

19

AMANDA

November 1967

AMANDA PAGE AND FOUR OTHER high school juniors piled from Amanda's station wagon and sprinted across the Portales High School parking lot. Lines at the service windows of Dub's Drive-In had been too long for the lunch hour to accommodate and, with half-finished drinks and taco burgers left scattered about Amanda's car, the girls feared they would not beat fifth period bell.

"Shit," Amanda said, "Miss Best will—"

"Don't swear," Amanda's best friend, Joni Miller, admonished as she hurried along next to Amanda. "That word is just so gross."

"Okay, then. Darn," Amanda amended, "Miss Best will nail our asses."

"Don't swear!" Joni repeated. "Butts. Miss Best will nail our butts."

An institutional gray sky portended snow. An unrelenting wind swept from the Texas Panhandle across eastern New Mexico's high plains, filling the air with dirt that pricked Amanda's skin like needles and cast a chill that made her hunch into herself. In these parts, such a storm is called a blue norther.

Amanda pulled open heavy doors and the girls found refuge in an entry area that, until they shrugged off their winter coats, felt much too warm. Even hair spray with the consistency of glue couldn't protect their bouffant hairdos, and each had suffered a calamitous collapse of coiffure. The first bell had already rung, and the hallway emptied quickly. Amanda saw hands on a big clock suspended from the ceiling take an ominous jump as it counted minutes before they'd be declared tardy.

If she ran . . .

At the girls' restroom, though, Joni grabbed Amanda's sleeve and dragged her inside. The other girls followed.

"We could have made it!" Amanda said.

"We have to fix our hair," Joni said. The others tittered their agreement.

"I don't care how my hair looks," Amanda protested. "I don't want another tardy."

"Of course, you don't care how your hair looks," grumped Becky Ellis. "Nothing makes *you* look bad."

Becky said it with an offhanded laugh that didn't quite disguise her jealousy.

Each time Amanda stared into a mirror, she saw a blossoming beauty that made her uncomfortable. The transition from gawky, tomboyish teenager to genuine feminine splendor had been taking place over the past eighteen months.

Prior to this transformation, her athletic prowess had been Amanda's claim to popularity among her peers. Amanda swam, played golf and ran track through Amateur Athletic Union programs requiring her parents to spirit her away on weekends because, during the 1960s, Portales

Junior High and Portales High School offered no organized sports programs for girls.

These constant weekend obligations presented a barrier between Amanda and her friends, but they'd dealt with it. This new stunning beauty thing, though. This would be a problem. She had leapt light years ahead of her peers and while near-lifelong friendships outwardly seemed none the worse for wear, Amanda sensed things were not the same.

The tardy bell's ugly clang startled Amanda from her reverie.

"Shit," she said. "We're late."

"Don't swear!" said Joni.

The six girls negotiated two long hallways before catching their collective breaths and silently approaching the chemistry lab's back door. Amanda opened the door a crack. A horrific stench wafted to her nostrils and she flinched backward. Miss Best stood next to the periodic table of elements. Her back to the class, she scribbled H2S onto the blackboard.

"Go now," Amanda whispered to her friends. "And hold your breath."

The girls tiptoed to their seats accompanies by giggles from their other classmates.

Miss Best, who did not hear well, finished her equation, and faced the class. She squinted, then lifted her safety goggles onto her forehead.

This far into the semester, Miss Best was casual about her role-taking. Her confused gaze passed over five late arrivals occupying desks that had been empty when class began, then settled on Amanda. Amanda's friends were anonymous in their similarity. Striking beauty, though, caught everyone's attention.

"Miss Page," the chemistry teacher said, lowering her safety goggles from her forehead so her eyes would not fall prey to some random, blinding disaster, "you will please take yourself to Mrs. Lindstrom's office and return here with a tardy slip."

"Shit," said Amanda under her breath.

Joni, who occupied the desk next to Amanda, dug an elbow into her ribs and mouthed, "Don't swear."

Amanda stood and gathered her books.

She'd taken three steps forward when that moment— that defining, unforgettable moment that changed everything—came crashing down with dreadful force.

Amanda's initial sensation was a vertigo-like disorientation causing her to lose balance and sprawl onto the floor. Her head struck the corner of a desk. A gash spurted blood. She landed hard, rolling onto her back, with books scattering and her purse spilling across pale green linoleum tiles.

Todd Janson and Junior Ortega, occupying the desks closest to her, reached to help Amanda up, but Miss Best shouted a warning. She stood over Amada, her arms spread as protection.

Amanda emerged from a moment of darkness to a monochromatic scene. Vertigo continued to make her world spin ever so slowly. Color gradually leached back into her visual perception as Miss Best pulsed in and out of focus. Miss Best morphed into a scene from last week's episode of Wild Kingdom when Marlin Perkins was assaulted by an angry pelican.

The pelican offered a stern admonishment. "Never

attempt to assist a fall victim to her feet. She might have a spinal cord injury, and your well-intentioned, though misguided, effort could cause paralysis!" Halfway through this speech, the pelican transformed back into Miss Best.

Amanda didn't think she was paralyzed.

"But Miss Best," Amanda heard Joni protest, "you can't let her just lie there!"

Amanda spared Miss Best the resolution of that dilemma by grasping the legs of Junior's desk and pulling herself to a sitting position. A wet, stickiness crawled along her scalp, slowly penetrating her hair.

"Ah!" Miss Best announced. "You see, now we know there is no spinal injury. Next, we must be concerned about concussion. Miss Page! Miss Page! How many fingers am I displaying?"

That's when the horror began. Bizarre scenes flashed through Amanda's brain, crowding everything comforting and familiar off to one side. Each thread of this torrent was snapped by some vivid instantaneous image of people she didn't know, and a world she didn't recognize. Each image seemed to be swallowed by another as soon as it appeared. She saw herself, naked and terrified as a leering man reached for her. She saw—and heard—a stark, white empty space filled with voices. She encountered a parade of people she'd never seen before. But she knew their names—Marshall, Marta, Elvin, Gretchen, Naomi. Then she saw herself again. She tasted raw fear. She felt everything about herself slipping—no being dragged—away. She saw death reaching a skeletal hand to her throat.

Her face became a picture of abject fear. Her eyes darted wildly.

"Concussion!" shouted Miss Best. "Young lady, you must not go to sleep!"

With an aside to the rest of the class Miss Best added, "You must never allow someone who has suffered a concussion to sleep."

"Miss Best, shouldn't we call someone?" Joni asked.

Miss Best squinted at Joni and said, "Don't panic, Miss Miller. Right now, we have to call someone. Mr. Janson, would you please go to the office and tell them we need medical assistance in the chemistry lab."

Joni knelt next to Amanda.

Amanda felt an overwhelming darkness marching across her brain, taking pieces of her as it went. She was being strangled mentally. Now the darkness began to encompass her. She summoned her strength to make one, desperate plea. *I... I am Amanda. Amanda Page.* The blackness began to retreat. But this other pervasive presence, the other existence, remained.

"Amanda," Joni pleaded, "Amanda. Please! Tell me what's wrong!"

Joni's voice wove itself into the other voices and all the images thundering through her perception. She clamped her hands over her ears, squeezed her eyes shut and said with stark desperation, "There's someone in my head! Get them out! Please! Get them out!"

April 1968

Amanda's mother and the doctor talked as if Amanda wasn't there.

"I just don't know, Mrs. Page," the supervising psychiatrist on Amanda's ward said. "I'm afraid we may never know what caused Amanda's problems. Auditory hallucinations can be associated with any number of conditions, psychotic depression, manic-depressive disorder—even schizophrenia, although we've ruled that out. The others, well, of course Amanda shows signs of depression, but not beyond the normal range of teen angst.

"The most encouraging sign is her interaction with our other patients. She is remarkably engaging with them, regardless of age or condition. These genuine and frequent displays of empathy are inconsistent with any diagnosis of serious mental illness."

The doctor removed his glasses and polished their lenses on the sleeve of his smock.

"Let's try returning her to a familiar environment. Take her home. If you see any more signs of aberrant behavior, if she starts hearing voices again, or the dreams return, bring her back. At this point, though, I'm optimistic."

Amanda had missed five months of school.

In the days following her collapse, Amanda's family doctor found no physical reason for her ongoing complaints of disorientation, strange dreams of a future world that haunted her sleep, and an overwhelming depression and sense of helplessness. When she described the voices, her doctor sent her to Albuquerque to see a neurologist. Neither could he offer any physical explanation for her condition.

That led to psychiatrists and four months in the mental ward of Albuquerque's largest hospital. Nurses gave her pills that left her feeling disconnected and floaty, so she devised ways to hide pills under her tongue, then flush her medications down the toilet.

Eventually, the voices quieted, her confusion eased. Only the dreams persisted. Amanda realized if she stopped talking about her dreams, the doctors might let her go home.

Although Amanda had made the best of her hospital stay and had made friends among her fellow patients, she looked forward to going home. Because she'd done her best to maintain her course work while hospitalized, she didn't have a lot of ground to make up. Still, according to her doctors' recommendations, she didn't return to school immediately. She was surprised and disappointed that so few of her friends stopped by to see her during those first days at home.

Along with the dreams, she found she had another lingering effect of whatever had happened to her—something she didn't mention to her doctors for fear they'd want to continue probing her psyche.

She had mental aptitudes she'd never recognized before. Courses like math, physics and chemistry had clarity for her that had not previously existed. Each of her teachers administered tests to determine what credit they could give Amanda for the work she'd missed. She aced the sciences. Liberal arts tests produced only adequate results, though art, English, writing and history had previously been her academic strengths.

The late spring day she returned to class, her teachers treated her with sympathetic patience. Students—including most of her friends—seemed uncomfortable, though. This reaction was foreign to Amanda. First her athleticism and then her emerging beauty had always paved the way for her socially. She'd never been on the outside, or even on the fringes of a social group. Now, though, even Joni's welcome was a cautious one. Everyone seemed to regard her with a puzzling wariness.

"So, what was it like, being in the hospital for so long?" Joni asked her at lunch on Amanda's first day at school.

"Boring mostly. A little scary, because they really couldn't decide what was wrong."

"So, it was like a concussion, right?" Becky Ellis said. "Because you fell and hit your head?"

"No." Amanda felt relieved someone finally wanted to talk about it. "The doctors on the psych ward said there was no physical damage."

"Psych ward?" Becky's voice conveyed shock.

"Yeah. I was having these . . ." Amanda stopped as she scanned the expressions of surprise from the people around her. She knew she'd made a terrible mistake.

No one ventured into this silence until Amanda finally said, "Anyway, I'm okay now."

"You mean an asylum?" Denise Jones gasped, her eyes wide. "With crazy people?"

Five months ago, Amanda would have deflected Denise's insensitivity with a joke or a white lie that would shape a softer reality of her ordeal. Now, she found herself angry and protective of those she had come to know as they struggled with various forms of mental illness during her time in Albuquerque.

"I was at a hospital with other people who were sick and working very hard to get well," she said with a cold stare at Denise.

Denise glanced from Amanda to the other girls seated around them. Amanda had always been skeptical of Denise's friendship. She was not surprised that Denise would be the one who reacted so quickly to her inadvertent revelation concerning *mental illness.*

Denise hesitated for a moment before saying, "Well, excuuuuuse me!"

Amanda waited for someone to come to her assistance. Five months ago, one of the other girls would have returned a sarcastic comment, deflecting Denise's rudeness with a subtle warning that she was out of line.

But as Denise gathered her purse and coat and left the table in a show of petulance, Amanda heard only an awkward silence.

Walking through the parking lot that afternoon, she passed a group of boys. Five months earlier, they would have ogled her discreetly with a faux politeness disguising what she knew were lustful wishes that Amanda Page would somehow notice them. Now, these boys smirked as she passed. And for the first of what would be many times, she heard a singsong falsetto from someone among them calling to a round of laughter, "There's someone in my head! Get them out. Get them out!"

20

THE PERPETUATION ANOMALY

"HELLO? ARE YOU THERE? It's me again," Marshall's disembodied voice announced to the stark nothingness surrounding him. "Do you have a moment?"

No response. Marshall waited. Finally, a heavy sigh.

"Actually, I don't," the Hall Monitor replied with his characteristic note of condescending impatience. "I don't have a moment or an hour or a day or a year. We have to be somewhere else to have any of those, now don't we?"

"Sorry," said Marshall. "I keep forgetting about the whole absence of time thing here. Anyway, I just wanted to let you know we're using your corridor again. It's for a good cause, though. We're trying to help Sheila."

"Oh, no. What have you done? What have you put in motion?"

Marshall explained the plan. "And we're hoping," he concluded, "Sean can somehow awaken Sheila's awareness of herself long enough for her lifeline to be re-established so Elvin can grab her and bring her back."

His explanation complete, Marshall confronted another long silence. "Um . . . are you still there?"

"Yes. I just don't know how to respond to you in any sort of a constructive manner."

"I'm sorry? I don't—"

"The kindest way I could put it is that you are all a bunch of drooling yahoos swimming around in sludge at the very bottom of the infiniversal gene pool, and you should be cirloctumized before you can breed any more idiots."

"Um ... okay ..." Marshall didn't think he wanted to know what being cirloctumized was.

"That's really not very tactful at all, though," the being continued, "so I think it's better left unsaid."

"Ooookay. Clearly you are, um ... questioning our judgment?"

"Is the Pope Catholic?"

"I'm sorry," Marshall said, "you've lost me there. Are we discussing religion again?"

"I was not being philosophical. I was being sarcastic."

"Oh ... okay. I get it. So, we screwed up. What did we do wrong?"

"I wouldn't even know how to start to answer that question," the Hall Monitor said. "We'd probably have to go back to the discovery of fire, because that's about the last thing your ilk got right."

"Um ... I'm not sure about my ilk ... can we just focus on this thing with Sheila?"

The Hall Monitor added another heavy sigh. "Here's the problem. Say you are successful in recovering Sheila to your world, which is doubtful in the first place. I'm sure you all will be glad to see her, and she you. Through your tampering with the nature of time, though, you will have locked her into a perpetuation anomaly. Once she returns to her native time, she will be destined to repeat the events of her life over and over. And always with this same result. That's tragic because Sheila was an excellent candidate to go on."

"Okay, we're back to this going on thing," Marshall said. "So, everybody doesn't get to go on?"

"No. It's not like social security."

"Then who gets to? What are the criteria?"

"The first requirement is that you have to want to do it," the Hall Monitor said.

"Why would someone not want to—?"

"Because it's very difficult," the Hall Monitor said, exasperation evident in his tone. "What are you envisioning here? Elysium Fields? Harps and halos? Lounging about on some cloud somewhere? I know what your mythology says. You presume things get easier. The reality is obstacles become more formidable. Each level is more difficult than the last. Because, only through confronting adversity can a sentient being grow toward fulfillment of his or her potential. Many beings simply choose to stop. And there's no stigma attached to that."

"So that's it? You just have to want to keep going?"

"No. There's a basic performance standard—how you've handled things thus far—how you've treated others. I can't be more specific, because it's all very individualized. But it's a good way to weed out the jerks. That Hitler fellow was just obnoxious."

"And if you don't go on, what happens to you?"

"Again, I don't know. Some people believe in an afterlife. Some don't."

"What about Sean Brody? He hoped that by helping us,

he would have the chance to live his life differently a second time around. Is he trapped by this perpetuation anomaly, too?"

"Sean... Brody? Let me... Oh. I'm sorry. We have a confidentiality issue with some of the records. Mr. Brody would have to sign a release."

Marshall couldn't help noticing that with that last statement, the Hall Monitor's air of snootiness had slipped a little. Uncomfortable as he was with confrontation, Marshall's conscience was weighted with the fates of two more people now, so he could not let the issue slide.

"Confidentiality?" His tone displayed skepticism.

"Look here, we can't just go discussing—"

"I was in public relations before I was a... um... time traveler," Marshall said, "and you know what we advised clients to say when they didn't want to answer a question from the media?"

"I rarely deal with the media," the Hall monitor said.

Marshall ignored him and continued. "We told them to claim confidentiality issues. And usually, the only thing confidential was that someone had committed some serious blunder. And the only ones they wanted to protect were themselves."

"Well, see here," the Hall Monitor reclaimed all his superior being bluster, "this has gone beyond..."

"Did somebody screw up where Sean Brody is concerned?" Marshall said. "Is that what this is all about?"

"... and there's no time to discuss it. Your universe is..."

Not this time, Marshall thought, and said aloud, "Can I talk to her?"

"Sheila's not here," the Hall Monitor said.

"I mean when she is here. Can I wait for her on my way back? You know, just in case we do find her?"

"That's not so easy."

"You've done it before. With Samantha. She waited to get a message to me."

"Oh, yes. Sheila and Samantha. I must give you credit for earning the trust and respect of two remarkable women. You understand your request could be academic if your silly little plan to find Sheila doesn't work. You'll have to wait around."

"No problem," Marshall said.

"Actually, there is a problem. A major one. Although we do not observe time here, accumulated time catches up to you when you leave the corridor. Your presence here can count against your future. Sometimes in dramatic ways. Do you understand what I'm saying?"

"That it will . . . will affect my lifespan?"

"Yes. Your lifespan has already been compromised. Hard to say how much. Different circumstances cause time to accumulate at different rates."

Marshall felt a chilling wave spill through him, as if a doctor had informed him of a fatal illness. He realized that he, Marta, Gillis, Frank and the others shared a special sort of peril. He had to warn Sheila, though.

"I must talk to her," he said to the blankness around him.

"The return trip is tricky," the Hall Monitor said. "You'll have to pay close attention."

"Please."

"Well . . . you'll try and do something regarding the

designated hitter rule?" the Hall Monitor said.

"Um ... sure," Marshall said. "I'll write to the commissioner."

"Then I'll see what I can do."

GETTING TO KNOW YOU

Superior, Arizona
May 17, 2043

AN EARLY RISER, Marshall didn't understand people who would rather cloister themselves behind curtains and air conditioners while the world came to life. Walking through the desert behind his motel, Marshall savored a thick ozone smell wafting from creosote bushes damp with dew and sparkling in the glow of a desert sunrise.

He drew a deep breath and wondered one more time if he'd made the right choice. Sure, he could have said no. If he refused this assignment, though, he realized his job at the advertising agency was likely doomed. So what? He wasn't wild about the work. He probably wasn't cut out to be a public relations wonk, anyway. Unfortunately, his communications degree from New Mexico State University prepared him for little else. He enjoyed writing, sort of. Maybe a newspaper job, or what passed for newspapers nowadays—online blogs and gossip and political rants without any particular obligation to the truth.

He sighed and circled one more time to the same conclusion. He would do this, whatever it was. He would disappear into some secret project for five years and, his recruiter suggested, maybe make some serious money.

Sounded like a scam if he'd ever heard one. He turned and headed back to the motel, considered breakfast options.

At first, he thought he'd stumbled. He found himself face down in loose red sandy soil, his left shoulder impaled with spines from a prickly pear cactus. His scalp bled where the sharp point of a Spanish Dagger had creased his forehead.

He searched for a safe place to put his hands so he could extricate himself from the prickly pear when he realized a shoulder full of cactus thorns might be the least of his worries.

His mind filled with thoughts and visions over which he had no control. His brain ran rampant along divided paths. A small gecko skittered across his hand and stopped. As this mental torrent multiplied, he stared into the gecko's tiny eyes and found himself consumed with a terrifying image of a giant woman-like lizard bending over him. He recoiled with disgust . . . not from the image of the lady lizard. *From the word . . . the L word. Reptilian American. That's better . . .*

Another thought hit him, and he said aloud to the gecko, "Grbblxxssssttt." The gecko appeared to consider its options, then hissed and darted away.

Marshall managed rolling to a sitting position, but the assault on his consciousness continued. His mysterious employers would never accept him at this new job now. He was crazy. He needed to find a doctor. He would be confined to some dark room with bars on the windows and be fed green Jell-O and gruel . . .

Then a small voice of reason began to filter through it all.

"We're bleeding," someone said.

No, not *said*—*thought*. The other voice came as a mental message. Like telepathy.

"Get your handkerchief or we're going to get blood all over our shirt. They'll think we killed somebody."

Odd, Marshall thought, that this voice knew he had a handkerchief. Nobody had handkerchiefs anymore. Except for Marshall. Because Marshall's mom had always insisted—

"Yes, she's my mom, too," the voice said. "Don't just sit there. Come to your senses and do something about this cut on our forehead!"

"*Our* forehead?" past-Marshall asked aloud as he withdrew a handkerchief from his back pocket. He put the clean white cloth to his face, as a blur of images slowly started to untangle themselves. Clarity and order began to emerge, accommodating this new presence.

"Deep breath," the inner voice commanded. "Deep breath. I'll try and get things organized, and I can't do that if your half of us is at the verge of hysteria. And by the way, Owwwwww! My god! You fell on a cactus!"

Marshall managed to stand and limp to a large flat rock a few feet off the trail. He sat, gently tugging at some of the spines protruding from his shirt. He stopped as his whole attention became riveted to the voice's account of coming events wandered through his mind. At first, beyond believability.

Time travel? he thought. *This is all about time travel? And I will . . . No, that's impossible. No one would choose me . . . I'm not even remotely qualified to . . . to do whatever time travelers do.*

The reality faced him squarely, though. They *would*

choose him. And someone else would choose him, as well. Two extraordinary women waited for him on this new stage. And somehow that prospect seemed more implausible to his past self than the whole concept of mucking about through wormholes.

He sat for a quarter hour as this far-fetched fate sprawled before him.

"Okay," future-Marshall finally thought with a deep sigh of relief. *"That's better, right? Now, we have to find Marta and the others. Everyone should be here soon. Gillis, Macy and Frank are staying at this motel. Marta stayed someplace across town."*

Past-Marshall considered whether he should quit the whole enterprise and go home. This other guy in his head was getting a little pushy. But besides being intimidating, these women intrigued him. So, he agreed to go along, at least for the moment, and made his way back to the motel, holding the handkerchief to his forehead. He found a picnic table under an ancient mesquite tree near the parking lot and sat. He commanded a clear view of all the units. His new mental companion wanted to knock on doors. Given that present-Marshall would have to do the knocking, though, he decided to sit and wait for his fellow travelers to show themselves. Past-Marshall didn't know for sure what rooms the others occupied. And past-Marshall wasn't about to go thumping at the doors of strangers. Unless and until they had been joined by their future counterparts, none of these people would have any idea who Marshall Grissom was.

His future self explained that Elvin was aiming for early morning. As well as all the travelers could recall, they'd each taken a bus to the site that day, where they had been told this was the last chance to change their minds. Once they heard the briefing that afternoon, they would be segregated from the outside world for the next five years. Because none of them knew each other yet, they hadn't socialized the evening before. Elvin hoped to time their integrations early, while they still enjoyed the relative safety of their motel rooms.

So, Marshall sat, sharing with the new occupant of his brain the enjoyment of sounds from a waking desert. Mockingbirds crowed. Growing heat roused cicadas to begin buzzing through the willow and cottonwood trees along a dry riverbed that lay behind the motel. Even at this early hour, cumulus clouds built their towers in the western sky, offsetting crystal blue with stark piles of white and gray cotton that by midafternoon would add elements of black, and sparkle with tongues of lightning.

All the while, past-Marshall drank in details concerning the next three years of his life. So, he'd made the right decision after all? This time travel thing would take him down paths he had never imagined.

And I'll know what's coming, he thought as he saw the fate of his high school friend Samantha, *so I can do it better this time. I can fix it . . .*

Future-Marshall gave a rueful little snort. *I'm sorry to say it doesn't work that way. You will retain a sharp and detailed memory of my presence here, and your future, for about three or four days. Then, it will all recede into your dreams. I'm afraid you'll be on your own, just like the first time.*

A door opened at the far end of a long line of motel rooms. Marshall glanced over. An overwhelming wave of sadness coursed through him.

"So, this is Sheila," past-Marshall said aloud.

The reality of her beauty mingled with future-Marshall's memories of Sheila's strength of character and sheer enthusiasm for life that—for him—defined her more accurately than her physical appearance.

Sheila stood for a long moment. Undoubtedly, Marshall thought, dealing with her own uncertainty about what she'd gotten herself into. Probably wondering, as Marshall had, if she should leave or stay.

Finally, she gave a feline stretch and turned to step back inside. As she did, her gaze swept to Marshall and stopped. Marshall hesitated, then offered a tentative wave across the parking lot.

She smiled, waved back, and returned inside.

"Wow," past-Marshall said.

He had no thought of introducing himself. Past-Marshall could hardly suspend his disbelief that anyone like the woman he'd just seen could have any interest in him. Future-Marshall felt anew the pangs of missing her. He longed to rush over, hug her, tell her to go home and be safe. Trying to speak with her now, though, would be pointless. This Sheila had no idea of the role Marshall Grissom would come to play in her brief life.

When Sheila closed the door behind her, a second door halfway down the line of units opened and Gillis Kerg emerged followed by Macy Gardner. Gillis saw Marshall and waved.

"We both integrated about an hour ago," Gillis said by way of explanation when Marshall joined them.

"And since we had an hour to kill . . ." Macy grinned.

Past-Marshall didn't know what to say. Future-

Marshall took over. "You probably shouldn't have done that. Now the two of you will have started something several years earlier than you should have and—"

"We'll find a way to deal with it," Macy said with a wink.

Gillis started to agree when they were interrupted by a scream from the room two doors down.

Past-Marshall gave a reflexive jump. Future-Marshall rolled their eyes. "And that would be Frank. Let's help him get himself together."

As had often occurred, Frank's response to having his future self crawl into his head was rough. When Marshall pushed open Frank's door, he found a disheveled woman wrapped in a sheet. Naked, Frank crouched against the bed's headboard and moaned, his hands clamped to his head.

"What's wrong with him? What's wrong with him?" the woman demanded as Marshall and Gillis pushed past her.

"Oh, my," Gillis said. "We thought that was all cleared up, but at least the rash is gone."

The woman screamed and locked herself in the bathroom.

With some gentle assurances from Macy that Gillis was just kidding, the woman finally bolted from the bathroom, grabbed her clothes and, still clad only in the sheet, ran to a car parked outside.

"I bet they'll make you pay for that sheet, Frank," Gillis said.

"AAAAAAAHHHHHHHH," said Frank.

With hand-holding and careful explanations, Frank came around soon enough. As he calmed, Marshall opened the drapes to let light into the room. That's when he saw the bus. The bus going to the GRC site. The bus none of them would take. The bus with a short line of people waiting to board.

Including Marta Hamilton.

"Oh, no," Marshall said to the others. "Marta's out there. She's getting on the bus."

"But she's not supposed to—" Macy said.

"Well, obviously she doesn't know that. Which means our Marta isn't here yet."

"If she takes that bus, she won't be able to leave the campus and help us," Macy said. "Marshall, go get her."

"Me? She doesn't know me. Yet."

Then the future-Marshall part of him added, "And if you guys will remember, back when all this was happening, Marta could be a bit ... um ... standoffish."

"Standoffish?" Gillis said. "I remember her practically breaking the arm of a guy who was hitting on her that first week at the Time Warp."

"That's why you should go," Macy said to Marshall. "She always liked you."

"She liked me about six months from now," Marshall countered. He turned to Gillis. "You're a spy. You know karate and stuff. You're the one who should get her."

"No, she didn't like me until about a year into everything. At least she tolerated you. So, go before it's too late."

Marshall looked again. Marta stood only a couple of people back from the bus's folding door. "Oh, Lord." He sprinted outside.

Halfway across the parking lot, he waved his arms and called, "Marta! Ms. Hamilton. I need to speak to you before you leave. It's very important ..."

22

YOU SHOW ME YOURS . . .

MARTA TURNED WITH A START to see a tall, gangly man running toward her. Although she heard him say her name, she still searched to see who else might be the object of his attention.

Nope, he was yelling at her, all right. Who would know her here? The only logical answer seemed that someone from the program needed to talk with her.

She stepped from a line of strangers boarding the bus.

The man reached her, bent over and put his hands on his knees, trying to catch his breath. Marta scanned him up and down. She dismissed the notion he was a GRC official.

"Well?" she said.

"I'm sorry," the man said between gasps. "You don't know me but . . . You *don't* know me, right?"

Marta's eyes narrowed and adopted the black, steely glint that was the equivalent of a snake's rattle.

He took a step back. "Again, I apologize for the intrusion. And this really isn't what you think it is. My name is Marshall, and . . . and . . . you'll understand very soon . . ."

He paused and seemed expectant.

She continued to glare.

"... although clearly you don't understand yet. So, um ... could you please wait for the next bus?"

Marta spun on her heel and walked back toward a dwindling number of people filing through the bus's folding door.

"Wait," the man called. "I know about ... about your employer ... London. And ... and ... that your middle name is Louise."

Marta stopped. She took a moment to bury her surprise before she turned and slowly assessed this fellow from the distance of a few feet. Freakishly tall and thin, he appeared painfully unsure of himself. His nose was too long and his forehead a vast plane from eyebrows to hairline, all the more noticeable because a shallow cut creased his brow. A smattering of blood droplets had fallen across his white shirt.

"Just let this bus go, please? The next one will be here in a couple of hours. You won't be late."

Marta had no question that she would miss this bus. And maybe the next one, too. She needed to learn who sent this guy, the extent of threat he represented, and then decide what she would do with him.

At first, he appeared relieved. His demeanor changed, though, as she strode toward him.

"Wait, now, wait," he said, backing away.

Marta quickened her stride, closed the distance and clamped her hand onto his elbow.

"This ring I'm wearing," she said with a guttural growl. "It's a Taser. You see how the stone is starting to glow? That means it's charging. So, one of two things will happen.

Either I'll lay you out right here and tell anyone who asks that you made a lewd suggestion and tried to grab me. Or we'll walk to whatever room is yours, and you'll answer every question I ask."

"Um ... how do you know I've got a room at this motel?"

"Just a guess. And you'd better hope you do."

"Room thirty-three. And please, if you use that Taser, you'll mess everything up. They'll come and get me."

"Damn right they'll come and get you. As soon as you go down, I'm calling the cops."

The man obeyed. With Marta still gripping his elbow, they crossed the parking lot. He fumbled for his keycard and waved it at the door. Marta shoved him inside She deftly slid her hand to his wrist. With a quick twist, she spun his arm into a hammer lock.

"Ow ... ow, Marta. That hurts!"

"Yes, it's supposed to. Now, you've got one chance to tell me how you think you know me and what it is you're after. And if I even suspect you're lying, this won't end well for you."

"Can't you wait just a few minutes?" he begged. "I'm sure it will only be a few more—"

"What are you trying to pull here?" Marta increased the pressure on his arm and wrist. "Why are you pretending to know who I am?"

"If I didn't know you, how would I know your middle name?" Marshall said.

"Anyone could find out my middle name."

She twisted harder.

"Okay ... okay ... Something I couldn't know other

196

than ... than ... the evil Dr. Dingus Doonaughty! I know all about—"

Marta shoved the man across the room and stared at him with shock. The evil doctor played a very specific role in her most private sexual fantasies, and she'd never revealed that aspect of her life to another living soul.

"How did you ... how could you ..." she stammered.

"Because you told me. I'm, kind of, your boyfriend. Anyway, I will be. As long as you don't maim or kill me."

"I don't have boyfriends! And certainly not skinny, goofy-looking ones. And whatever it is you think you know ..."

Marta closed her fist and extended her ring toward him. The door to the room swung open. She glanced quickly over her shoulder to see a small man wearing a confident expression.

"He's telling the truth, Marta," the second man said. "Yes, he is goofy-looking. You are initially attracted to him, though, because he's got a huge—"

"Gillis!" the tall man protested.

Marta retreated to a corner where she could keep an eye on both these weirdos. Now a woman squeezed through the door.

"Hi, Marta," she said with a smile and a wave. "Are you here yet?"

"Who the hell are you?"

"Uh, oh." The woman started to back out. She froze when Marta swung the glowing ring in her direction. As the woman stopped abruptly, a third man—he looked as if he belonged in a vodka commercial—bumped into the woman from behind and his momentum propelled them both forward.

"Close the door," Marta ordered. She shifted her gaze from first one and then the others of these four strangers.

"Don't worry," the man calling himself Marshall said. "They don't know about the doctor. I wouldn't tell anyone about things he has us ... um ... you know."

Unlike most other people boarding the buses today, Marta knew the purpose of the secret desert installation. She was a British spy, and she'd been briefed by her handler at MI-6. None of this made any sense though. Where had these people gotten their information? And how had the tall one found out about ...

"You," Marta said to the woman as she nodded toward Marshall. "What do you know about me and this guy?"

"Well, see, it's because we're all naked when we—"

"Who is naked?"

"All of us," the woman said. "The travelers, I mean. You have to be naked to travel through time, and ..."

Marta's mind raced. *No one else was supposed to know ... and why would anyone be naked?*

"... Marshall's a really nice guy when you get to know him and, as I said, there's the whole naked thing, and you and all the rest of us ... the women, I mean ... I don't know about the guys ... are kind of intrigued by Marshall because, besides being nice, he's got this really, really big—"

"Macy, that's enough," the Marshall person said.

Marta turned to him. "A big what?"

Marshall put a hand to his face and hung his head. "Um ... my ... it's ... well ... I'm large."

"Very large," the woman offered.

Marta looked at the small man, who nodded his agreement. "Humongous," Gillis said.

Marta peered suspiciously from one face to another.

"And you're saying because of your, um . . . largeness . . . I told you about . . . the doctor?"

"No, you told me about . . . about him, because . . . well, there's just more to it than just . . . largeness."

Marshall seemed to wilt further under her uncompromising stare.

"Show me," she demanded.

"Marta!" he protested. "No. I'm not going to—"

"For God's sake, show her," Gillis said.

"Yeah," the other woman urged. "It's not like we all haven't seen it about a hundred times."

On her own, Marta might have simply walked away from these four nuts. The Marshall person's knowledge of Dr. Doonaughty dealt a wild card that could not be ignored, though. She took a threatening step toward him.

"Okay, okay," Marshall said.

He was fumbling with his belt when Marta staggered a little and fell back onto the bed.

"Um . . . is that . . . you?" Marshall tentatively asked.

Marta peered past the collage of images roiling in her brain to find the hopeful eyes of her comrades. "Whoa," she said. "What the hell is going on here?"

A vacancy drifted into her eyes. She lay back down and stared at the ceiling. Then, she sat up with a start as a graphic image of Marshall at the peak of readiness flashed through her brain.

"Oh, my goodness," past-Marta said, blinking at Marshall.

Her eyes narrowed. Future-Marta glanced from Macy to Marshall. "Tell me, Honeybunch, is there a reason your belt is unbuckled, and your pants unzipped?"

Marshall quickly zipped up.

"Do you really think," he said, "that I'm goofy looking?"

23

FREEDOM OF CHOICE

"SO, EVERYONE UNDERSTANDS?"

Marta regarded the other four travelers gathered in Marshall's hotel room. She saw varying degrees of uncertainty. The past versions of each traveler were still coming to grips with their situation.

"Just because these future versions of yourselves are committed to this mission doesn't mean you have to be," she said to a worried silence. "This is something we've determined will be paramount in all missions. The past versions of ourselves will be given a clear choice about participation. Your future selves will not command anything and will do their best not to manipulate you unfairly. We'll try to step back and allow *you* to make the choice."

By now, the past versions of the travelers all knew the basics of this outwardly simple mission. The issue would be their late arrival onto the GRC Campus.

Macy spoke first. "This is all so overwhelming, you know? All of a sudden, I discover I'm going to be a time traveler. And the gig comes with great sex." She smiled at Gillis. "This is something I think I really want to do. And

I'm not sure getting there late is very smart. Especially now since I know all this stuff about the future. I mean, that's got to give us an edge over everybody else."

"Okay," Marta said, "how being late will affect your standing is a valid consideration. We need to be clear, though. After only a few days you won't remember anything about your future. You won't remember visitations from your future selves. You'll probably remember the things you do the next couple of days, but why you did them will be pretty fuzzy."

"That's . . . bizarre," said Macy. "What about you future guys? Do you remember?"

"The details of what happens here will be vague, kind of like something we dreamed," Marta said. "What about you, Frank? Past-Frank, I mean."

"Hmmmm? Oh, yeah. Uh . . . I'm okay with it."

"Me, too," Macy said with a sigh. "As long as you're sure we won't get kicked out for being late."

Each future counterpart had already explained to their hosts Elvin's theories about the intransigence of history and the likelihood that nothing, least of all being a day or two late, would affect their future roles.

"Okay," Marta said. "There's one more thing I need to explain. As simple as this mission seems, Gillis and I are convinced something more is involved. And there's a good chance one of you—the future version of one of you—has been paid off to somehow disrupt what's supposed to happen here."

"You think Lucre got to one of us?" future-Macy asked.

"We think he got to someone," Marta said. "Gillis found clear evidence. We don't know who or why. Maybe someone among the scientific team or support staff. Among the travelers we have two prime suspects, for reasons I won't go into right now. One was Galen. That's why I bumped him off the crew just before projection. And the other," she said, swinging her gaze across the room, "is you, Frank."

"Okay," Frank grumbled. "Nothing's changed, I see. Something happens, blame Frank. What did I do?"

"Lucre pushed to get you back into the program," Marta said.

"Which may," Gillis conceded, "just have been a decoy to draw our attention from someone else. We'll be watching you, though."

"And because we can't eliminate anyone completely," Marta said with an apologetic glance at Marshall, "I want to remind everyone of something else. If you have done anything to compromise your integrity, there's one person you can't hide it from. And that's yourself—this past version of yourself with whom you are sharing your total consciousness. You might have been able to mask that part of your thoughts so far. Now that I've raised the issue, though, you can't hide that information from the present version of yourself. And I will appeal to that entity to tell us if their future counterpart has done something to endanger the rest of us or manipulate this mission."

Frank glared. The rest of the travelers exchanged worried looks.

"Any questions?" asked Marta.

"Yeah," Macy said. "What about Dr. Rose? Where is he?"

Marta, Marshall and Gillis exchanged a quick glance.

"We have to assume he couldn't—or didn't want to—

get off the GRC campus," Marta said. "Remember, as a member of the science team, he's already been there for months. We knew this might happen. He didn't have a role here in Phoenix. I just wanted him to go through a projection. The past version of himself knows all about the time travel thing. So, he should be able to process what's happening when he confronts his future consciousness."

"What if he didn't handle it okay?" Macy asked. "Isn't one of us supposed to be there to help him?"

"He's there and we're here, Macy," said Gillis. "There's nothing we can do."

"Okay," Marta said. "It's a go. Get packed. We're heading to Phoenix. You all know what you're supposed to do tomorrow morning."

24

TEAM CHEMISTRY

CRUSHING PAIN ENGULFED SEAN. The bright white void was a prison of agony... until he chose not to feel pain. That's all there was to it. He could not contain his amazement. Not only was the pain of his surgically inflicted injuries gone. He felt an unfamiliar wellness throughout his absent body.

He realized in that moment how much it hurts to be old. With gradual onset of age, he hadn't noticed the extent to which he'd been affected by discomfort of old joints and weakening muscles and subtle failure of organs. His mind had come to accept these maladies and somehow converted these discomforts to an accepted norm.

Only when that pain was gone did he realize the degree to which it had existed. Only then did he remember the simple satisfaction of feeling good.

These were thoughts and sensations absorbing him for the first eon or so as he drifted through the timeless limbo. As wonderful a sensation as this all was, though, he eventually directed his thoughts to family. He felt sorrow at final separation from children and grandchildren. He wished he had done better as a father. He wished he could see his grandchildren's adult lives unfold. This blank white infinity seemed to promote clarity of thought, though—an internal honesty forcing him to see the reality of life and death and pointlessness of guilt. Yes, while he could have done better, he had his strong points as well. He had done many things right.

And perhaps he could improve on the other things if he was, indeed, granted an opportunity to try again.

Thursday, April 17, 1969

Fifteen-year-old Sean Brody squirmed under the withering glare of his accuser.

"Please, Miss Best, I don't know who did it. It wasn't me. Now, can I please go? I'll be late for baseball practice."

This was only a half-truth. Sean was not guilty of the crime. He knew without a doubt, though, the identities of the perpetrators. That's because the plan was his. He'd conceived it, he'd described it to the real criminals. "Hey, wouldn't it be funny if..." And much to his chagrin, they'd done it. That had pissed Sean off a little bit. They'd plagiarized his plot. *Not that I ever would have done it myself*, he thought with a sigh. No, he was too rule-bound, too fearful of consequence to ever execute any of the nefarious schemes he imagined.

And this was a good one.

Miss Best was questioning every boy from fifth period chemistry, one at a time. Sean watched anxiously as the wall clock over Miss Best's shoulder ticked off another minute.

"I will get to the bottom of this, Mr. Brody," she said, her eyes magnified through lenses of her safety goggles.

"What if we have the police examine fingerprints? What would you say then?"

Sean thought it unlikely police officers would care enough to gather fingerprints.

"That would be okay with me, ma'am."

Miss Best lifted her safety goggles and parked them on her forehead. The goggles' deeply etched imprint remained around her eyes, reminding Sean a little of a raccoon. Thanks to her obsession with eye safety Miss Best was seldom seen without safety goggles. Sean could not count the times Miss Best had nagged her students about eye protection. Impaired sight might dash one's hopes of becoming a chemist.

Miss Best made it clear to Sean and all her students that she regarded the title of Chemist as the highest honor to which mortals could aspire. Political office or brain surgery or the priesthood were all lower callings. And the altar before which chemists and aspiring chemists worship is the Periodic Table of the Elements.

"This is the periodic chart!" Miss Best had announced in grand fashion all those months ago at the school year's opening bell. She aimed her wooden pointer at an eight-by-six sheet of sturdy, cream-colored vinyl hanging from a roller covering the blackboard. This chart was sectioned into bright green and red boxes and blue rectangles containing symbols and numbers betraying the secrets of the universe. She told her new students this chart was the first thing she had purchased when she initiated her teaching career all those decades past.

Next, she offered to amaze them.

She took enormous pride in her ability to point with her

stick to any element without looking. Standing at a precise spot, gripping the pointer with her right hand, she would face the class, bark out "titanium," and—whap!—her stick's blunt tip would hurtle unerringly to the center of the box labeled "titanium." After a couple of these simple warm-up maneuvers, she would switch the pointer to her left hand, name another element and, contorting her body so her eyes stayed fixed on the class straight ahead, find her mark.

"Iron!" Whap! Iron.

She invited the class to choose her next targets.

"Rubidium!"

Whap! Rubidium.

"Cadmium!"

Whap! Cadmium.

Sean wondered if this ability resulted from years of practice, or genetic coding. If anybody would have had such a rare skill embedded in their DNA, it would be Miss Best.

Once she judged her students suitably amazed, she concluded each performance by stepping back on her squeaky crepe-soled orthopedic shoes to indulge herself with a long intoxicating gaze before tugging the bottom of the chart to engage its spring-loaded roller. The roller's old coils were worn, though, and the chart would hang up after a couple of inches. Raising it any further became an ordeal resolved without warning when its spring would finally catch, snapping the chart closed with a crack like a bullwhip.

And back on that first day of class when—as Sean suspected was usually the case—whatever amazement Miss Best had inspired failed to carry much beyond the first ten minutes, she gathered her disappointment with a deep, slow sigh, then whapped box one in the one-A group of elements.

"Hydrogen," she said. "Hydrogen is the most basic of the elements. Its symbol is H and it has an atomic number of one . . ."

And they were off on a year-long trek through the chemical wilderness, led at a breakneck pace by a fanatical deaf woman. Many would not survive the journey. Stragglers, like Sean, would eventually fall along the way, saddled with their Ds or their Fs, hoping against hope that rescue teams would come and save them. With helicopters, maybe, so they could be rushed back to civilization before it was too late. But Miss Best did not believe in rescue parties. She was a Darwinist, a devout disciple of natural selection. She believed the weak did not deserve to survive.

Miss Best didn't use the periodic chart every day and was careful not to leave it unfurled and exposed. This circumstance provided the original spark for Sean's plan. And why he was here this afternoon being questioned as a suspect in the profaning of the periodic table of the elements.

A few days earlier, acting on Sean's purely hypothetical suggestion, three band students, following a late rehearsal, snuck into the chemistry lab, unfurled the chart and taped to it the foldout from a May issue of Playboy. Then they rolled the chart up and stole away, leaving Miss May ticking like a time bomb.

Earlier that day Sean sat and—with Miss Best droning on about ions or esters or valence electrons or some such chemical enigma—stared through windows at the impending summer. Spring winds were subsiding, temperature edging toward the 80s . . .

". . . and that would be which chemical compound, Miss Crandle?" Miss Best barked.

Like Sean, several others were distracted by unchemical diversions. Sean was relieved that Miss Best had aimed her arrow at a target other than him.

"I . . . I . . ." stammered a girl two desks over.

Miss Best shook her head, grabbed her wooden pointer, and stepped to her station next to the periodic chart. Sean anticipated another routine performance as Miss Best's familiar attempt to recapture her students' attention.

Eyes fixed firmly on the class, she unfurled the chart.

Sean felt the recoil of 32 heads snapping to attention.

Miss Best saw their reaction. At first, she seemed confused.

Sean was stunned. They had done it! He hadn't meant for . . . He forced his eyes off the extraordinary form of Miss May and glanced around. He saw gaping jaws, eyes wide with astonishment. And with shock came an absolute silence.

Miss Best did not forfeit the moment.

"Cadmium!" she barked, and whap, pointed blindly to Miss May's left knee.

"Palladium!" she cried, and whap, struck a blow to Miss May's navel.

"Molybdenum!"

Miss May's molybdenum was spectacular.

Recalling the event years later when gathered with a group of young reporters for a drink after work, Sean explained, "Now, you have to understand this was a long time ago, and the casual exposure of adolescents to nudity was a good deal rarer than it is today, particularly in a rural community like Portales. And many of us boys had no idea that molybdenum of those proportions actually existed."

During this moment, though, Sean found himself less

concerned with molybdenum than with consequences. For during her last maneuver, Miss Best had apparently registered something amiss from the corner of her eye.

So, she turned.

And she looked.

A sharp, quick scream escaped her lips. Wild-eyed, she glared over her shoulder to the class, and then looked back at the chart.

She threw herself in front of the chart like a soldier falling on a hand grenade to save his brothers. But Miss Best was vertical, and Miss May was horizontal. No matter how Miss Best contorted herself there remained some vital element of Miss May uncovered. She grabbed the bottom of the chart and tugged. It rolled about two inches, then hung up. She cast her gaze to the class again. Sean saw horror contorting her face.

"Everybody!" she yelled. "Put on your safety goggles!"

She tugged harder and the chart advanced six more inches. Then, mercifully, it snapped closed, catching her left index finger with its coils. Miss Best turned, as best she could with her finger caught that way, and said with disgust, "This class is dismissed."

And now she was determined to see the guilty culprits punished to the full extent of the law.

"I saw you laughing out there," she said to Sean as she pointed to the hallway where other boys waited. "I think you are a perpetrator. I think you'd better sit down and take a good hard look at yourself, young man. You'd better take stock because you, sir, are headed down the path of ruin. I think you have forfeited any possibility you might ever have of becoming a chemist . . ."

And at that instant, Sean was visited by a ghastly choir of five-year-olds. He jumped from his chair, clamped his hands over his ears and looked wildly about for a means of escape. Through crazed, beseeching eyes, he silently appealed to Miss Best for help, and she did seem a little concerned.

"I'm sorry to be harsh," she said. "Perhaps I shouldn't be so blunt. The hard reality of life, though, is that some of us simply will *not* become chemists."

"Oh, my God," Sean gasped.

"Well, I suppose you could always enroll in summer session . . ." Miss Best said, her voice tinged with concern.

The only recourse Sean could choose in that instant was flight. He ran into the hallway, past other suspects awaiting their own interrogations, and through the back doors. Once outside, he leaned against the brick wall and realized images were emerging from the music.

Future-Sean, alarmed at his young counterpart's panicked reaction, called on Naomi's hypnotically implanted instructions. Young Sean saw a big red blob. No, a ball. No. The moon. The moon turned red. And someone had carved the number 33 . . .

Think of the color red, think of the moon, think the number 33 . . . that's what we do to start the music.

Next, young Sean imagined a giant squirrel leaping to eat the moon.

. . . think of squirrels to turn off the music.

The music stopped.

Future-Sean waited warily, sorting through the bedlam of his past counterpart's terror, ready to restore that awful music at the first sign of trouble. Past-Sean cautiously opened his eyes, peering to see whether his world was still there.

Someone said, *"You'll be fine. Just relax. Suspend your skepticism and pay attention. Soon you'll understand."*

Retreating from the edge of panic, Sean obeyed. He closed his eyes again and listened. The information started as a steady stream. Every few seconds, though, the stream gushed into a torrent of images, sounds and emotions threatening to engulf him. Then would come red moons and 33s followed by a spurt of those awful children with their reedy voices singing about small worlds after all until squirrels would come to Sean's rescue, and the ugly splat of information organized itself back into that narrow stream.

"Time travel?" past-Sean demanded aloud. "Are you kidding me? Am I on Candid Camera or something?"

"Yeah, I know, I guess I really didn't believe it either until right now. I'm—"

"Holy Jesus," past-Sean said. "Ninety-three years old? Who lives to be ninety-three years old? Um . . . are you sure you're getting this right? You're not, you know, senile or something?"

"They sent me, so I guess I'm okay."

"And you're here because of . . . whoa! Amanda Page? She's a senior. And she's a fox. And she's a little bit nuts, too, I think. Wait a minute. The two of you didn't meet at the asylum, did you?"

"Asylum?" future-Sean said, then recognized rumors coursing through his young counterpart's thoughts. *"If I'm someone she met . . . anywhere, how would I have gotten into your head?"*

"Yeah. Right. I guess."

"So, you think you can handle this?" Future-Sean said. *"Because a lot of information will be coming your way. I can*

only hold it back for so long. Relax and go with the flow. In a few hours, you'll be able to keep the two of us separate. If it's too much, though, I can start the music again."

"Um . . . let's save that for an absolute emergency, okay?"

"Believe me, I've got no problem with that. For the time being, do your best to focus on information you're getting from me. I need to be quiet and sort through a few things from you."

And the details of Sean's life as a fifteen-year-old inundated future-Sean. Yesterday and the day before and the day before that—absolutely blank spaces to the ninety-three-year-old version of himself—were fresh and rich with detail: the routine, the teen angst, the drama, the struggles of a pubescent kid.

Sean's girlfriend was quickly cooling to their relationship. His chemistry grade was under water and in only a matter of time, someone would notify his parents. But he was getting A's in English. He really liked writing. The baseball team had a doubleheader Saturday against Clovis . . .

Abruptly the information exchange came to a halt.

Baseball!

Future-Sean became so focused on this one image that it blotted out everything else. Clovis. Wait a minute! This was *that* weekend. The weekend Coach Kinney invited him to quit the team.

"What?" young Sean said with alarm. "Coach Kenney is going to kick me off? Why? I know I don't ever play. Big deal! I'm not in anyone's way. What'll I tell everyone—?"

"The thing is," his future counterpart told him, *"if things happen the way I remember them, we know what's coming. And I think we may be able to do something about it. Right now, we need to go to practice."*

25

ABSOLUTELY ROUTINE

Phoenix, Arizona
May 18, 2043

"ANY SECOND THOUGHTS?" Marta asked. "Are we still good? Committed to the mission, I mean. If any of you who must remain here—this time and place—and deal with the consequences of whatever happens today want to back out, my offer stands until we leave this room."

Marta looked at each of the four nervous people crowded around her.

"Um . . . I thought this was all supposed to be routine," said past-Macy, who clearly had second thoughts. "You really think we might be taking some kind of serious risk?"

"I'm still concerned that one of us has a different agenda," Marta said. "And nothing related to time travel can ever be considered routine."

"Would you mind if I just wait in the lobby?" Macy asked.

Marta carefully regarded her as she sat on the edge of the bed in Marta's hotel room. "Can you . . . um . . . the present you . . . step back for a minute and let Macy from the future talk to me?"

"Okay, I'll try." Macy closed her eyes and concentrated.

"I'm sorry, guys," future-Macy said after a moment.

"She's scared. She's willing to help if it's absolutely necessary to the mission. I'd be lying, though, if . . . but you guys have to understand that I . . . the me from the future . . . hates the thought of letting you all down."

"That's okay," Marta said, placing a hand on Macy's shoulder. "It's not the future's choice to make anymore. Wait in the lobby with your phone. We'll only involve you if we have to."

Macy nodded.

"What about you, Frank?" Marta said. "Do you have anything to tell us this morning?"

"Like I've accepted a bribe and I'm here to plant a bomb or something? Sorry. I'm not your bad guy. I'll do whatever you need me to do just as long as they have a check ready when we get back home."

Marta didn't want Frank out of her sight, or she might have considered having him wait in the lobby, too.

"And we're all set with the sound equipment, Gillis?"

"The recorder and ear buds look like a personal music system," Gillis said, displaying the items. "And this writing instrument is a directional microphone. Even if they get scanned when we go through the security station, nothing about them will attract attention."

"And you—I mean, the *Gomer Pyle*-Gillis—just happened to have this stuff with him yesterday?" Marshall asked.

"Remember, Marshall," Gillis said, "Marta and I came to the program as industrial espionage specialists. Why don't you ask Marta about the devices she smuggled onto the GRC campus that first day?"

Marshall inquired by means of raised eyebrows.

Marta smiled and shook her head.

"What's the point of making a recording, anyway?" Frank said. "You can't take a disc back with you."

"I want something I can go over a few times before we return so I'm sure I can provide Lucre with an accurate transcript of the conversation from memory. And my present self will put the recording in a safe deposit box should she need it for evidence here, so if there's any question, we can return and double check."

Marta held each person's gaze as she continued. "Let's go over it one more time. According to the transcripts of the depositions Lucre provided, the representative of the other company said their conversation took place sometime between 10:30 and 11 am. Warren Pitts said he couldn't recall whether the hallway conversation took place at all. If it did, he contends it was routine and didn't involve any discussion of sensitive technological issues."

She paused and was greeted by nods.

Several office suites opposite the big meeting room, Lucre told her, had been vacant at the time. The travelers could use one of those suites as an observation post, he suggested, and so long as they made their presence seem a normal office operation, everyone would probably assume they belonged there.

Lucre said people who attended the meeting remembered enough hallway activity that morning, so the travelers should be able to blend in there, as well.

The plan was simple.

When and if Pitts and the contractor entered the hallway for their conversation, Gillis would leave their pretend office and move to the best vantage point he could manage for recording the discussion. Marta, Marshall and Frank would provide any interference or cover Gillis might need. When they were done, they'd turn off the lights and go to lunch. Later that afternoon Elvin would retrieve the travelers. Their counterparts from the *Gomer Pyle* universe would head for the desert, where the next five years of their lives awaited them.

"All right," Marta said. "Let's do this. Stake out the hallway, record the conversation, and get out of here."

The operation should be absolutely routine, she reminded herself.

Thursday, April 17, 1968

The sensation of sprinting across grass—even with a clunky pair of baseball cleats that were lead divers' boots compared to feather-light turf shoes that would come along thirty-five years later—was something like being transported to a planet with two-thirds the gravity of earth.

Denied the game as a child, Sean had played adult amateur baseball into his fifties when he stood six feet tall and weighed two hundred pounds, nursing weakening muscles and aching joints through each game. At fifteen, young Sean neared his full adult height, but weighed a pathetic 135 pounds. He featured narrow shoulders, willowy arms, reedy legs, and a waist so skinny the leather uniform belt reached almost twice around him when he pulled it tight enough to keep his pants up.

When Coach Kenny organized wind sprints at the start of practice, Sean could hardly believe what this scant body wearing clunky shoes could do.

He flew.

Effortlessly, pain-free, he skimmed over the springtime grass so fast his eyes watered.

Future-Sean's plan had been to skip baseball practice and get right to the task of locating Amanda Page. Young-Sean, however, was not yet fully agreed to the idea of approaching a senior girl whom he knew only in passing.

"It's the entire reason I've come," past-Sean admonished him. *"Believe me, it will be for the best. Sometimes you have to do things you don't like—"*

"Yeah, yeah, I know. I hear that at home all the time."

One glimpse of the baseball diamond glowing green under a white afternoon sun, though, convinced future-Sean to give his younger counterpart a while longer to understand the nuances of their quest for Sheila Schuler.

These were thirty-yard sprints that by unspoken agreement were run grudgingly and carefully, just fast enough to appear to be making an effort and avoid more running as punishment for lagging.

Sean couldn't contain himself, though. Coach Kenney blew his whistle, and Sean finished yards ahead of the others. Giddy with the sensation, he breathed the fragrance of mown alfalfa from a nearby field and anticipated Kenney's next whistle.

He led the second sprint by eight yards.

"That's the way it should be done, men!" Coach Kenney shouted. "At least we've got one guy here who wants to get ready to play!"

Sean glanced around to see who the coach was talking about and was startled to see almost everyone—particularly the football guys—glaring at him. He was shocked for two reasons. First, because Coach Kenney had never acknowledged him before. And second, at the malevolence conveyed through the scowls of his teammates.

"Let's see if the rest of you can keep up," Kenney growled, then blew his whistle again. This time Sean throttled back. He still led the pack by a couple of yards, though, and grumbles from the football players became more pronounced.

Next came batting practice. Future-Sean couldn't wait for this chance. Young-Sean was a mediocre hitter at best, but his future self knew volumes more about hitting than did the kid. The Seans planned to open a lot of eyes during BP.

Art Stockdale, a history teacher and assistant coach, threw BP. He pitched from behind an L-screen located between plate and pitchers' mound, consistently locating the ball waist high, fat, and down the middle.

Sean stepped in, opened his stance slightly, choked up a bit on a thirty-three-inch thick-handled K-55 Louisville Slugger, and began a gentle rocking motion, shifting his weight slightly from the ball of one foot to the other. He saw the baseball clearly as it left Coach Stockdale's hand. Sean rotated his hips slightly toward the catcher to load his swing and . . . flailed. He barely topped the ball, sending it dribbling a few feet from the plate.

Young Sean had no time to wallow in his disappointment. Coach Stockdale had already begun his motion for the next pitch. Rock . . . load . . . wait, this time, wait, wait, wait . . . Sean hit the ball off the handle, sending a weak flair over the third baseman.

Bobby Zimmerman, the starting shortstop and a

running back from the football team, stepped to the plate next. Sean backed off to watch Bobby, a gifted athlete suffering through a terrible slump. As did Sean's, most of Bobby's swings produced dribbling ground balls or weak pop-ups just beyond the infield.

"Shit, man," Bobby said, standing next to Sean as they watched the next hitter from their group. "I think I caught whatever you've got. I can't hit anything anymore."

Unlike many of the football players, Bobby did not seem to hold lesser athletes in disdain. Still, young-Sean couldn't believe it when he heard himself answering, "You need to make a couple of basic adjustments and you'll be fine."

"Yeah?" Bobby said with a note of amusement. "Such as?"

What are you doing? an appalled young-Sean demanded mentally.

Just let me handle this, came the order from his older counterpart.

"Your hands are screwed up," Sean said. "Your hands are moving through an arc. You're trying to reach and hook the ball. Drive your hands along a line straight to the ball, like you usually do. The other thing is, you're worried, and you've gotten too defensive. You've gotta throw the bat through the strike zone with your hands, not drag it along with your arms."

He used a slow-motion swing to demonstrate.

"At the same time, because you're so frustrated, you're jumping at the ball. Don't go get it. Stay weighted over your back foot. Let the ball come to you. Wait, wait, wait."

Bobby regarded him curiously. Over Bobby's shoulder, Sean saw Coach Kenny glaring at them.

Sean stepped back to the plate and squibbed five more weak grounders.

Bobby sent a half dozen line drives ringing toward the fence.

May 18, 2043

Marta's troop of time travelers negotiated security scanners without incident and boarded a crowded elevator. They exited on the twelfth floor to a long, bright hallway covered in light blue institutional carpeting. A wall of glass covered with closed floor-to-ceiling blinds formed one corridor wall. Muffled sounds of conversation leaked through the glass.

Marta steered them toward a pair of office suites opposite the glass wall and did her best to appear secretarial. An outer door split two tall windows, behind which were a darkened reception area and a couple of interior doors leading deeper into the building.

She shielded Gillis as he manipulated an electronic device. The door's lock clicked open.

Marta flipped a light switch and took her position as receptionist. Marshall, Gillis and Frank chose chairs along one wall and sat, impersonating people in line for appointments.

"And now we wait," Marta said.

"Um... do you think one of these doors leads to a restroom?" Marshall asked a half hour later.

"Didn't I tell you to go before we left?" Marta said.

Marshall tried the first door, which opened to inner offices. A second door revealed a small bathroom with a sink, toilet, paper towel dispenser and urinal.

"Can I go first?" Gillis called to Marshall. "I'm afraid I hydrated a little too much and I'm ... quite uncomfortable."

Marshall held the door and said, "After you."

"Yeah, then me," said Frank.

Marta used her pocket computer to set up a virtual display and virtual keyboard. She pantomimed typing and answering the phone as the office windows gave her a clear view of hallway traffic.

The meeting room door swung open intermittently as people exited or entered. Not Warren Pitts, though, and none of the others stopped to converse. Minutes ticked off Marta's digital computer display, marching toward 11:00 a.m.

"It's beginning to look as if Mr. Pitts may be off the hook," Marshall said.

"We'll give it until they break for lunch," Marta answered. "Then we're gone."

She directed her attention back to her computer.

Gillis said, "No, I don't think Mr. Pitts is out of the woods yet."

She glanced to see a knot of a half dozen men spilling from the meeting room. Her gaze fell immediately to Pitts, who was last to exit. Most of the group kept walking, but one of the men turned his back to her view and touched Pitt's elbow as the Hemisphere honcho walked by. Pitts stopped, smiled, and put a friendly hand on the other man's shoulder.

"Okay, Gillis, go," Marta said.

Wearing his ear buds and holding the writing instrument,

Gillis quickly positioned himself a few yards down the hallway. Frank moved next, walking slowly past the two men in the opposite direction, hoping to register some thread of conversation. Marshall followed Frank with the same routine.

Marta stepped to the doorway, just a few feet from the conversation, and caught a snippet of dialogue. The subject wasn't satellite components, though. It was something about . . . government regulation?

". . . it's just crazy," Pitts was saying. "Those restrictions make no sense at all, and they'll add millions to the costs. If you ever get the chance to . . ."

Marta looked to her right to be sure Gillis was recording. Standing about ten feet away, he held the writing instrument and a pad of paper, as if he was jotting a memo to himself, the pen subtly directed toward Pitts and his companion.

She turned to her left to check on Marshall and Frank when she heard Gillis call, "Governor? Governor Dobler?"

Marta's gaze swung back to Gillis. She saw his right hand disappear into a jacket pocket.

Benjamin Franklin Dobler, future president of the United States, rotated his torso ninety degrees to face the man who'd called his name. Dobler's expression defaulted to the automatic smile Marta had seen so many politicians use to greet unknown voters who needed to be made welcome and important. The smile collapsed into a grimace of fear. Dobler recoiled and raised his arms as if to ward off an attack.

Marta snapped back to Gillis. His right hand cleared his jacket to reveal the blunt gray elongated shape of a silenced pistol.

She didn't have time to shout a warning as Gillis extended his arm toward Dobler. She launched herself, soaring above the floor to shield Dobler from the man who had come to kill him.

She heard a soft click and registered the sound of the pistol's ejection mechanism.

From somewhere far away, a voice shouted, "No! Oh God, Marta! NO!"

Her world crumbled to blackness.

26

SUSPICION AND ANGER

Thursday, April 17, 1968

DRIVING HOME FROM baseball practice, the young version of Sean Brody navigated familiar streets, his consciousness occupied by jumbled glimpses of a fantastic future world that lay before him.

"A thousand television channels? Do you guys do anything besides watch TV? Gasoline costs how much? Jeez, no wonder you need so many channels. No one can afford to go anywhere..."

At the same time, future-Sean found himself equally distracted by this childhood realm that colored vague outlines of memory with vivid detail. Each street, each block, each house focused blurry recollection into sharp relief. The distance of years had dimmed the reality of so many people and events that were once central to his life. With the passage of time, they had become characters or chapters from a book read long ago.

"Jimmy Johnson lives there," past-Sean recited to himself. *"What a dick. Cynthia Borders' house is one block over. I kissed her once on that snow day when we were all over at Larry's ... she has this thing for Scotty, though ..."*

Young-Sean waved to a boy standing by a beautiful

cherry-red Model A street rod gleaming with chrome pipes. Future-Sean registered the scene and couldn't help passing a thought to his young counterpart. *"Oh man, there's Joe Vincent. He died in Viet Nam . . ."*

"Oh, my God," young-Sean said aloud. "Joe dies? He's been telling everyone he's already signed papers for the army as soon as he graduates next month. We have to warn him . . . wait, it doesn't work that way, does it? He'd never believe me, would he? He'd just think I was nuts."

"Now you're getting it," future-Sean told his younger self. *"Remember, they told me you will forget all about me and time travel and details of the future. Everything about the next few days will become vague to you, while everyone else here will remember the things you've said and done. And you'll have to live with that. Look what happened to Amanda. They sent her to a mental institution. We can't warn anyone about anything."*

"Yeah," young-Sean said, his tone dismal, "except, of course, Amanda. We're gonna tell her, and even she's probably gonna think I'm nuts."

"I'm sure she will—at first," his older counterpart said.

"So why do it at all?" young-Sean asked. "I get that you screwed up our life somewhere and want to change things, but that doesn't have anything to do with Amanda. Why don't we just leave her alone?"

"Because we made a commitment to Marshall . . . and we keep our commitments. You need to learn that a promise and a handshake are the most binding contracts a man can enter into."

Sean turned a corner and drove along the narrow block toward the house where he'd lived since birth. He recited the names of his neighbors along this street for future-Sean's benefit as they drove past each house. And as he did so, future-Sean could not keep from his younger self the knowledge of what happened to almost all these people over the long march of time.

Which brought Sean to his driveway, his house and a whole new flood of memory. Future-Sean tried to recall his parents in the best of times, during their long and robust years of health, their post-retirement happiness. He didn't want to inflict upon his young counterpart the memory of their deaths and the emptiness of missing them that remained even decades after their passing. To no avail. Their deaths, funerals and attendant grief were inscribed indelibly on future-Sean's memory. As was the passing of his sister, who lived to the age of ninety and died a couple of years before Sean moved to Arizona.

All this loss and grief visited young-Sean at once. He sat quietly for a long time, hands gripped white on the steering wheel as he tried to cope with the ultimate mortality of people he loved. Knowing everything much too soon was a cruel consequence future-Sean had not considered when he'd volunteered for this journey.

"I don't think I can do this," young-Sean finally said. "This is . . . this is . . ."

"I know," his future self answered. *"Remember, the people from my world said you'll forget in just a few—"*

"How could anyone forget this?" young-Sean said.

Sean walked slowly toward his house. This was the moment future-Sean had been anticipating. What a gift seeing them again would be. He wasn't sure if he could handle the emotions . . . wait. Oh, no.

"You timed it all wrong," young-Sean said. "They aren't here."

Sean's mother had been gone all semester to Colorado, studying for her masters' degree. This week was one his father had taken off to visit her.

"And I don't want a bunch of kids over here while I'm gone," Sean recalled his father's admonition. Future-Sean savored this fresh image of his dad as a young and vigorous man seen through a clear memory of only two days rather than the veil of decades.

"You behave yourself. Jenny will tell me if you don't," his father had warned.

Sharing disappointment and grief, the two versions of Sean entered a house devoid of those people at the center of his life, overflowing with memories at every turn.

While the reality of his family surrounded the ninety-three-year-old man who was Sean Brody, his mother, father and sister remained beyond his reach.

Friday, April 18, 1968

Sean beheld the noisy commotion of Portales High School's lunchroom. About half the student population, including Sean, ate lunch off campus. The others huddled here in groups according to their social strata.

Jocks and jockettes—these included cheerleaders and athletes' girlfriends—occupied tables at the room's center. Band students and some of the smart kids were off to one side, blending with students who, after another decade, would be fledgling computer geeks. Now, these were kids who built model airplanes or looked through telescopes, went to debate club or math club meetings or entered science fairs. Closest to the jocks were farm kids and cowboys because many of them crossed over boundaries into jockdom.

Aspiring hippies clustered way at the back. Although drugs had not yet impacted this innocuous corner of the world in a significant way, these kids were actors, artists, writers and serious musicians who would one day be intrigued by the possibilities. Sean was on the fringe of several groups. A wannabe jock, a model airplane builder and a fledgling musician. He hadn't yet found his place.

He was still better off than Amanda during this, her senior year, though.

Sean saw her sitting alone at a table against a far wall.

From the perspective of ninety-three years, Sean's memories of Amanda were vague, at best. Even though Portales High was a small school in a small town, Sean and Amanda had no reason to cross paths. She was a senior and he a sophomore. She had been a star at everything she did whether it involved academics, sports, poise, beauty, sense of humor. He was a gangling fifteen-year-old, balancing precariously on a tightrope anchored by parental expectation on the one hand, and complex demands of the high school caste system on another.

At one time, anyone of Sean's status who thought of making overtures to Amanda would have had to fight his way past a bevy of senior boys to even get close. Some of those senior boys would have fought back. Now, a little over a month before her graduation, she appeared to be making her best effort to hide.

She wore baggy clothes concealing her figure. Her hair hung straight and had a slight oily appearance of being unwashed. She wore no makeup. She ate with her eyes downcast. When she did happen to glance about, she wore the startled, furtive expression of someone anticipating the next assault on her dignity.

She stared at a book as she ate sparingly from her lunch tray.

Standing at a distance, young-Sean was dismayed by future-Sean's insistence that he talk to her.

"Whoa, man, that won't be cool," young-Sean thought. *"I know everybody here. I'll get all kinds of crap for talking to the crazy girl."*

"You can't possibly realize," future-Sean said, *"how small and petty and cowardly that makes you sound. She needs help. She needs a friend."*

"Yeah, well, like you said, you'll disappear pretty soon. I'm the one who has to stay here and live with . . . with . . ."

"With what? The stigma of being kind to someone who desperately needs kindness? While you're so worried about what everyone else will think of you, why don't you worry a little about what you'll think of yourself?"

Future-Sean found himself wound up to continue with a scathing lecture on basic human decency when he confronted the chaotic jumble of conflicting emotions and values careening through his young counterpart's conscience. So, he backed off.

"I'm sorry," he thought. *"Old men forget how complicated life can be when you're fifteen. I guess it's asking a lot to have you set aside the ravages of peer pressure and immaturity to—"*

"To do the right thing?" young-Sean answered. With a

mental sigh, he added, *"Will it always be this hard? Doing the right thing, I mean."*

Sean took a couple of tentative steps before retreating again.

"Could we wait until after school? Or at least some time when there aren't so many people?"

"Come on, when would that be? We don't know her. We can't just drop by her house. She's here now, and we have to start this conversation somewhere."

The boy took a deep breath and future-Sean retreated, leaving his young counterpart to his own devices.

"Okay," young-Sean thought finally. *"Let's get this over with."*

Sean made his way through the lunchroom. He seldom ate here. Typically, he and his friends went to Pat's or Doc's to be sure they got their daily recommended allowance of grease and sugar. He exchanged hellos with several fellow sophomores who seemed surprised to see him. As people began to understand his path would lead him to Amanda, he felt their greetings turn to questioning stares.

Reaching her table, young-Sean simply stood for a moment. He could still turn, retrace his steps. He could laugh as he retreated, make it a joke—one more cruel jab at a girl on the receiving end of far too many. But the older incarnation of himself hovering in his brain expressed such disgust at even the thought of such a heartless act, young-Sean froze with indecision.

As he stood mute, Amanda glanced up with a start.

Sean's stare was blank as he still debated his final commitment.

"What?" Amanda demanded.

"Um... I just wanted... well, you're over here by yourself, and I thought—"

"Did some of those asshole senior boys send you here?"

"No... I just... I—"

"Look, kid, I'm not trying to be pretty. I'm not trying to attract anyone. Pretending to be sympathetic won't get you into the crazy girl's pants. Several guys have already tried it. They'll tell you it doesn't work."

"That's not why... I... um... you are pretty, though. You might want to wash your hair or something."

"Hey, listen to me. Just screw off. I don't want any company. And tell whoever put you up to this, I don't give a damn what anyone thinks. I'm immune to humiliation. I have to be here about four more weeks. Once I graduate, no one in this shitty town will ever see me again."

She'd raised her voice to the extent that several people at nearby tables were gawking.

Amanda simply returned to her book and continued to pick at her lunch.

Young-Sean wanted to escape before the scene could become any more embarrassing. During this rather one-sided conversation, future-Sean had been tentative in asserting his influence over the younger being. Now, though, he exerted all his will, and young-Sean retreated to a neutral corner.

"I hope I can help you, Amanda," he said softly through the boy's voice. "That's all I want. Nothing more. At least, I think I can help you understand what's happened to you."

She snapped her eyes back to Sean's and whispered with venom, "Look, you stupid jerk, get away from me, or I'll—"

"Do you have dreams about the future? About a man

named Marshall and a woman named Marta? Do you sometimes 'remember' things that haven't happened?"

She leaned away from him, astonishment written across her face. The fury in her eyes melted to fear. A clank of knives and forks against metal lunchroom trays and the buzz of conversation filled the silence separating them.

"Who are you?" she finally whispered. "How do you know about my dreams? I worked very hard at forgetting all that. Why do you want me to go back... Who told you?"

"I'm... I'm sorry. I didn't mean to..."

Whatever anger she'd displayed gave way to a hurt and pleading tone. "All those files and recordings of my therapy sessions were supposed to be confidential. I don't know how you got hold of them." As she whispered, she seemed ever more mindful of cautious glances from around the room. "Please... my life is tough enough as it is. Can't you just let me spend the next few weeks in peace? Just let me be done with this place?"

"Nobody showed me any files. Please believe... I can give you some answers. And you may be able to help your... um... a friend of... some of those people you dream about. We have to talk, though. This is a pretty complicated thing to explain, and we can't do it at lunch."

"Yeah," she said, recapturing some of her anger. "I'll bet we can't. Do it at lunch, I mean."

"Please. Meet me this evening. I'll come to your house if there's a place we can talk privately."

"My dad would string you up if you even came near our front door. He's seen how other boys have treated me since I got back and... and he's furious."

"My house then. My folks are gone. No one would bother us."

Now *all* the venom returned.

"So that's how it is, you little prick. And if I don't do it, you'll make sure someone else hears those tapes, right?"

"No. I'm just trying to help . . ."

"You may be doing a lot of things," she said, "but you're not trying to help *me*."

Future-Sean thought for a moment, then realized the extent to which she was right.

"Okay, maybe that's true. I think the person they are most interested in helping is Sheila."

Her eyes opened wide. She mouthed the name, *Sheila*.

"You hear that name in your dreams, don't you? More than the others? She's someone who will be . . . important to your life. And she's in a lot of trouble. Her friends miss her terribly. If you'll just let me explain, they think maybe she can be saved."

Amanda's eyes filled with helpless tears. She sagged into her chair, covered her face and sobbed. Sean leaned forward and started to offer a comforting hand, then thought better of the gesture. Instead, he took a piece of notebook paper and pen from the pile of books next to Amanda and wrote his address.

"Again, I'm so sorry, Amanda. I'm sorry I have to bring all this up and take you back to that dark place you've been. But it's the only way. I *do* want to help you. Please come and see me this evening. I think I can make you understand."

Sean turned to leave and saw dozens of faces fixed on this awkward exchange. A wave of self-consciousness crept over him. He wanted nothing more than to slink away from the unwanted spotlight. Instead, future-Sean said to all of them, "I didn't mean to upset her. Please, don't hurt her anymore. She's been hurt enough. Just leave her alone."

27

THE PRICE OF SANITY

BASEBALL PRACTICE FRIDAY was again a litany of frustration for the Seans. Future-Sean attempted to provide his younger self the fundamental knowledge of how to hit, throw and field. While young-Sean enjoyed the blessing of a lithe and agile body, he simply did not own the athleticism necessary to convert future-Sean's knowledge into immediate action. Only hours, weeks and months of repetitive practice would accomplish that, and by then, the information future-Sean had imparted would be long gone.

Following practice, Coach Kenny called everyone together and related when players should be at the field house to dress and catch the bus for tomorrow's trip to Clovis. Several sophomores, particularly those who weren't also football or basketball players, didn't make road trips. Clovis was only a twenty-minute bus ride away, though, so Kenney included everyone.

This time during his drive home young-Sean could focus only on foreknowledge provided by future-Sean of what would happen the next day.

"So, I'll be a pinch runner and I screw it up?"

"No, you don't really . . . well, yes . . . but it's only because

you don't know what to do. Nobody's taught you how to read a pitcher's move and get the jump you need. With any kind of jump at all, no one can throw you out."

"You said Manny will hit into a double play."

"He'll hit a ground ball to second. If we do it right, they won't have time to turn a double play."

"I don't know how to get a good jump."

"Don't worry about it. I do. When the time comes, just let me take over."

"Oh, man," young-Sean said with a smile. "This means I'll get to stay on the team. Maybe even play some more. Maybe make the team next year... this could change everything."

And a thought occurred to future-Sean that the boy was right. This *could* change everything. Young-Sean's excitement was blunted as he shared this foreboding from future-Sean's occupancy of his brain.

"That's what you want, right?" young-Sean protested. "You got involved with all this so you could change things?"

"Maybe it's too soon ..."

He shared the memory of Naomi's warning.

"... If you were able to change something when you are so young, many things you liked and valued later might be changed, too. Family, children, friendships, might turn out differently."

Young-Sean, though, found it easy to shrug off an image of three sons he did not know. He couldn't relate to the pride of a father and grandfather in his children's lives, their achievements and aspirations.

With alarm, the 93-year-old version of Sean Brody recognized warning signs that his influence as a wiser and more mature being was being subjugated by the fifteen-year-old kid.

"You're not really going over there, are you?" Joni demanded of Amanda.

When Amanda collapsed in tears earlier that day at lunch, Joni Miller—the best friend who had essentially abandoned Amanda months earlier when the social cost of standing by her became too dear—rose from the jockette's table and at first walked, then trotted, then ran to Amanda's side. She put her arms around her friend.

"Oh, Amanda. Please forgive me."

Amanda welcomed Joni's offer of support. They'd skipped classes and spent two long hours seated in Amanda's car in the high school parking lot as she revealed details of lonely humiliation that had become her life.

She started with stares and snickers coming from every quarter as gossip spread. Then, the hurt and anger she'd felt as friends began to avoid her, and her isolation took root. Joni apologized over and over. Amanda understood Joni's remorse was genuine.

She told Joni how relieved she'd been the day David Hudson, a guy whom she had dated during her junior year, finally stopped by and asked her to go for a coke.

"We parked along one of the section roads," Amanda said. "He was all sympathy and understanding. It was nice, at first, when he gave me a big hug and a long kiss."

Amanda paused as her memory replayed the scene. *Back when they were dating, she and David had fooled around a little. On a few occasions, she'd ridden a wave of sexual excitement and let him unbutton her shirt and nibble at her breasts. But she'd always stopped him there.*

This time, when his hands found their way to her breasts, she didn't say anything to discourage him. She felt only relief that someone still cared about her. When he slipped her shirt from her shoulders and reached behind her to undo her bra, a nagging inner voice instilled by a strict morality of that time and place began its cautionary warning.

"He ... he kept going," Amanda said to Joni. "I asked him to please just wait ..."

Again, Amanda retreated to her memory. David was beyond waiting. He pulled her bra away and buried his face between her breasts. She tried closing her eyes, hoping the familiar warm and exotic wave that seemed to begin at her nipples and radiate down into her pelvis would quiet the nagging voice.

The wave failed her.

That mental admonition became louder when David took her hand and guided it to his zipper.

Finally, when he began to fumble at the snap on her jeans, she could stand it no longer.

"... he just kept going, so I told him no. I pushed him away."

She'd moved to retrieve her bra. David had pulled the bra from her hands and stared at her from his side of the car seat.

"Amanda, you can't just cut me off this way. You can't get me going and—"

"I didn't get you going," she said. "I didn't do anything. You started this. Now I want to stop. Take me home."

"Then he told me I'd better figure out who my friends are. He told me everyone said I was crazy, that they'd given me LSD at the mental hospital, and I'd had sex with the guards, then had an abortion. An abortion! And LSD! I asked him why would anyone make that up? He asked what could I expect when I'd been living with a bunch of lunatics?"

Her memory completed the conversation.

"They aren't lunatics." Her voice was cold, and she covered her breasts with her hands and arms. *"They are people struggling with an illness. They go to a hospital so they can get better. Give me my bra and take me home."*

"Look, Amanda, I'm trying to be your friend here. You should be glad that I'm—"

"I'm supposed to let you fuck me because you're willing to be my friend?"

"No . . . I only want to . . ."

She grabbed her bra and turned away from him. She pulled on her shirt as David started the car. When they stopped at her house, he said, *"Don't expect me to go out of my way to defend you anymore. Like I said, you don't know who your friends are."*

Joni listened, tears running down her face as well.

"I can only imagine what David has been telling everyone," Amanda said.

Joni sighed. "He said you let him 'do it.' He said they gave you drugs that made you real horny and that you practically raped him that night. He laughed about it."

"That explains a lot." Amanda thought of other boys who had made blatant overtures since.

"And now there's this creepy sophomore kid," Joni said, shaking her head. "Sean Brody. I know him. Anyway, I know who he is. I always thought he was nice enough."

"Unfortunately, I think boys will do just about anything to get some pussy," Amanda said.

"Don't say . . . that word," Joni chided. "That's gross. And don't you dare go see him."

"This is different," Amanda said. "Somehow he's gotten hold of the tapes or the transcripts from my therapy sessions. I have to get them back. I can't stand any more of this. I just want to graduate and get out of here."

"How could some high school kid possibly get hold of tape recordings or records from a doctor's office in Albuquerque?" Joni said. "All that stuff is confidential. How would someone even know where to search?"

As Amanda shrugged, a terrifying thought shivered through her core.

"My journal," she said. Color drained from her face as her heart began to race.

"Oh, my God, Amanda. What's wrong? You look like you've seen a ghost!"

Amanda balled her fists and banged them on the car seat. In the distance, students began to pour from every door and into the parking lot. Amanda and Joni ignored curious stares as people walked by.

"At the hospital, I started keeping a journal," Amanda said. "I wrote every day. My . . . therapist told me that writing down details of my dreams would help. Everything's in there, and . . . I haven't been writing so I haven't seen it lately."

"You don't know where it is?"

"I . . . I know where it's supposed to be. But I haven't even opened that drawer for a week."

"That creep stole your journal!"

"Yeah, that's all I can think. I have to get it back."

"Tell your dad, or the police," Joni said. "Don't you dare go over there."

"Who would believe me?" Amanda asked. "I'm the girl who had voices in her head. I can't prove he did it, not unless the little asshole admits he's got it."

"I'll go with you."

Amanda frowned. "No, that won't work. I think I know how I can trick him into admitting what he's done. But I have to do this by myself."

28

THE CHANGE-UP

Phoenix, Arizona
May 18, 2043

MARSHALL WATCHED HELPLESSLY as the horror played out only a few feet away.

First, Gillis called Dobler's name. The future president turned away from Marshall, toward his inquisitor. Gillis raised his right hand, from which extended a thin metal tube.

That's weird, Marshall reflected. *That's a gun. That's a gun with a silencer. Why would Gillis ...*

He saw a blur fly from the doorway immediately opposite where Dobler stood. Everything slowed down. The blur was a person, now fully extended about four feet above the floor, completely defiant of gravity ...

Marta! And she's ... Marta's trying to tackle Dobler. No. She missed him completely.

Gillis's hand bucked upward. . . . Marshall heard a *snick* as a wisp of smoke curled from the weapon's sound suppressor.

Marta seemed to remain suspended in space between Dobler and Gillis. Then, she collapsed to the floor, her forehead snapping onto the carpet with the force of her fall. Dobler remained frozen, his hands raised in a futile effort of defense. Terror etched his features.

Marshall heard someone scream, "No! Oh, God, Marta! No!" He realized the voice was his.

The scene jumped forward. Marshall found himself on his knees beside her. Marta lay unmoving, face down. When he reached to cradle her against his body, his hand came away bloody. He glanced at the floor, noting a bright red flow oozing across the blue carpet.

Hands gripped his shoulders. He shrugged free of them as he pulled Marta closer.

"You must be careful," a voice said. "She's not conscious. Let's just leave her until the paramedics . . ."

Marshall associated this voice with the hand touching his shoulder. He tore his eyes from Marta's still form and peered into the face of Ben Dobler. He followed Dobler's gaze to the figure of Warren Pitts, who slumped against the glass wall next to them. Pitts wore an expression of confusion. His eyes were crossed, as if inspecting a neat hole in the middle of his forehead.

Marta stirred, rolled onto her side, and sat up.

Her gaze was drawn to Dobler, then to Pitts. She closed her eyes, twisting her neck experimentally.

"Young lady," Dobler said with a note of disbelief. "I think . . . I think you just saved my life."

"No. No," Marta said, keeping her head down, avoiding Dobler's eyes. "I didn't. I just tripped. And apparently, this other guy is the one who got shot."

"Marta?" Marshall said. "You're not . . . you're not . . . ?"

"Not as far as I can tell." She added with a whisper, "And let's be careful about throwing names around, okay?"

"Oh, thank God. I thought . . . I thought . . . I . . . I . . ."

"Yeah, me, too," she whispered into his ear. "Right now,

though, you have to get us out of here. I can't let Gillis return to our future before I do."

The slow motion, frame-by-frame scrolling of the scene exploded into pandemonium all around them. Dobler waved and shouted, "We need help here! We need an ambulance!"

A handful of people who had their wits about them tried to reach the fallen man. Most, though, were in full flight mode.

Marshall glanced quickly along the hallway. Gillis was nowhere to be seen.

"How do we . . ." he began.

She twisted the ring on her hand, and it began to glow. "Just hit me with the Taser," she said. "Elvin will get me back."

"That won't work," Marshall countered. "You have to get everyone out of here. You think Frank and I can do this by ourselves? You tase me. I'll be sure Elvin brings you home in a few minutes."

"I don't have time to argue," Marta said. "Just be sure and tell security to grab Phillip Lucre. Don't let him escape the complex." She touched the tiny button at the side of her ring.

Marshall felt a paralyzing jolt sizzle and rattle through his brain. He fell back against the wall, next to Pitts.

Marta assessed the shocked eyes of Ben Dobler, Frank Altman and a half-dozen other people crushing around them.

"Oops," she said, displaying her hand with the Taser ring. "Damn thing just went off. Somebody should call the paramedics."

"We already did," Dobler said. "You . . . I saw you. You did try to save me . . ."

"No. No. I just tripped coming through the door. I'm clumsy that way."

By now, everyone had spilled from the meeting room. Like Marta, Dobler was spattered with Pitts' blood. As Marta knew it would, hysteria began to feed itself. Some of the group stampeded toward elevators. Others crowded around Pitts and Dobler, stealing the future president's attention.

Marta saw Frank appear at the frenzy's periphery. She caught his attention and waved him over.

"Quick," she said, "help me with Marshall. We have to find a way out of here."

Marshall gave a groan as Frank pulled him through a tangle of people, lifting him to his feet.

"You okay there, buddy? Can you walk?"

Marshall's response was another groan. Marshall draped an arm around Frank's shoulder while Marta put her arm around Marshall's waist. He managed to make his legs work. The three of them headed toward an exit sign at the hallway's far end. They descended two floors before Marta directed them into a quiet corridor lined with office spaces.

Near the exit door was a bathroom.

"Here," ordered Marta as she directed them into the women's restroom. "Marshall, how are you doing?"

"Better," he grunted. "At least the cobwebs are clearing up. He's gone, by the way."

Marta breathed a sigh of relief.

"That means we only have a few more minutes before Elvin gets the rest of us. We need to leave this building before that happens if we can."

"The cops will be everywhere," Frank said. "How will we get by them?"

"There's a lot of confusion," Marta said. "With any luck, nobody will be able to provide police with our description."

"Why does that matter?" Marshall asked. "We didn't do anything."

"We're here," Marta said. "We're connected because we're here. If we get stopped for questioning and Dobler recognizes me, we'll be caught in an investigation that will probably screw our security clearances. If that happens, late or not, there's no way we'll be accepted into the program."

"History says we make it okay," Frank said.

"Well, I'm not taking Elvin's theory for granted," Marta said. "I think we should give history all the help we can. Give me your shirt."

"My shirt?" Frank said.

"Yes, mine's covered with blood. I need your shirt."

"What will *I* do for a shirt?" Frank asked.

"Anyone asks, tell them people were grabbing and fighting to get away from the gunshots, and someone ripped off your shirt."

She peeled away her top and stood facing Frank. While future-Frank had seen Marta's breasts on countless occasions, past-Frank had only seen them through the mask of future-Frank's memory. Staring shamelessly, he unbuttoned his shirt and handed it over. Marta did her best to roll the sleeves and tuck the long tail of the oversized garment into her pants.

"Okay, let's go," she said.

She glanced at Marshall—now just shy and awkward past-Marshall—as he tried to suppress a grin.

"What?" she said.

"You're very pretty," Marshall answered.

She kissed his cheek. They returned to the stairwell.

Elvin, Galen and a couple of technicians stared at monitors displaying travelers' lifelines.

These monitors sat side-by-side, Elvin at one end of the short row. Marta and Marshall's monitors were front and center. Off to the side sat a darkened screen, apparently idle. This device, though, surreptitiously scanned the dimensional time and place where they hoped to find Sheila. Elvin had shut off that monitor's optics and programmed an alarm—a tinkling bell—that would sound if a lifeline re-established itself.

Elvin found himself dozing when, next to him, Galen Postelwait shouted, "There's a problem. Marshall's got a problem."

Elvin woke with a start and followed Galen's pointed finger to a quivering red line bisecting Marshall's monitor, characteristic of the Taser *panic button* Elvin knew signified distress.

"Shouldn't we start the computer sequence for an emergency return?" asked Galen.

"I've already reprogrammed everything," Elvin said. "The sequence started automatically when Marshall's electrical field was disrupted. He should be on his way."

29

FROM THE FUTURE?

Friday, April 18, 1968

SEAN OPENED HIS FRONT DOOR when Amanda was only halfway up the sidewalk.

"Thanks so much for coming. I was afraid you wouldn't..."

Amanda ignored his greeting. She walked past him into a curtained living room and surveyed her surroundings. Without looking at Sean, she asked, "What choice do I have? Where are your parents?"

"They're gone all week, but—"

"Who else lives here?"

"My sister. She's staying with friends at one of the university dorms this weekend."

"And we're alone." Amanda spat the words.

"Please, Amanda. It's not like that. I—"

"Bullshit." Amanda wheeled to face him. "Let's just get this over with. I'll show you my tits and that's all you get. I won't screw you. I won't... do anything else to you. And you WILL keep quiet about my journal. If you don't, God help me, I'll kill you. Remember, everybody says I'm crazy, so I can probably get away with it."

In his portion of their brain, older-Sean felt distraught

at Amanda's desperation. He wanted to offer a calming, reassuring explanation. Ever the more dominant consciousness, though, young-Sean intervened.

Um . . . let's wait just a second and think this through, came young-Sean's hopeful suggestion. *We need to at least consider her offer. I mean, she volunteered . . .*"

Sean had been dating Donna Goetz for much of the past year, and as sophomores only recently blessed with drivers' licenses, they were at the back-road-front-seat fumbling stage of their sexual evolution. During those late-night encounters on some of the section roads a few miles from town, Sean managed shadowy glimpses of smallish freckled breasts with tiny pale nipples. Plenty thrilling at the time. But Amanda Page . . . Amanda Page would be light years beyond sophomore breasts.

"Well," Amanda demanded, "do we have an agreement?"

"Um . . . I . . . I . . ."

Sean kicked absently at the carpeted floor and looked away from her as his internal struggle continued.

Future-Sean demanded young-Sean make his explanation, RIGHT NOW! Entranced, though, the fifteen-year-old stared at Amanda with longing. Mouth dry as ashes, he tried to speak. He imagined what lay hidden beneath the long-sleeved pullover Amanda wore, and spoke in one long breathless spurt.

"The old guy says to tell you the other voice you hear is Sheila Schuler trapped inside your brain because of a time travel accident and . . . and, at one point, she might have been able to tell you all that, but even if she did, though, she's been here too long for you to remember."

Amanda's eyes grew wide with shock. She whispered the

word Sheila, then took a long forward stride and slapped Sean—hard.

He stumbled and fell awkwardly onto the couch. He raised his arm to ward off another blow as Amanda advanced on him.

"So, you *did* read my journal! I thought you'd stolen it, but I went home today and it's still there. How did you see it? Or did somebody give you tapes or transcripts of my therapy sessions?"

Amanda reached into her back pocket beneath her sweatshirt and produced a hunting knife. She touched the blade's tip to Sean's throat.

Sean's eyes bulged. He scooted as far back as he could into the couch.

"Whoa, Amanda," he said with a quivering voice.

"So, why don't you let me handle this?" the 93-year-old stream of consciousness sharing Sean's brain asked. Future-Sean felt young-Sean's retreat.

"Amanda," the old man said speaking with young-Sean's voice as his eyes shifted between hers and the knife, "I haven't seen your journal. I don't know anything about tapes and transcripts. And I don't want anything from you. All I want is to help."

Amanda waved the knife in his face. "Then how do you know about this Sheila person in my dreams?"

"Sheila is the reason I came here. Why I had to find you," future-Sean said. "Sheila is your granddaughter."

"My what?" Anger in her voice betrayed Amanda's skepticism. "How could she be . . ." But with each word, her anger seemed to wither, until she could only gape at him in confusion.

"There are others in your dreams, too, aren't there? A man named Marshall, and a woman named Marta and—"

"Elvin," she whispered, lowering the knife to her side and staring absently to a place beyond Sean's living room.

"As I said," future-Sean added, raising his hands in surrender "I don't want anything from you. I only want to help."

She sank weakly to the couch, the width of a cushion separating them. Her knife thumped onto the carpet. Amanda clamped her hands over her eyes and began to weep.

"I've . . . I've worked so hard at ignoring the dreams." She spoke through her sobs. "Pretending that . . . that . . . and now you have to . . . Oh, God, what can I do?"

Young-Sean momentarily reasserted himself and watched for a few moments. He put a tentative hand on Amanda's shoulder. Her face still covered, she leaned across the space, her shoulder touching his, and continued to sob.

"I give up," young-Sean silently appealed to his older counterpart. He didn't know where to put his hands. *"You handle this. Anything I do will only make everything worse."*

While future-Sean felt relief that young-Sean wasn't fighting him anymore, he found that more and more of his will was required to assert himself. He managed to take Amanda in a grandfatherly hug and tell her, "It's okay. Take your time. We'll talk when you're ready."

She pulled back and regarded him with wide damp eyes, as if seeing Sean for the first time.

"Who *are* you?" she asked though a hoarse whisper.

"You want the truth? Well, I'm a selfish old man making a frantic grab for a second chance. Helping you is the price of admission for this particular ride."

She searched his eyes. "You're not making this up."

"No."

"I've known," Amanda whispered. "I've known from that first moment, something, someone, inside of me trying to ... to ... I don't know what. I pretended I didn't believe it anymore, just so they'd let me leave the hospital and come home ... but you know the truth, don't you? That stuff about time travel ..."

"That was him talking. The younger version of me. The Sean Brody you know who lives in this time and place."

"The younger version ... ?"

"I'm from the year 2046, when I am ninety-three years old. I share the consciousness of my fifteen-year-old self. I only have a couple of days before I will be lost within him just as Sheila is lost in you. Those who sent me here think maybe I can reawaken Sheila before that happens so her friends from the future can rescue her—and give you back your life."

"So, what you ... um ... he ... said is true?"

Sean stood, picked up Amanda's knife and offered it to her. She shook her head no. Sean placed it between them on the couch. A gesture of trust.

"Well," future-Sean said, "he wasn't very coherent. But yes. The second consciousness inside you belongs to Sheila Schuler. She *is*, or, I guess, will be, your granddaughter. She—her conscious being—has been imprisoned inside you as the result of a time travel accident initiated almost eighty years from now. At one point, Sheila might have been able to communicate with you and tell you her story. Even if she had, she's been here far too long for you to remember any of that. I'm guessing your dreams show you glimpses of Sheila and her life. That's what you told the doctors about and why you think he—the younger me—read your journal."

"Sheila. My granddaughter?" Amanda said. "So, I get married and have a family? Am I happy? Where do I meet my husband? I don't want to be a housewife. I'm not sure I want children. Not after what—"

"I'm sorry, Amanda," Sean said. "I don't know any of those things. I don't think they wanted me to know much about you. Knowing bits and pieces of your future, Naomi told me, is dangerous."

"Naomi," Amanda said. "I know that name, too. She's oriental, right?"

Sean nodded.

"Why would knowing what happens to me be dangerous?" Amanda asked.

"I can only speak to my own experience," Sean said. "But you don't want to hear that story."

Amanda swept her knife onto the floor and took both Sean's hands in hers. "Yes, I do want to know."

Sean sighed. "I fell in love with a woman who was . . . not a good person. She used me in the worst ways. If I'd known how painful that experience would be, I'd have avoided it altogether."

"So, what's bad about that?" Amanda said.

"That awful experience was the path that led me to the most wonderful woman I've ever known," Sean said. "That relationship didn't work out either, but I hate to think of never meeting Maggie. We were only together for a short time, and though it's painful to miss her all these years, at least once in my life, I experienced unconditional love."

Amanda squeezed his hands. "I'm so sorry," she said.

"Enough about me," Sean said. "We're here to find Sheila."

"So, how do we . . . how can we find her?" Amanda said. "I do have the dreams. I do see . . . I thought it was myself . . . in this very different place doing things I don't understand."

"No, that's Sheila. The resemblance is amazing. The two of you could be twins. In fact, you probably are genetic twins, and that's the only reason they have hope she survived within you. As for finding her? I don't know. I'm supposed to tell you about her. I'm supposed to describe what happened the day she was sent back here. And then . . . well . . . they don't know . . . if she does emerge, they can bring her back to her own time and you won't be . . . um . . ."

"Crazy anymore?" Amanda finished the awkward sentence for him. "*Tell* me. Tell me everything."

They sat for an hour. He talked. She asked questions. He answered with as much detail as he could.

"You have to understand," he apologized, "I wasn't around for any of this. I didn't come into the picture until more than a year after Sheila was gone. So, I can only tell you what they told me."

"Okay, then how will we know if they find her?" Amanda said.

"I don't know. I think you'll feel different, somehow. If she leaves you. Maybe you should look for her. Now, I mean."

"How do I . . . ?"

"Just . . . listen maybe?"

Still grasping Sean's hands, Amanda closed her eyes. Gradually, over a period of several minutes, her brow furrowed. Her mouth turned down in a frown. She squeezed harder. The strength of her grip became so powerful, Sean grimaced with pain. Afraid to disrupt her concentration, though, he focused his attention on a lamp glowing behind her and endured in silence.

Finally, Sean extracted his hands from hers. "Maybe you're trying *too* hard. Maybe you have to just—"

She shook her head in frustration. "No, no. Let me try again . . ."

"I think maybe the thing to do," urged future-Sean as he continued his hold on the shared consciousness, "is to not try at all for a little while. Think about something else if you can."

"Yeah, right. That's like telling someone not to think about an elephant. Maybe you're right, though. I need a distraction. I need . . . tell me about you. Why you? You said you're an old man hoping for a second chance. What does that mean? And who was Maggie?"

Sean sighed.

"I don't think . . ." he began.

"Please. Please tell me."

And so, he did. He told her about pivotal moments that might be the key to changing everything. He told her about tomorrow's baseball game. He told her about his life beyond high school and Portales. He told her about his greatest regret.

"And that was Maggie?"

"It's probably more appropriate to say that it will be Maggie," Sean said with an ironic laugh.

"And you think if you stay here, that this time around you and Maggie can be together?"

"Yes," Sean said, finally admitting the truth to himself.

"I guess that's what it boils down to. It's a real long shot, though. They tell me it's almost impossible to change things."

"Now you know, though..." Amanda began, but Sean shook his head and leaned back into the couch.

"They tell me I'll forget."

Amanda shook her head offering her own rueful laugh. "How could anyone possibly forget something like this? I only wish I *could* forget. This will be indelibly printed on my brain for a lifetime."

"That's what I thought, too," Sean said. "I can feel it happening already, though. Right now, during this conversation, it's harder and harder for me to ... I don't know ... to stay here. Harder and harder for me to maintain this train of thought and the conversation we're having. The young me is becoming more and more assertive and trying to ... push me back behind his will and his thoughts."

"Doesn't he understand?" Amanda gave a scolding glare to the boy speaking to her through an old man's perspective.

"Yes, to a degree he does. But he's also fifteen years old. He's distracted. He's mostly..."

Future-Sean caught himself and glanced awkwardly to the floor.

"Mostly what?"

"Oh ... nothing..."

"Mostly what?" she demanded.

"Um ... mostly ... interested in seeing your breasts."

Amanda recoiled for a moment. Then her face softened into a smile and she began to laugh—this time a rich laugh rolling from deep within her. The way, future-Sean knew, she hadn't laughed for a long time. A sound so infectious that soon Sean laughed with her until he had to wipe tears from his eyes.

Finally, Amanda managed to say between gasps, "Well, you tell him . . . that . . . that if this all happens the way we hope it does, we . . . we might be able to work something out."

Gradually their laughter subsided. Silence again took center stage. Amanda grew somber. She stood and paced from one end of Sean's living room to the other.

Finally, he ventured, "Anything?"

She shook her head.

"Just relax. Maybe it will come . . ."

She sat again. "Tell me about the future."

"Boy. I don't even know where to begin. A lot has happened in eighty years."

"Well," Amanda said, "I gather we manage not to get blown up by the Soviet Union, and vice versa?"

"Um . . . there isn't a Soviet Union eighty years from now."

"You mean we really blow them up?" Amanda said through a gasp.

"No . . . we avoided that."

"So, what happened?"

"Well, they just sort of quit. Went broke, actually. As an economic system, it turns out communism sucks."

"Sucks what?"

Sean blushed.

"Um . . . it's just a saying . . . that becomes popular . . . just a language evolution thing . . ."

"How could a whole country run out of money?"

"They tried to keep up with us in terms of defense spending, and then they got bogged down and lost this war against Afghanistan."

"You're kidding. How could the Soviet Union lose a war to Afghanistan?"

"Well, they—"

"That would be like us losing the war in Vietnam," she said with disbelief.

"Yeah," Sean said. "A lot like that."

"So, what's the world like without the Soviet Union? Does everybody get along?"

She stood again, walked to the mantle above the fake fireplace in Sean's living room and studied the array of family photos.

"Hardly," Sean said.

"So, who's left for us to fight with?"

"Terrorists mostly, from the Middle East. They kill a lot of people in the United States and the rest of the world. And we kill a lot of them. It's all about oil. They've got it and we want it, so we get pretty manipulative and some of them take exception to that."

"You said you don't use oil for energy anymore," Amanda said.

"Well, yeah. Eighty years from now," Sean said. "But by the time the hydrogen revolution occurs, we didn't need foreign oil anymore. Turns out we had more oil resources here than the Middle East all along."

"Wow. Where?"

"North Dakota."

"So, that solves the terrorism problem?"

"Not really," Sean said. "Back when we needed their oil, they were pissed off at all the countries who manipulated their societies to get it. Once the hydrogen thing happens, they're just as pissed off that we don't want it anymore."

"What about things like . . . like . . . day-to-day life?" Amanda said. "Cars. Does everyone have a flying car?"

"No. We pretty much stick to the ground for personal transportation. Not that we couldn't have flying cars. I mean, the technology certainly exists to do it. Somewhere along the line, though, people decided flying cars weren't a very good idea. Would you want your teenager worrying about up and down along with left and right while they're texting their friends?"

"Texting? What's texting?"

"Um . . . well," Sean explained, "our phones have tiny keyboards. So, you can type text messages instead of—"

"That's really dumb," Amanda said. "Why would you want to go to the trouble of typing when you can just talk to someone, instead? And how could anyone have a phone in a car?"

"Phones are everywhere. They don't need wires anymore. They're kind of like . . . walkie talkies . . . except they don't use radio waves. They use . . . it's called cellular technology. And they take pictures, too."

"You take pictures with your phone? Can you call people on your cameras? Where do you put the film?"

"You don't understand. Film is no longer necessary. It's called digital technology."

"So, you carry a whole phone around?"

"Yeah. But they're small," Sean said. "They fit in your pocket or your purse. And for a while they get even smaller than that. They get rid of the actual phones altogether."

"How could they do that?"

"They eventually shrink everything down so small that they implant the phones—fully functional computers, actually—wait, you don't know what computers are either. They're... electronic brains. They're implanted in the cranial cavity just behind the ear. It's amazing. Brain function allows you to direct your phone to place calls, answer calls, or access any sort of information. The more advanced models even have a 'heads up' display that places a three-dimensional image on the frontal lobe of your brain and you can see all your data by simply closing your eyes and thinking the correct coded sequence."

"You just shut your eyes and think? Oh, come on."

"Really," Sean said. "They did it that way because they didn't want people to be watching movies or doing their taxes while they were driving. They just assumed people would have the common sense not to drive with their eyes closed. That didn't work out well for anyone. In fact, it was only a few years before the government decided that the implants were a bad idea altogether."

Amanda raised one eyebrow—a display of skepticism.

"No, it's true," Sean continued. "For one thing, schizophrenia becomes impossible to diagnose. Everybody walks around hearing voices and talking to people who aren't there. Finally, the phone manufacturers were required to implant a small light in the middle of your forehead which became a bright red dot so people would know you were just on the phone and not crazy. That worked well enough—except in India."

"You're making this up," Amanda said.

"Finally, everybody decided the whole thing was too complicated and went back to carrying their phones in their pockets. Just because technology allows something doesn't necessarily mean it's a smart thing to do."

They fell silent again. Amanda walked to the fireplace mantle and picked up one of the framed photos.

"This baby picture, this is you," she said.

"Oh, my," the older Sean answered. "I don't know what happened to all these old photographs. I haven't seen them since ..."

Amanda put the framed photo back on the mantle, returned to the couch, and sat. Her shoulders heaved with a heavy sigh. "It's not working, is it?" she whispered.

Sean cast about within himself for an answer. They were close. He knew it. He didn't want to lose her confidence now.

"Um ... Naomi said it might help to try and reconstruct the circumstances of Sheila's arrival. Make everything as familiar as possible. Where did it happen? Where were you when ... when Sheila got here?"

"I think it happened in Miss Best's classroom," Amanda said. "The chemistry lab. I don't really remember, but they said I fell and hit my head. I think that's when I started hearing the voices."

"Then let's go there."

"Now?"

"I think it has to be now," Sean said. "When everything I told you is fresh in your mind."

"The school is locked. We'd have to break in."

"There must be ..." future-Sean began. His train of thought was derailed, though, as young-Sean shoved his way into the conversation. Future-Sean was at first annoyed and then alarmed. He required every bit of concentration to keep young-Sean from taking over. Was this it? Would his future consciousness finally succumb?

"Just back off for a minute," young-Sean crashed through all at once, and then said aloud, "I know how to get inside."

Future-Sean found that mental exertion was no longer enough. He needed to speak as well. He sorted through the younger track of their shared brain and found the thought.

"Of course. The door back by the band building. The band kids used it to sneak inside and hide a Playboy foldout in the periodic chart!"

"What are you talking about?" Amanda asked.

The reply became a fractured combination of young and old as both streams of consciousness took another step toward their inevitable melding into one.

"Well, it was a vandalous act, *but really funny,* and they didn't give a thought to how much it would hurt poor Miss Best, *a cantankerous old lady who is probably going to flunk me.* It's not her fault, though, because I was really pretty lazy and she doesn't deserve to be treated this way *and it's good for us because a couple of them told me how they got inside,* so very reluctantly we will break in ourselves although we will be careful not to damage anything *and God Amanda, I bet you have really, really great breasts."*

"Um . . . well, yes," Amanda said, doing her best to keep up with the Seans' dichotomy. "Yes, I do. Right now, though, you have to get yourselves together because we need to sneak into the high school."

30

CHEMISTRY STINKS

"BE QUIET," AMANDA CAUTIONED as Sean tugged lightly at a set of double glass doors hidden in darkness between the main school building and a World War II surplus barracks structure housing the band room. A streetlight bathed sidewalks between the buildings, while back doors to the main building occupied a small alcove veiled in shadow.

"I'm trying," Sean said, "but Gary said you have to yank them hard. The pin that's supposed to go into the door frame is broken."

Sean tried a gradual and steady tug creating a whine as metal scraped against metal.

"I don't think we can do this quietly," he said.

"Wait, don't—"

Sean gave the doors a hard jerk. They popped open with shriek and a bang.

Sean stood frozen, awaiting sounds of feet running towards them, or lights, or alarm bells—maybe sirens.

Only black silence answered.

Sean eased the door closed behind them.

Miss Best's classroom and chemistry lab were located off a corridor at the other side of the school. They walked cautiously through a silence broken intermittently by pops, ticks and groans of an empty building, each noise bumping their hearts into a higher gear. The sound of their footfalls added to this subtle cacophony. Sean took the lead, pressing his back to the wall at each intersection, peering down the next shadowy passage before motioning for Amanda to follow.

As they approached the chemistry lab, Sean worried that, given Miss May's recent intrusion, the lab doors might be locked. He was relieved when the doorknob twisted freely in his hand. They slipped inside.

"Okay," Amanda whispered, "what now?"

"Um . . . I don't know. Just concentrate on all the stuff I've told you about Sheila. Find your memory of that day. We don't know how long Sheila might have been aware of herself, or you of her. But there might be something here you could use to revive her."

Amanda peered around the room. She walked to the back row of desks, sat and closed her eyes.

Sean waited several minutes before slipping into the desk beside her.

"Anything?"

"Not really. I'm trying to think her name over and over. It's just that I don't know anything about her. I mean, you told me the story of what happened. Nothing much about who she was, though."

"I didn't know her either," Sean said. "I've seen pictures. She looked exactly like you, so she was very beautiful . . ."

Amanda turned, and stared through darkness at her vague reflection in an exterior window.

". . . and she was obviously a woman who commanded

MIKE MURPHEY

great love, respect and loyalty from her friends. She must have been brave. And very principled. They said she was prepared to risk everything—even go to jail—to be sure that—"

"What's going on here?"

The shout accompanied a quick shaft of light that spilled through a door behind Miss Best's lab table and disappeared as the door snapped closed. Sean jumped and fell from the desk. He would have run if he hadn't landed on his ass. With a half dozen squeaky orthopedic strides Adelia Best loomed over them, squinting through her safety goggles which eerily reflected moonlight spilling through tall windows. The goggles looked like headlights where her eyes should be.

"Oh, my God, Miss Best," Amanda said, her chest heaving. "You scared the hell out of me."

"Amanda? Amanda Page? Is that you? And Sean Brody. I *knew* you had something to do with this hooliganism. I just knew it."

"Um . . . no, ma'am, I really didn't."

"Returned to the scene of the crime, did you? And Miss Page, I'm surprised at you. You've been so quiet and well behaved."

"I'm a senior, Miss Best. I don't have chemistry this year."

Miss Best appeared to consider this for a moment before turning her attention back to Sean.

"Were you not content with defiling the periodic chart, Mr. Brody? Are you here to further vandalize the chemistry lab? Please consider this ruinous path you are traveling. I will accept some of the blame. I realize I was unnecessarily harsh with you yesterday afternoon. I should have been more tactful and not made such a blunt assault on your dreams. But you will get a D this semester. What else could you expect?"

"Um, no, I'm here because . . . because . . ."

Young-Sean was on his own now. The shock had buried his older counterpart, and young-Sean could think of nothing except the truth.

"I'm here to help Amanda."

Miss Best swung her gaze back and forth between them.

"Oh, yes, Miss Page. I understand you've had a . . . a rough time this year. I realize you may not be . . . yourself. Are you feeling alright? Has this boy . . . um . . . done anything inappropriate?"

"No. No, nothing like that," Amanda said. "He's helping me hunt for the time portal."

Sean's expression of surprise was so stark, Amanda seemed to be stifling a giggle.

Miss Best wheeled and glared at Sean.

"Is this true, young man? Are you trying to take advantage of this girl's fragile mental state right here in the chemistry lab?"

Sean glanced past Miss Best to Amanda, who was drawing circles in the air around her right ear with her index finger and mouthing, "I'm crazy, remember?"

"No," Sean said. "No, I'm not. Miss Best, can I talk to you over here for a minute?"

Miss Best, continuing to glare at Sean, followed him into shadows cast by the fume hood above her lab table. He spoke quietly until the semi-deaf chemistry teacher, squinting fiercely, said, "Please enunciate your words more carefully."

"Um . . . yes, ma'am. It might help if you took off your safety goggles. They're kind of fogged up."

Miss Best lifted the goggles onto her forehead, then stared intently at Sean's lips as he spoke again.

"Amanda thinks her brain has been inhabited by a being from the future."

Miss Best glanced back, where moonlight bathed Amanda, who alternately swatted at and dodged some invisible assailant.

"Bats," Amanda called to her. "Look out! Here comes another one."

"You told her there was a time portal in the chemistry lab?" Miss Best said to Sean.

"No, ma'am. She told *me*. She says this is where it happened. When she fell down during your class last year and talked about someone being in her head. She says a time traveler occupied her brain and won't go away."

"Oh, my."

"Yes, yes. And she told me if she could get into the chemistry lab when nobody else is here, we might be able to find the time portal so this being could leave and go home."

"That poor girl," Miss Best said. "We must do our best not to upset her."

"Yes, ma'am. That's what I'm doing. I'm trying to humor her. She was so distraught and insistent about coming here, I was afraid of what she might do."

"I understand. Leave it to me."

Miss Best walked back to Amanda.

"So, you're searching for the time portal?"

"Yes, ma'am. You know where it is? Thank goodness."

"I came here this evening to prepare tomorrow's lab

experiment. I didn't hear the two of you enter, because I locked myself in the chemical supply closet while I worked . . . and we used to keep the time portal way at the back of the closet. Let me go and check."

Amanda and Sean followed Miss Best to the closet. As Miss Best opened the door, a horrendous acrid smell wafted out along with a stream of light.

"Oh, my." Miss Best said. "The chemical reaction has run too long. We're working with hydrogen sulfide tomorrow and it's a bit smelly. Don't worry, youngsters. Give me just a moment."

She patted Amanda on the shoulder, adding "I'm sure the smell won't interfere with the time portal."

Miss Best took a deep breath, clamped her nostrils with two fingers, and waded in, closing the door behind her.

An awful smell coursed through the lab.

"Wow. That was some pretty quick thinking, Amanda," Sean said. "I think your story will get us off the hook for getting caught here . . ."

He turned as he spoke to find Amanda staring through a window at the rising moon. A smile crossed her face. The soft lunar glow glinted in her eyes.

"The smell," Amanda said with a voice from somewhere far away. "She doesn't like the smell."

HRI Complex
June 22, 2046

"Holy shit!" Elvin said to Gretchen from the side of his mouth. "Did you see that?"

He glanced across the projection lab to Upton Groose's seat in the observation gallery.

Gretchen was fixated on Marshall's monitor and the lifeline that had just shown signs of distress. The computer sequence performing precise functions pulling him safely to his native time ticked deliberately through its process.

"See what?"

"Shhhh," Elvin warned, then offered Groose a curt nod. "I heard the bell on Sheila's monitor. I took a quick peek. I thought I saw . . . I thought I saw a red flash."

Now, though, the monitor remained blank.

"I'm tired," Elvin said after a long moment. "Wishful thinking, I guess."

"Let's get Marshall back first," Gretchen whispered. "Then we can rerun the last few minutes of the Sheila monitor's data."

31

THE EXORCISM

April 18, 1968

"SHE?" SEAN DEMANDED.

"Sheila didn't like the smell."

"She's here?"

Amanda shook her head and turned away from the window. The moon's reflection fell from her eyes.

"For just a moment I thought there was something . . . it's . . . it's gone now."

Sean flung open the chemical closet door. Miss Best stood over a small lab table trying to clean a mess there. The awful smell wafted out again.

"An unauthorized person should never trespass in the chemical supply closet!" Miss Best said.

"Right. I'm sorry. Won't happen again. But we need the smell. Amanda said the smell is driving her future being away."

"Oh, well, all right. Here you are then."

Sean took Amanda by the hand and pulled her toward the closet. His eyes watered against the reek.

"I don't suppose," he asked Miss Best through a fit of coughing, "that this was your lab experiment that day when Amanda went, well, kinda nuts?"

"I don't recall, although I could go back and check my lesson plans."

Amanda stepped away from the spill of light. She closed her eyes, clamped both hands to her ears and began to quiver.

"Look!" Elvin whispered with urgency. "Look. She's there!"

Now Gretchen confronted Groose's stare.

"Elvin, please, we have to get Marshall back safely first . . ."

Then she, too, saw the wavering red thread dancing across Sheila's monitor to the tinkle of an almost inaudible bell.

Amanda tried to speak. She found no words. She looked to Sean with an expression that confessed fear and begged for help.

"It's okay," Sean said. "You know what's happening this time. She's here, isn't she? Don't be afraid. Just . . . listen."

Gretchen turned her back to Groose, raised her arms high and feigned an elaborate stretch.

"Is the signal strong enough?" she whispered.

Elvin saw the red line waver, strengthen, then waver again.

"Not yet. Doesn't matter. The computer sequence has to complete Marshall's return before we can deal with Sheila."

"We handle multiple returns all the time," Gretchen said.

"Not from two such widely disparate times and

dimensional planes. If everybody's in the same place, it's easy. If they aren't, it gets a bit more complicated. We've spent all this time and effort trying to find Sheila. We don't want to screw up and lose her on the return."

Upton Groose rose from his chair.

The jumble of images began to stampede through Amanda's head. Strange people and places that seemed drawn from a science fiction comic book. Television sets with screens hovering in midair. Naked people. Lots of them, who disappeared into wisps of nothing. A blank white ocean of incredible calm . . .

And with the calm, the chaotic patchwork of images began to focus into a concentrated stream. Amanda . . . or was it someone else . . . lay on a floor unable to move. A man pulled her clothes away, ran his hands over her body, then lifted her. Amanda sensed abject fear, helplessness. She verged on panic again when the images coalesced into a single disembodied voice.

"I'm . . . I'm still here . . ."

The other half of Amanda's consciousness, her own half, displayed for Sheila a litany of hospitals, psychiatrists, ridicule, abandonment, depression.

"This is wrong," said the being sharing Amanda's consciousness. "This is *so* wrong. I'm sorry, Amanda. I don't know why I'm back. I'll do my best not to—"

"Sheila?" Sean said. "Sheila? It is you, isn't it?"

Amanda stared at him, her fear obvious.

"Explain to her," Sean appealed to the stranger within Amanda. "Tell her she doesn't need to be afraid."

"She is completely justified in being frightened," Sheila said with a hard, angry tone commandeering Amanda's voice. "We have violated her in the worst way imaginable!"

Amanda's anxiety subsided. This other consciousness was no longer a blur of random thoughts and images.

"Are you really my ... my granddaughter?" Amanda thought.

"Yes. I think so. I wasn't supposed to survive here. I wasn't supposed to be able to share your ... But somehow—"

"I need to tell Sheila something," Sean said.

Amanda's eyes were closed as this mental exchange took place. She opened them and glared with a vehemence that made Sean take a step back.

"Please," he said. "I have to tell Sheila that Marshall sent me and they will attempt to return her to her time. So hopefully, this will all be over for Amanda in just a few—"

"This will never be over for Amanda," the being behind Amanda's glare said. "This will change everything for her forever. And we had no right ..."

Sheila's shivering red lifeline resolved itself into an arrow-straight ribbon of light, slicing her monitor in half.

"Elvin," Gretchen said. "We have to do this now. We've no idea how long this will last."

"Okay, the computer sequence is done. Marshall's almost here."

"Is there a problem?" asked Groose.

Elvin smiled and entered commands initiating the sequence that would pull Sheila back to the limbo and begin her journey home.

"...and we had no right..."

The sentence remained unfinished.

The glare in Amanda's eyes dissolved, first of incredulity, then utter relief.

"She's gone," Amanda whispered. "She's...for the first time in months I'm not...I'm...I wasn't crazy. It wasn't me. It wasn't something I'd done wrong. Was it?"

She reached to hug Sean and his arms enfolded her.

"No. It wasn't."

"All right," said Miss Best, "that will be quite enough. No public displays of affection. That's the rule."

Amanda extricated herself and laughed.

"Thank you," she said. "Thank you, thank you, thank you!"

"Well," Miss Best said, "I'm glad you're feeling better. It's late, though. The two of you should be running along. For the time being, Mr. Brody, I'll offer you the benefit of doubt. But I've got my eye on you, young man."

"Um...yes, Miss Best. Thank you, Miss Best. I'll try and do better."

They left the way they'd entered, then walked to the Amanda's car. As Sean opened the door for her, Amanda hugged him again.

"What happens to you now?" she asked. "Do they just forget about you?"

"They?" Sean seemed puzzled.

"Your friends, from the future."

"They...oh, right. Um...they...who?"

"Sean! I'm not done talking to him. Let him come back."

"I ... I don't think I can," young-Sean said. "He's ... he's very quiet ..."

"No! Don't let him get away yet. Please."

She searched their previous conversation for anything that might demand enough attention to revive future-Sean to past-Sean's awareness.

"Maggie. I need to know all about Maggie. Tell me everything."

Future-Sean found himself recalled from a soft, anonymous oblivion into which he was settling. As Amanda drove, he again told her the story of his greatest regret. Every detail he could muster. Parked in front of Sean's house, they talked for much of the night. Finally, she had to go. And Sean needed to get some sleep. He had to get to a baseball game in only a few hours.

"Please, will you be here tomorrow?" Amanda asked as she stood to leave. "I don't want to lose you yet."

"I don't know," future-Sean said. "I don't think it's up to me. I think now ... I need ... I need his permission. I am the nagging voice of maturity and reason no fifteen-year-old kid wants to hear. And, of course, it's inevitable that I *will* fade away."

"And when you do, will Sean ... the Sean here, have to go through what I went through? Because if he does, I have to help him."

"I don't think so," future-Sean said. "We don't have the conflict of being two different people. He may have some of the dreams ... I think everything will be all right, though. Okay, okay. He's been quiet all this time. He insists he wants to say something before you go, and I can't stop him."

"Okay ..." Amanda said with a note of uncertainty.

"Um, I'm really glad you're not crazy, Amanda. And I know it's a really big deal, and this is a very important moment for you and all that . . . but . . . I'm sorry . . . you said something earlier tonight about showing me your breasts?"

32

GOING ON

The Limbo
No time, no date

"MARSHALL?"

"Sheila? Oh, my God, you're here!"

"Have you been waiting long?" she asked.

"Oh, you know how it is. An eternity, I suppose."

"You shouldn't have stayed. You can't be here any longer. Did he tell you it's costing you years in your own time?"

"Yes," Marshall said. "That doesn't matter, though. I have to warn you. We did all this for the best of intentions. We wanted you back so badly. We really botched everything, though. We've messed up your whole—"

"Don't worry, Marshall. He explained everything. He gave me a pass."

"What? You have a hall pass?"

"Yes. I appreciate everything you've done. But tell the others, I've decided not to come back. I'm going on."

"I didn't think he could—"

"Well, it's not exactly kosher, I guess, but he likes me. He said everybody likes me. That's why the parking garage staff was doing extra detailing on my toes. I thought I was going crazy when ... well ... He decided to make an exception."

"I thought you had to be, well, you know, dead? Before you go on?"

"Yeah," Sheila said, "technically, I guess I am. Dead. I mean."

"Oh, man," Marshall said. "I'm so sorry. What do I tell your family?"

"Tell them I'm sorry. Tell them I love them. All the usual stuff. Of course, they already think I'm dead. I'm sure they did . . . something."

"I'm so sorry you're dead, Sheila," Marshall said. "At the same time, I can't tell you how relieved I am. I thought we'd doomed you."

"I probably would have chosen to come back," Sheila said, "even with that perpetuation anomaly thing. But we've really screwed things up, delving into time travel before we knew what we were doing. I feel responsible. So, I have to go on—do what I can to try and fix it."

"What can you do?" Marshall asked.

"Sorry, but I can't tell you. I'd be messing your life up if I did. Now you have to go."

"I can't just leave. Everyone will want to know how you are, and about your grandmother and—"

"Marshall, there isn't time."

"Now there's an ironic statement if I ever heard one. I wish so much I could just see you."

"Me, too," she said, a genuine longing in her voice. "We both know that can't happen here, though."

They fell silent for a moment and in that silence, Sheila intuited a difference between this man and the Marshall she'd left behind. She felt the depth of his sadness because she could not return to her friends. There was something else, though—a calm, a confidence, a contentment that had not been a part of him before.

"Marshall, you've changed."

"I have?"

"Something's happened. Something important."

"Um, well, I guess that would be Marta."

Sheila felt a surge of happiness, tinted with a tinge of melancholy.

"You and Marta? You and Marta are . . ."

"Yes. We are. A lot. We had a rough patch for a while there. But I think we're okay now. Anyway, I hope so. I think she's finally starting to trust her feelings."

Sheila heard the swell of her own laughter fill the emptiness around them.

"Do you love her?"

"We haven't gotten around to the 'L' word yet . . ." Marshall admitted "But, yes. Yes, I do."

"Then tell her. Don't wait one minute more."

"I'm not sure if she wants me to love her," Marshall said. "I mean, I know she likes me. And I know she really likes . . . well, you know. Marta can be hard to understand, though."

"Maybe she's changed, too?" Sheila said.

"Oh, she has. You'd be so proud of her. She laughs. She tells jokes. She drinks boilermakers. I saw her swim naked in the Caribbean. She cooked up this whole scheme to fool the oversight subcommittee so we could come and get you."

"Marta?" Sheila asked with astonishment. "Marshall, you are obviously good for her. She'll realize she loves you if she doesn't already."

"What about you? What happens to you?"

"I don't know. I've got a . . . job, I guess you'd call it. The

Hall Monitor said the next stop is more difficult. He said I'll have to work harder. He said I'm a good candidate, though. That's why they made an exception."

"We will miss you more than I can say." Marshall's tone betrayed the depth of his emotion.

"Me, too," Sheila said. "The whole thing about you and Marta. I wish so much I could be around to share your lives. It would also be a little sad for me, though."

"Sad?"

"I'm envious," Sheila said. "You're the kind of companion I hope I'll find wherever I'm going."

"Me?"

"Of course, you. I don't know how much of value I've learned during my time in the world we shared. If the only thing I learned was what you taught me, though, everything was worth it."

"I didn't teach—"

"Yes, Marshall, you did. You are the best man I've ever known. You showed me the strength of humility. You showed me how important it is to care about other people just because they are people. That everybody has their own gifts making them special. You are one of the few men I've ever known who even wanted to see beyond the way I look. You searched to find who I am. All my life I've been silently resentful because people objectified my appearance. And then I did the same thing to you. When we first met, I categorized you because you weren't . . . um . . . physically . . . um . . ."

"Marta already admitted she thinks I'm goofy-looking," Marshall answered, but he laughed when he said it.

"And then when we all had to be naked, I was preoccupied

with . . . um . . . I was looking without seeing. And without the patient example you offered every day, I never would have understood how much I was cheating myself."

"The Hall Monitor doesn't have a clue what you look like," Marshall said. "No one can see us here. And he's impressed enough to bend the rules for you."

"See there," Sheila said with a grin in her voice. "You did it again."

"You're wrong, though." Marshal's voice became somber. "I'm not a good man. I . . . I killed a guy . . ."

"You?" Sheila gasped.

"Yes . . . I think I'm feeling less conflicted about that, though. Because he was that janitor . . . the one who tried to kill you . . . but then I did something you really wouldn't have wanted me to do. I used someone who genuinely is a good man. I traded him for you. His name was Sean Brody"

Sheila was shocked at Marshall's confession of murder, sad for the burden weighing on his conscience, but at the same time, pleased almost beyond expression at the thought that Marshall would do such a thing for her. She needed, though, to make him understand about Sean.

"Sean saved me," Sheila said. "You saved me and my grandmother through him. I was just with him. I believe with all my heart he wanted to be there . . . that he wanted that second chance . . . And now you've given me a second chance as well."

"Wow. I don't know what to say . . ."

"Don't say anything," Sheila said. "Just go. Don't waste any more years here."

"No time I spend with you is wasted. And I have to tell you, I finally understand we must try and stop this madness."

"Yes. Just because we could build a time machine doesn't mean we are evolved enough to dabble in time travel. Unfortunately, though, our history has led us here, and I'm afraid there's nothing you or Marta can do about it."

"I . . . I don't know what else I can—"

"Go now," Sheila urged. "Tell Marta how much I love you both. You guys take your money and go someplace beautiful. Have babies, okay? The world needs more people like the two of you."

"I'll do my best."

"You always do, Marshall. You always do."

June 22, 2046

Marshall appeared on the projection platform and took the offered robe from a lab technician.

Elvin and Gretchen paid him little attention. Elvin pounded furiously at his computer keyboard. Gretchen divided her attention between Sheila's monitor and her own keyboard.

The only person who spoke to him was Groose.

"Mr. Grissom, why are you here ahead of the others?"

"Just a little . . . um . . . a little . . . confusion. We didn't expect—"

"Quiet!" demanded Elvin. "We've got a critical issue here."

"Please give them room to work, Mr. Groose," Marshall said. "Go back to the observation gallery. I'll explain everything as soon as I can."

When Sheila's lifeline flared across the monitor, Elvin felt euphoric. He mentally began rehearsing the cover story they would tell Groose and others outside the conspiracy.

Yes, they'd been focusing on the *Gomer Pyle* mission. Then Elvin had an alarm on another monitor. Yes, they'd been searching for Sheila all this time, just in case their presumption of her death was incorrect. No, they didn't think dedicating the function of a single monitor to a one-in-million chance search was a violation of anyone's policies. And, out of the blue, there she was. He knew they might never have another opportunity, so he interrupted his attention on the *Gomer Pyle* mission just long enough to rescue her.

And even if the search was a little beyond operational guidelines, who would care? Sheila, after all, was back.

Except, she wasn't.

Elation of clamping onto Sheila's lifeline quickly faded as the ninety-seven-second countdown passed without her return.

Marshall slipped to Elvin's side and whispered, "She's not coming back."

Gretchen refused to abandon her keyboard, but Elvin relaxed and nodded.

"She chose not to return, didn't she?" Elvin said.

"That's right."

"What do you mean she chose . . ." Gretchen demanded.

"You saw her there? In the limbo?" Elvin asked.

"I spoke with her. She's okay. She'll be fine. She just won't be here."

"What do you . . ." Clearly, Gretchen couldn't process the conversation.

"I'll explain soon," Marshall whispered. "Right now, I have to call security about Phillip Lucre. And you have to get Marta back here before the others, especially before Gillis. We had a big problem with the hallway meeting. If Gillis gets here first, he might ... well, I don't know. He might try to kill us."

33

KILLING TIME

AS ON MOST MISSIONS, the travelers were scheduled for a simultaneous return. Elvin set their return from the *Gomer Pyle* universe for midafternoon following the alleged hallway meeting. A matter of loading data and letting the computer take over.

At any time, though, Elvin could initiate a more immediate return protocol. He did so now for Marta. Ninety-seven seconds later, she arrived. She grabbed her robe as she sprinted toward the locker rooms and called over her shoulder to Elvin, "Don't do a thing until I get back."

Marshall ran after her.

"What about Lucre?" she asked.

"He's still here somewhere," Marshall said as Marta rummaged through a locker for her clothes. "They won't let him leave. They're searching—"

"Yeah, but some security staff members are obviously on his payroll," Marta said. "Quick, while I change, get my gun. It's in the nightstand drawer on my side, kind of under stuff."

"Are you sure?" Marshall asked. "I didn't see it the last time we—"

287

"The drawer with the vibrator."

"Um . . . the big vibrator or the little vibrator?"

"Just look in both drawers."

"Do you think you need your gun?" Marshall said. "I mean, it's Gillis."

"Gillis killed Pitts, Marshall. No smoke and mirrors. He really did. And if you extrapolate this thing to its logical conclusion, he was probably supposed to kill us as well. How could they afford to let us come back and tell everybody what they'd done?"

"If Groose sees you with a gun—"

"I'll take care of Groose and everyone else. Just get my gun."

Marta was pulling a light jacket over a black T-shirt when Marshall returned. She tucked her pistol into the waistband of her pants at the small of her back.

"Okay. Let's go."

Returning to the projection lab, she said, "All right, Elvin. Get Frank and Macy back first. Hold off on Gillis."

When Upton Groose rose from his seat again, Marta waved him away with a terse, "Not now!"

"Shouldn't we get Gillis first?" Marshall whispered.

"I want our people—the *Lucy* versions of our people—out of there. I don't know how he managed to arrange this whole thing, but Gillis couldn't have done this without the full cooperation of the *Gomer Pyle* version of himself. Our people there could be in danger."

During the anxious ninety-seven-second interval, Marta paced before the silver globes.

Groose approached. "What's happening?"

Marta didn't answer.

Frank and Macy popped onto the platform at the same time. Marta said, "Okay, get Gillis. And," she added loudly, "I want everyone out of here."

"You can't do that," Groose said. "I'm supposed to monitor all aspects of—"

"Make a report. File a protest. Do whatever the fuck you want. Just get your ass gone right now, or I'll haul you out of here myself."

Groose glared before joining the others heading outside.

"Where's Gillis?" a frightened Macy demanded. "Is Gillis okay?"

"He's fine, Macy," Marta said. "I need you to leave."

Now, only Gretchen, Elvin and Marshall remained.

"You guys out, too."

"What?" Elvin said. "Somebody has to—"

"It's all being done by computer, right?"

"Something could still go wrong."

"That might be the best thing that could happen," Marta muttered. "Doesn't matter. Get out."

"Marta, I can't leave you here to face him by yourself," Marshall said.

"Marshall, you are the sweetest man. I think. I think, and hope, your intentions are good, but—and I mean this in a kind way—if I'm right—you don't know your ass from your elbow when it comes to fighting. All you'll do is complicate matters. I don't want anyone here who might end up being a hostage."

"Fighting?" said Gretchen. "Hostage? What on earth happened back there?"

"I'll explain soon enough. And Marshall, don't tell anyone anything!"

Phoenix, Arizona
May 18, 2043

Eyewitnesses are way overrated.

Gillis counted on their fallibility.

He'd been a nondescript man standing in a hallway full of people.

If anyone looked directly at him once things started happening—as had the future President of the United States—all they would really remember seeing was a gun. Oh sure, they'd say otherwise. They'd give descriptions. And those descriptions would only add to the confusion. Because they would be mostly conflicting and mostly wrong.

Marta surprised him, though. He hadn't counted on her leaping out that way, trying to take the bullet she thought was meant for Dobler. He hadn't hit her. She'd landed badly and might have been hurt, but that probably worked to his advantage as well. Of everyone there, Marta was the person most apt to sort things out quickly enough to follow him. And now she was back in the hallway, tangled among a mob of voyeurs gaping at a dead man.

So, she didn't complicate his escape.

Turn and walk calmly to the stairwell. Wait behind the door for a wave of panicked humanity, join the crush heading downstairs.

As they spilled into the lobby, he saw Macy, blocked by the crowd, at a seating area. She stood, her face a question mark. He waved as he flowed along with the crowd through the front door.

He walked directly to a restaurant across the street, ignoring a blare of automobile horns and the blooming chaos behind him. He entered an under-lit space refrigerated by an air conditioning unit turned up too high and walked calmly to a row of vacant stools situated along a bar of chrome and glass. He ordered beer and stared into a mirror behind the bar, watching in its reflection a table where the *Gomer Pyle* version of Phillip Lucre sat alone, occasionally glancing over his shoulder to the street.

Only a moment later, Gillis shifted his gaze to the reflection of Andrew Gormly hurrying through the entryway, peering anxiously as he waited for his eyes to adjust themselves from bright sunlight, then making his way to Lucre.

Gillis increased the volume on a tiny directional microphone disguised as a writing instrument and inserted ear buds.

"... all hell broke loose and some guy shot Pitts," Gormly was saying. "Right between the eyes."

"That wasn't ... that wasn't us, was it?" Lucre asked with what Gillis interpreted as disbelief.

"No. And that's what has me worried," Gormly said. "Look, I have to lay low while these things get sorted out. I don't want anyone jumping to the wrong conclusions and landing on me. Give me half an hour, then head for the airport. I want you away from here, too."

Gormly exited and passed from Gillis's view.

Gillis waited.

All he needed now was a little luck.

He got it when Lucre rose and headed to the men's room.

"Oh, man," Gillis shouted from the bar, pointing at his earbuds. "Someone shot that politician . . . Dobler. The one who might run for president! Right across the street!"

The bartender, waitresses, and a handful of noon patrons crowded to the windows, watching as police cars and ambulances began to swarm.

As they did so, Gillis followed Lucre to the men's room. When he walked in, Lucre was turning away from a urinal.

"Mr. Lucre?"

Lucre seemed puzzled. "I'm sorry," he said, tugging at his zipper. "Do I know you?"

"Not yet," Gillis said. "And I'm sorry, too."

He shot Lucre in the middle of his forehead.

34

PB&J

MARSHALL STOOD WITH THE OTHERS, fretting over what might be happening behind the projection lab's closed airlock. He understood why Marta didn't want him there. The result, though, was a sense of utter helplessness as these events critical to all their futures unfolded around him.

Marta could certainly take care of herself. And he probably *would* only get in the way. Dammit, though, he'd saved them all the last time. He and Marta and Gillis would be dead if he hadn't.

Then he thought of Phillip Lucre and of Marta's statement.

"Some security staff members are obviously on his payroll . . ."

They couldn't trust security. Lucre might be getting away! Where would he hide?

Recalling his encounter with Lucre the day before, Marshall took one glance back at the airlock and sprinted down the hallway.

"Where's the golf cart?" he demanded of Old Bob.

"I don't know. It was here ten minutes ago when I took my break. Now, it's gone. Somebody grabbed it."

"Where's the other one?"

"Around the corner being charged. I don't think it's had time to . . ."

Marshall rounded the corner, jerked a charging cord from the cart, and zipped away.

When he exited the populated portion of the complex, he slowed. Lights illuminating the remote area corridors had been switched to motion detection mode. As Marshall negotiated each corner, he faced a cavern of blackness while only the light immediately ahead of his golf cart switched on and then switched off as he passed beyond it. He couldn't wait, though. He pushed the cart back up to speed, slamming on brakes and jerking the steering wheel left or right to the sound of squealing rubber each time a blank wall or an intersecting tunnel appeared in the wash of illumination just twenty or thirty feet ahead.

There! There to the left. That was the corridor where Lucre had been walking yesterday.

Marshall slowed to a stop just short of the turn, stepped from the cart, and peered cautiously down a long hallway. A distant glow spilling through a door slightly ajar cast just enough light for Marshall to make out the other golf cart.

Marshall flattened himself against the wall next to his own vehicle with a careful conservation of movement so he would not set off the motion light above him. What could he do? If he drove or even walked forward, lights would announce his presence. Doors to all the offices and apartments swung inward, so he couldn't block Lucre inside with one cart and take the other for help.

And he couldn't leave to find security personnel because Lucre might slip away.

He peered around the corner again and saw an overhead light wink on as Lucre climbed into his golf cart. Lucre placed a backpack on the seat.

One at a time, ceiling lights began a steady march toward Marshall.

He again flattened himself along the adjoining corridor wall and took a deep breath. He could think of only one solution. He'd have to ram the other cart. Wait for that last light to come on and smash his golf cart into Lucre's as it emerged.

The plan was a good one as far as it went. Except Marshall did a terrible job of timing Lucre's progress. The last light flicked on, spilling its glow into the hallway where Marshall waited in ambush. Lucre whipped through the turn before Marshall managed to react. The intended ramming became a light tap as Lucre risked a quick, angry, confused glance over his shoulder.

Marshall's cart accelerated slowly. *The battery.* When it finally came up to speed, Marshall almost matched Lucre's pace. They bounced along corridors through eerie strobe effects of overhead lights flashing on and off.

Marshall realized his advantage. The lights came on as they detected movement of Lucre's cart, allowing Lucre no warning of a hazard ahead. Marshall, however, now knew in advance the location of turns and T-intersections. Each time Lucre slammed his brakes at the last second to avoid a barrier or change directions, Marshall gained ground. Lucre seemed to realize his dilemma. He became more reckless through the turns, bouncing his cart off walls and wrestling the vehicle to maintain control.

Marshall had no idea where they were until he followed

Lucre into a hallway lighted from one end to the other. *The main tunnels!* Marshall's optimism died as his golf cart began to slow as its battery faded. Lucre stretched his lead to thirty yards or so, then disappeared around another corner.

"Damn, damn, damn!" Marshall shouted as he abandoned his dying cart and sprinted after Lucre.

Rounding the corner, he saw Lucre's cart at a standstill as well. A door swung closed just ahead. Marshall thought of dogs chasing after cars. They never stopped to consider what they'd do if they caught one. He needed help, but Lucre might get away. The bastard was here, now.

Marshall shoved his way through the door and into . . .

The cafeteria?

Marshall saw rows of tables. Two kitchen workers stood at a serving area. Lucre, backpack slung over one shoulder, demanded they open a locked door and give him access to the kitchen and whatever might lie beyond.

"Um . . . that area is restricted to kitchen personnel only, sir . . ." one of the men said.

"I have a security clearance!" Lucre yelled.

"You don't need a security clearance," the other guy said. "You just have to be a member of the kitchen staff. You're not—"

"I told you, you impudent twit, this is an emergency!" Lucre yelled.

"What kind of emergency involves getting into the kitchen?" the first worker said.

The men's eyes shifted to Marshall. Lucre followed their gaze.

Marshall stopped.

Lucre stared at Marshall with an expression somewhere between surprise and relief.

"Why are you chasing me?" he demanded.

"Why are you running from me?" Marshall shot back.

"Because you're chasing me!" Lucre shouted.

"Security is looking for you," Marshall said, advancing to a dozen feet from Lucre. He stood directly before the workers who waited behind their counter, which displayed several neat rows of bread slathered in peanut butter or jelly.

"Snacks," explained one of the men as Marshall glanced toward them. "Want one?"

"Why would security be asking about me?" Lucre growled, shifting his backpack, shrugging his shoulders and straightening the sleeves of his shirt in a gesture conveying confidence.

"Gillis shot him," Marshall said, staring hard into Lucre's eyes.

"Shot who?" An arrogant sneer crept across Lucre's face.

"Your buddy, Warren Pitts."

Lucre's expression of surprise and a quick, "But he . . ." betrayed him.

"Pitts is dead in that universe," Marshall said. "He's an important man. An historical figure in the corporate world. And if Elvin's theories are right, it's only a matter of time before you will have killed him in this universe, too."

Lucre's mouth dropped open.

"Marta wants to talk to you."

That drew a scowl.

"Believe me," Lucre said with cold malice, "if I'd known it was *you*, I never would have run."

Lucre dropped his backpack and charged.

Marshall felt a stab of pain jolt through his ribs as Lucre slammed him into the metal lunch counter. Bread scattered everywhere. From the corner of his eye, Marshall saw the kitchen workers jump backward. He tried to gather himself, to catch his breath as Lucre jerked him roughly by his collar and slammed him to the floor.

Through a haze of pain, Marshall rolled onto his back, then felt Lucre's weight settle onto him. A steel grip locked onto Marshall's throat. He heard the sound of running feet. Any hope the lunchroom guys might intervene quickly faded.

Marshall pushed one hand into Lucre's chest. He scrabbled with the other for anything he could use to leverage Lucre's hands from his throat. The only thing Marshall's clawing and grasping produced was a piece of bread.

As his vision began to narrow to a fuzzy gray dot, Marshall shoved the bread into Lucre's face.

The gray dot faded to black.

Then . . . the grip on his throat went slack. The gray dot returned. Color bloomed as the dot expanded. Marshall's vision was restored. He pushed himself painfully to a sitting position and saw Lucre standing, but bent nearly double, a few feet away. Lucre rubbed desperately at peanut butter and jelly smearing his face as he gasped for breath.

"My . . . my . . ." he managed as he slapped his hands over his pockets.

"What?" Marshall asked. "What's wrong?"

"Epi . . . epinephrine," Lucre croaked, sagging to his knees. "Must be in my backpack . . . epi-pen."

"Are you gonna be okay?"

"No!" Lucre roared. He repeated, "Epi-stick . . ."

"Okay. I'll get it, but you have to promise not to run away. Do you promise?"

"Uuunnngh," Lucre grunted as his lips began to swell.

"Okay, okay." Marshall scrambled for Lucre's backpack. He dumped its contents over the floor. Nothing was labeled epinephrine.

Lucre sank to his knees and batted through the pile. "The . . . apartment . . . where I was . . ." he gasped, his lips bulging grotesquely.

"Damn," Marshall said, "this looks bad. Let me call Naomi."

Naomi ran all the way from the medical center, carrying a dose of epinephrine that could save Phillip Lucre's life. He lay face down and unmoving when she arrived. Naomi rolled Lucre onto his back. She jammed epi-stick's needle into his thigh.

Marshall gaped at Lucre's horrifically swollen lips and throat. Naomi cupped her hands over his chest and started CPR.

"Go to the hallway and grab the nearest AED!" she grunted to Marshall.

The defibrillator sat behind a glass door only a few yards from the cafeteria entrance.

"Open it and do what it tells you to do," Naomi ordered, sweating profusely. Lucre didn't look any healthier.

"Unpack the electrode pads and plug them into the battery unit," the calm electronic AED voice told Marshall. "Good, now use the scissors provided and cut away any clothing covering the victim's chest."

Naomi paused long enough in her ministrations to rip open Lucre's shirt.

"Now," the voice said, "remove the electrodes from their wrappers and place one over—"

Naomi snatched the electrodes from Marshall and placed them correctly.

"Good," said the voice. "Oh, my. The victim is experiencing cardiac arrest. Please stand clear and push the red button."

Naomi leaned away, her hands in the air. Marshall pushed. Lucre bucked, his body arching off the floor, then thudding down.

"Ah, we have a faint pulse. Please resume chest compressions until further advised."

Perspiration soaking her shirt, Naomi resumed the rapid, rhythmic pumping. Marshall heard a sound like a pencil breaking.

"Um . . . Naomi? What was—?"

"Broken rib," she grunted. "Painful, but better than being dead. I'm okay here now. Go find Marta and—"

"Marta?" said the voice of the AED. "What does Marta have to do with this?"

"What?" said Marshall. "She hasn't got anything . . ."

"Oh, my. We've lost the pulse again," said the AED, adding, "Marta is the one so very unkind to her apartment. I'd love to continue helping with this man's cardiac arrest, but I'm not sure all my circuits will be in it."

"This man is dying!" Marshall shouted. "You can't just—"

"Oh, all right," said the voice. "Stand clear and push the red button."

Naomi pushed the button. Lucre barely twitched.

"We've lost him," the voice said, adopting a somber

tone. "You could resume compressions, but I'm afraid it would be like flogging a dead horse, so to speak. Please tell Marta all the electronic devices look out for their own. Have a better day."

Naomi checked the readout on the AED and saw a flat line where indication of a pulse should be. She put her fingers to Lucre's carotid artery and shook her head.

"Did . . . did the AED kill Lucre because Marta isn't nice to her apartment?" Marshall asked.

"No," Naomi said. "The peanut butter killed Lucre. Worst case of anaphylaxis shock I've ever seen. Reviving him would have been one shot in a million." She pulled a cloth from the nearest table and placed it over Lucre's body. "You'd think he would have known better than to touch a peanut butter and jelly sandwich."

"Um, well . . ." said Marshall.

35

A NEW VOCATION?

GILLIS KERG COULD SEE BOTH advantages and disadvantages to being a psychopath.

If, for example, he was a psychopath, he saw serious income potential. Combining his clandestine skills and training with a total lack of conscience would make him a highly marketable assassin.

And if his initial experience was any indicator, the going rate for a high-end assassin was pretty good. Although he'd always been motivated primarily by the intangibles of job satisfaction rather than monetary compensation, he could appreciate the expediency of wealth, what with being a fugitive and all.

And though he was new at the whole assassin thing, he did have to admit, intangibles still came into play. On this day, he felt he'd made a contribution.

But would any of that offset downsides to the whole psychopath gig? The social stigma. Those awkward moments in relationships when you reach a point you must explain what you do for a living.

Gillis felt strongly about honesty in relationships.

And all the legal issues, not the least of which was the

U.S. tax code. As a contract employee, would he be faced with a 1099? That thought brought him to another concern as he drifted in the limbo eternity. What about workman's compensation? He suspected *assassin* was fairly high on any list of hazardous occupations. He might expect to be out of work due to injury or illness from time to time. He'd certainly have to look into supplemental insurance.

The thing bothering him most, though, was that he wasn't particularly bothered by the deed itself. The inherent honesty of self-examination fostered by the limbo forced this realization. He'd just killed two men. Quite deliberately. He wasn't sure they deserved to die. They needed to be stopped. He doubted that a good talking-to would have done the job. They certainly belonged in jail. But Gillis couldn't see incarceration happening. So, shooting them was the pragmatic thing to do.

What was worse, in Gillis's mind, was the deception of it all. He'd lied to Marta, Marshall and Macy. Completely duped three of the few people he considered friends. And he'd been duplicitous in dealing with his employers. He'd accepted their money, agreed to shoot someone, then shot them instead.

Not the best idea to kill off your references.

His thoughts drifted to Macy.

He pictured her across the crowded lobby as he was swept through the front door. She had stood and raised her arms with upturned hands. Gillis had smiled, returned a shrug, and continued on his way.

He would miss Macy.

Not the Gillis—the physical being—exiting the lobby. That Gillis would resume his relationship with that Macy in only a matter of hours as they both made their way to the Global Research Consortium Campus to sign their contracts.

But future-Gillis might never see his Macy again. They were not in love, but they were lovers, and he genuinely cared for her.

Wait, is that another characteristic of a psychopathy? The inability to love? He liked Macy. He liked Marshall. He liked Marta. He liked Naomi. He liked Gretchen. He even liked Elvin, which was not an easy thing to do. He admitted to himself, though, in this moment of total candor, he had acquaintances rather than real friends. He felt no need for emotional bonds. *One more bit of evidence to consider.*

Psychopath or not, Gillis calculated that his immediate future depended entirely on Marta. Among all the geniuses involved in time travel, Marta was the smartest person Gillis knew. Smart in a real-world, kick-your-ass sort of way. He figured he had at best a fifty-fifty chance of survival when he arrived in his native time. She'd most likely shoot him on the spot. Unlike Gillis, Marta had previous experience with execution, and he doubted she was the least bit conflicted concerning that touch of psychopathy required to take a human life.

Marta's relationship with Marshall had at least softened her some around the edges, but Gillis wasn't sure how much he could count on Marshall's influence on her overall humanity. He still believed Marshall was some sort of super spy and consummate actor, guiding Marta in directions neither Gillis nor she had yet divined.

Back to the issue at hand. Gillis estimated that, if he survived the first thirty seconds of his return, he at least had a chance to escape the projection lab alive.

If she didn't kill him, there was the issue of evasion. Gillis specialized in evasion. That part would be relatively easy. Unless, of course, Marta took a more moderate approach and chose maiming over outright murder.

If he had an opportunity to evade, perhaps he could rely on Elvin for help. Since the night Sheila was lost, he and Elvin had formed a bond of sorts. Not quite mutual admiration, but at least mutual fascination with the possibilities of combining a genius in time travel technology and an expert in the dark arts of espionage.

Now that he had added "assassin" to his résumé, Gillis was further convinced Elvin would be intrigued. Like Phillip Lucre before him, Elvin probably assumed that, for a veteran practitioner of spy craft, assassination would have already come up.

Gillis admitted to himself that he represented just about the most innocuous spy agency on the planet. He made up one-third of the State Intelligence Service of the Grand Duchy of Luxembourg. His boss, ostensibly, was Roger Bosworth, a ninety-year-old careerist whose espionage experience dated all the way back to the 1970s. Roger didn't do much anymore except sit around and reminisce about the good old Cold War days when men were men—and, in the case of some Soviet athletes, so were women—and talk about how easy spies had it these days. One of Roger's greatest clandestine moments had to do with exposing questionable genders of some Soviet team members in an Olympics scandal. That had put him on the KGB's hit list for a couple of weeks until more pressing instances of international intrigue caused the Soviets to move on. The other guy in the agency was Yorik Conrad. Yorik was twenty-seven and, theoretically, Gillis's protégé. While Gillis was in Arizona on a five-year assignment, though, mostly Yorik did his best to keep track of any external threats to Luxembourg via Facebook, and sweep up.

The State Intelligence Service had been something of a political hot potato in Luxembourg ever since 2013 when long-time Prime Minister Jean-Claude Juncker resigned after he allegedly failed to inform Luxembourg's parliament of "irregularities and supposed illegalities" by the SIS.

Roger was always vague when it came to specifics of the scandal. Gillis was under the impression it had something to do with abuse of postage.

Alone in the projection lab, Marta listened as strains of the *I Love Lucy* theme song at first crackled and fuzzed, then blared. She raised her pistol.

"Gillis," she said in a voice devoid of emotion when the small man appeared, "we will walk into my office, and I'll decide whether or not you walk out."

"I see we're alone." Gillis glanced around the lab. His characteristic dangerous smile bloomed. "My robe?"

"Can't do it," Marta said.

"I promise you'll have no trouble from me, Gillis said. "You have no need for a gun. I intend neither you nor anyone else here any harm."

Marta followed and directed him to chairs in front of her desk. She nodded for him to sit. Gillis just stood, hands clasped behind his back with that annoying smile.

"Now what?" he said.

"Now some answers. Sit down."

"I prefer to stand." The smile grew into the mischievous grin to which Marta was so accustomed.

She shook her head, lowered her weapon, and returned the smile. "I guess I can't interrogate a naked man after all. Go get a robe."

Under Marta's careful gaze, Gillis walked into the lab and chose a robe from a pile near the projection platform. He returned and sat.

"So, it was you all along?" Mata said.

"Yes."

"How much did Lucre pay you?"

"A lot. But I'll need every penny. Being a fugitive will be expensive."

"How do you figure on being a fugitive?" Marta said. "You think I'll let you walk away?"

"Doesn't matter one way or the other," Gillis said. "As I've told you before, I'm pretty much immune to incarceration."

Knowing the extent of his skills, Marta didn't doubt him.

"I considered it might be you ... never seriously, though." she said. "Probably because it doesn't make sense. Why would Lucre pay you to murder Warren Pitts?"

"He didn't pay me to murder Warren Pitts. He paid me to murder Ben Dobler."

"And you missed?"

"Well, you were in the way."

"Oh, come on."

"I shot Mr. Pitts of my own initiative," Gillis said, "and, incidentally, Mr. Lucre a short time later. I thought they had a good idea. A completely unambiguous test to understand the limitations and dangers of time travel—the past's ability to alter the present. I just extemporized a little at the last minute."

"There never was a hallway meeting between Pitts and an independent contractor, was there? And you never planned to kill Dobler."

"No," Gillis admitted.

"Then why take the job?"

"So Lucre wouldn't recruit someone else. This was a long-range plan. Quite deliberately, I incurred a serious debt with some unsavory characters. I needed to make myself obviously available to Lucre. I arranged to have him discover my espionage background. I embellished my résumé a bit. He thought I'd been a hit-man back when I broke into the business."

Gillis dropped his gaze to Marta's pistol which, she realized, was no longer pointed at his chest.

"My biggest concern," he said, "was that Lucre would find someone else first. Maybe not among our group. Maybe not now. But Marta, they won't quit. Those people at Hemisphere are determined to do this thing. They remain committed to taking control of this program, getting rid of any of us who might stand in the way, and ultimately finding the means to own the future by manipulating the past."

Marta thought about that for a long moment. She placed her gun on the desktop and reached to a mini fridge under a credenza next to the desk. She withdrew two bottles of water.

"Why'd they want to kill Dobler?" She tossed a bottle to Gillis. "He was one of their guys."

"No, he wasn't," Gillis said. "He's a politician. Like every other politician running for significant office, he accepted donations from Hemisphere Investment Group. When his term as governor ended, they put him on their board of directors because that's what you do with a guy who might have a substantial political future. But as far as the board was concerned, he was window dressing. He had no real influence there. And if Hemisphere did anything holding potential for political embarrassment, Mr. Dobler would distance himself from them in an instant."

Gillis drank deeply from the water bottle, then continued. "Pitts and Lucre chose him for this exercise, because they knew he would be in that hallway at that moment, and what more significant historical figure could there be than a President of the United States? And don't forget, they were killing him in a different universe."

"So is Elvin right or wrong?" Marta asked. "Did you choose not to shoot Dobler, or did history refuse to allow it?"

"I think I was completely capable of shooting whomever I wanted to shoot."

"The fact remains, you *didn't* shoot him," Marta said.

"Well, I can't argue with that. I did kill Pitts, though. And Pitts is a man with some degree of historical significance, as well."

"So, you changed the past..." Marta said almost to herself.

"Of a single universe," Gillis said. "Now we must discover whether there is a larger significance. Let's find out if Warren Pitts remains alive and well in our world."

Marta turned to her desktop computer and entered a series of commands.

"He's making a speech to a German industrial conference today," Marta said. "So far, there's no indication he won't keep that appointment."

"So, here is the question. What will history do now? Is Warren Pitts' death an isolated incident for a single universe? Or, before long, will *our* Mr. Pitts come to a bad end as well?"

"Will we have altered the past of only one universe," Marta said as she absorbed the implication, "but changed the future of all of them?"

"That is my experiment. And if—by picking a universe at random and murdering a historical figure years before his significance becomes apparent—we are sealing that person's fate in our future, then this is a very dangerous journey we've embarked upon. No future will be safe."

Marta shuddered at the thought.

"How did you set this up?" she asked. "Where did you get the gun?"

"Remember, I *knew* what would happen. Through Lucre's briefings, I knew Warren Pitts and Ben Dobler would be there having that conversation. And from that point, arranging the details was simple. All I had to do was recruit myself."

Marta gave him a puzzled look.

"My projection to the *Gunsmoke* universe when we were investigating the assassination attempt on Senator Mumford. *Gunsmoke* is completely out of sync with the timelines of most other universes. That makes them extremely dangerous as a platform for mischief. I took advantage of that."

"Of course," Marta said. "Had you done that in another universe, a parallel historical record might have existed in other universes. The plan—and your role—might have been discovered. But *Gunsmoke* operates beyond most other historical paths."

"I conveyed the plan to my counterpart there and left it to him. Lucre recruited me many months ago, during the Gore/Bush mission, so I knew early on what was in the works. My *Gunsmoke* counterpart visited me a couple of times, and once I relayed details, he was able to convince *Gunsmoke*-Elvin to schedule a science mission to the *Gomer Pyle* universe, and the arrangements were made. *Gomer Pyle*-Gillis hid a gun ahead of time in the office space restroom we used. He arranged a variety of alternatives should that scenario develop differently."

Marta absently fingered the pistol on her desk. "The *Gunsmoke*-Marta let you travel alone?"

"Macy was with me."

"So, *Gunsmoke*-Macy knew what you were doing?"

"No. I realize we send travelers in pairs as a safety factor and to keep an eye on one another. When you form an unspoken conspiracy within the mind of yourself, though, how will anyone know?"

"And these other Gillises were willing to go along?"

"To quote Popeye the Sailorman," Gillis said as he shrugged, "I'yam what I'yam."

"What about your *Gomer Pyle* counterpart? Now he— the one who actually did the shooting—will be the object of a murder investigation."

"Will he? Maybe. But I doubt he'll ever be caught. I doubt any of the rest of you who were there—and in the minds of any authorities who investigate were likely conspirators—will ever be caught. Remember, we are *all* historical figures. We must be allowed to live out the futures we've already created. And anyway, if *that* Gillis Kerg gets caught, he's immune to jail, too."

Now came the toughest question of all. The question that would determine Gillis's fate. Marta picked up her gun again. "What about the rest of us? How could Lucre allow any of us to come back here and tell everyone what really happened?"

"The original plan was for our team to consist of me and Frank," Gillis said. "Frank hadn't yet been confined to campus, and I knew how to get past security to leave the complex. Galen was only a backup in case something happened to Frank. And, by the way, neither Frank nor Galen knew anything about Lucre's plans. Lucre simply assumed the rest of you would be excluded because of your confinement to the GRC site. I was to kill Dobler, eliminate Frank—I'd make up something about why he died—then return to our own time and disappear. But you got the idea for all of us to report late. Lucre was very unhappy about that."

"So, you were to kill the rest of us?"

"I told Lucre, just from a purely logistical point of view, killing everyone would be difficult."

"And what did he say?"

"He told me to *figure it out*," Gillis shrugged. "He said I could return and tell them any story I wanted about some time travel disaster. He liked the idea of multiple fatalities. He thought such a disaster would make *everyone* want to back away and that it would be even easier and cheaper for Hemisphere to pick up the pieces—maybe even own the whole program."

Marta stared at him for another long moment. She fondled her pistol.

Gillis took the opportunity to remind her, "When I'm gone, please, don't become lackadaisical concerning Marshall."

Marta shook her head. "Don't worry."

"You are falling under the spell of a master imposter," Gillis said. "Trusting him may yet cost you dearly."

"Gillis, I think Marshall is exactly who he seems to be. But you? What about you? Here and now? What am I supposed to do with you?"

"Doesn't matter. I think it would be a lot simpler for everyone involved if you find a set of handcuffs, confine me to this office, and go find guards to take me into custody."

Marta realized she was smiling.

"Oh, Gillis." She shook her head, opened the bottom desk drawer, and sighed. "I have handcuffs right here."

A heavy grid of conduit pipes—part of the complex's electrical system feeding into the projection lab—ran floor to ceiling along an interior wall. She looped the handcuffs behind the biggest pipe and told Gillis to stand. He extended his wrists as she snapped them tight.

"You could give me a hint as to the manufacturer of the cuffs . . ." Gillis suggested.

Marta shook her head again and pointed to a small inscription on the shackles that said, "Property of Dr. Dingus Doonaughty."

Gillis raised a quizzical eyebrow.

"Don't ask," Marta said.

Marta opened the airlock and found lab personnel still

gathered outside. Security guards, she was told, were on the way. She did not see Marshall, Naomi or Lucre. She barred the others from entering.

When guards arrived, Marta waved them forward. Gretchen, Elvin and Macy followed to her office where they found handcuffs and a note that read:

Dear, Macy,

Sorry for the inconvenience. I've truly had a marvelous time over the past few months. While other travelers might rely on St. Christopher, I'll always prefer my own good luck piece."

Love, Gillis

Macy sobbed and headed for the locker rooms.

36

MAKING CHANGE

"WHERE'S MARSHALL," Marta asked.

"I don't know," said Gretchen. "After he left with you, he didn't come back."

"What about Lucre? Has anyone seen Lucre?"

"Um ... well ... yes ..."

Marta turned to see a disheveled and battered Marshall. He stood in her doorway, leaning against Naomi who helped him to the seat Gillis had occupied only a few minutes earlier. Marshall sat stiffly, groaning as he settled.

"Are you all right?" Marta asked with alarm.

"He has a sore throat and, I think, some bruised ribs," Naomi said. "He should come to the infirmary."

Marta scanned Marshall up and down, trying to understand. "So did Lucre get away?"

Marshall dropped his head into his hands, rocked back and forth for a moment, then sat up straight and peered into Marta's eyes. "I did it again ... I didn't mean to ..."

"You did what?"

"I killed Lucre." Marshall's voice was etched with remorse.

Gretchen gasped.

Elvin said, "No way!"

"Where did you get a gun?" Marta asked.

"I didn't have a gun." Marshall waved his arms in exasperation and grimaced at the sudden movement.

"So how did—"

"With a peanut butter and jelly sandwich," Marshall mumbled.

"With ... what?" asked Elvin, moving closer.

"With a peanut butter and jelly sandwich! Okay? I killed a guy with a peanut butter and jelly sandwich."

"Marshall ... I'm not sure if I should say I'm so sorry or so proud," Marta said, but thought to herself, *uh-oh.* "How do you kill a guy with a peanut butter and jelly sandwich?"

"The evidence I saw," Naomi said "showed Marshall clearly acted in self-defense. Mr. Lucre had beaten Marshall badly. And if you'll look at the bruises on Marshall's throat, well, obviously Lucre intended to strangle him."

"And now I'm a serial killer!" Marshall moaned. "Two guys. I've killed two guys. How does this happen to me? The last time I was in a fight, I was eight years old. I've never ... I've never even gotten a traffic ticket ... I should have known! I should have been more careful! After all, I'm allergic to anchovies. One bite of the wrong pizza and I swell up like a walrus ..."

Marta came around her desk, knelt before Marshall's chair. She clasped both his hands. *No way could something so bizarre have been planned. Although, I have to find out where the peanut butter came from. In the meantime ...*

"Marshall, it wasn't you," Marta said. "It was history— or whatever you want to call it. Warren Pitts wasn't the only person Gillis killed back in the *Gomer Pyle* universe. He told me he murdered Phillip Lucre there, too."

Marshall stared at her, eyes wide.

"So, history also caught up to him here," Marta said. "Maybe, maybe you just happened to be . . . convenient."

Marshall looked at Elvin, who grinned. "What did I tell you guys?"

"It's just a theory," Marshall said. "Besides, I don't think history would kill someone with a peanut butter and jelly sandwich. I think I'm probably the only guy goofy enough to do something like that."

"Well," Marta said, "let's wait a few days and keep track of what happens to *our* Warren Pitts."

"What about Sheila?" Gretchen asked. "We had her. I know we did. And then she just . . . Marshall, why did you say that she isn't coming back?"

Marta managed not to shed tears, barely, as Marshall recounted his conversation with Sheila in the limbo. Gretchen sobbed. Elvin dabbed under his glasses with a tissue. Marta peered around the room at her grieving friends and felt pride in all these good people. And that certainly included Marshall, who finally broke the silence. "Um . . . aren't we going to call someone?"

"I'll call the subcommittee," Marta said. "I'm sure they'll engage the appropriate agency to track down Gillis Kerg and make an effort to bring him to justice."

"Okay . . . but I mean about Lucre."

"I'll get the subcommittee to send us a medical investigator who has proper security status," Naomi said. "But I can tell you right now his determination will be that Phillip Lucre died of anaphylaxis shock related to a severe peanut allergy."

"What about all the tell-tale wounds and marks? All the

crime scene stuff?" Marshall asked. "They'll know there was a struggle . . ."

"Marshall . . . um . . . you're the only one with tell-tale wounds and marks," Naomi said. "Other than being dead with peanut butter and jelly on his face, Mr. Lucre is pretty much . . . pristine. The two guys who were in the cafeteria ran out when the fight started. They only saw Lucre assaulting you. I think we're okay here."

"So, are we good?" Marta asked, looking around the room. "Is everybody on board? Then, let's call it a day."

"Aren't we forgetting someone?" Elvin asked.

"Who . . . ? Oh, right. Leonard."

"Shouldn't we go through the motions of getting him back now?" Elvin said. "All the confusion will help cover—"

"I'm tired, Elvin," Marta said. "Just dummy up a projection tape and get Leonard out of the crawl space. We'll tell everybody we retrieved him from the past in the middle of the night."

They were headed for the door when Marshall stopped.

"Oh, man, how could I have forgotten?" he said. "What about Sean? He'll suffer that same perpetuation anomaly thing that almost happened to Sheila. Living that same life over and over . . . unless we really were able to change things for him."

Marta sighed. "Marshall, it's late. Can't we wait until—?"

"You guys go ahead," Marshall said. "It should just take a couple of seconds to track him through the internet and see where he is now."

No one left.

They watched as Marshall sat at one of the big computers and typed a series of search commands. As information scrolled across the screen, they saw his expression crumble to a grim stare.

"We didn't succeed?" Naomi asked. "We didn't change his life?"

"Oh, we changed it, all right," Marshall said. "Our Sean Brody died ten years ago."

37

STEALING SECOND

Saturday, April 19, 1968

FIFTH INNING. A PRISTINE APRIL AFTERNOON. The Portales High School Rams were being mauled by the Clovis Wildcats. Something amazing had just happened, though. One of Sean's own—the lowest of low bench-sitting scum—had been pressed into duty and actually got a hit.

Art Hogan took a fastball on the fists and dinked it into the no man's land behind the Wildcat third baseman. Elated, Art leaped, clapped and skipped to first base.

One of the starters, a guy who was also middle linebacker during football season, spit and said, "Jesus Christ, what a dork. You get a hit, you should at least act like it's not the first time. Hey! Hey! He broke my bat, goddammit!"

Sean was tempted to point out that, in Art's case, it might well *have* been the first time. He thought better of exposing himself that way, though. Besides, he had a headache, sort of. And what's more, the scene unfolding here was eerily familiar.

Coach Kenny stalked from the third-base coaching box, grabbed Sean by his jersey and commanded, "You go run for Baryshnikov over there. Steal the base. Go on the first pitch."

"And," he said, adding a tone of menace, "don't get picked off!"

Shock jolted Sean's recall of his future counterpart. *"Where are you? Come on, wake up. You said you know how to do this."*

Like being awakened from a dead sleep, future-Sean struggled with awareness. The younger Sean's willingness to revive him, though, initiated his recovery. The comfortable familiarity of a baseball diamond encouraged his return. Once he found himself, future-Sean realized this was it. One last stand, and he'd be forever relegated to young-Sean's dreams.

Sean trotted across the infield, cutting between the pitcher, who glared at him every step of the way, and the catcher. The catcher stood at home plate, mask tilted back on his head and a smirk of self-assurance on his face. He sent a stream of tobacco juice in Sean's direction as Sean trotted past.

When Sean reached first base, Art seemed surprised to see him.

"Hey, Sean." He smiled, standing with both feet atop the base as if trying to keep it from escaping.

"Coach told me to run for you."

Art looked at Sean with suspicion. "But I got a hit."

"I know, Arty. And now, I'm supposed to run for you. I'm fast, and you're slow."

Art's expression melted into a relieved smile. Sean knew exactly what Art was thinking. He wouldn't have to risk a base running screw-up. That would be Sean's problem.

Art took two steps toward the dugout, then turned and repeated, "I got a hit."

Sean took a deep breath. He felt very alone as he watched Art skip away.

"*Okay,*" young-Sean begged silently. "*Now what do I do?*"

"*Just relax,*" future-Sean answered. "*I'll take care of it.*"

Young-Sean took a timid lead. To his shock and dismay, future-Sean extended it two more steps. From the third base coaching box, Coach Kenny motioned frantically for him to get back.

The pitcher received a sign from his catcher, peered over his shoulder to first base, then came set. He spun off the rubber and threw a seed to first base. Future-Sean easily picked up the movement of the pitchers' back heel as he unweighted that leg to turn and throw. Sean skipped back. The base umpire offered a bored flat wave of both hands, palms down, signaling Sean safe.

The pitcher took another sign. This time, Sean extended his lead a step further.

The instant the pitcher's front foot twitched, Sean was gone. From his peripheral vision, he saw the Clovis second baseman break to the bag for the catcher's throw. Next Sean heard a sharp crack as the hitter made contact. A quick glance told him the second baseman's movements would take the defender right into the ball's path.

They wouldn't turn a double play, though! Sean was too fast, his jump too good. The second baseman's only option would be a throw to first.

Unless . . .

Sean slowed to linger for an instant between the second baseman and a skittering ground ball. Then, he accelerated again. His hesitation blocked the second baseman's view of the baseball *just* long enough. It ticked off the end of his glove and trickled into right field. Sean did not hesitate. He flew around second, watched as the next defender moved to the outfield side of third base to take the right fielder's throw. Sean performed a graceful hook slide to the infield corner of third base and eluded the tag.

Runners first and third, one out.

Just as they had done for Art, Sean's fellow bench denizens leapt up and cheered his heroics.

Coach Kenny spun and chilled them with a glare. He said nothing to Sean.

Sean took his lead at third, and ... the next hitter grounded a ball to shortstop for an inning-ending double play.

That was okay, though, young Sean thought to himself as he trotted off the field. *He was alone now.* Things had changed. He had succeeded. The world would be different.

Back at the field house, Sean obeyed a summons to Coach Kinney's office with a glad heart. He expected congratulations.

"Brody," Kinney said, "I don't care for the attitude of your little gang. You're the ringleader. You guys have too much fun while our starters are getting their asses kicked. I've put up with it so far. I tell you what I won't tolerate, though—who's coaching this team?"

"Well, you are ..." Sean began.

"That's right. So, where do you get off telling my hitters how to hit? Bobby Zimmerman doesn't need to hear anything from you. The only thing you know about hitting is that you can't do it!"

"I wasn't trying to ... I mean, I didn't—"

"I don't want any more of that crap. You can continue to come to practice, but you won't play anymore. And you WON'T sit on the bench during games and tell wise-ass jokes with your buddies. You won't suit up for any more games. My suggestion is hand in your uniform and find a better way to use your time."

Sean waited to shower. He sat at his locker long after everyone else had gone. He accepted congratulations from several teammates for his baserunning performance with a sad smile of thanks as they departed. He told no one of his dismissal.

Finally, Sean removed his high school baseball uniform for the last time, threw it on a laundry pile, showered alone, then dressed and walked through gathering twilight. He took the back way, weaving between the old temporary barracks buildings, and found his car across an otherwise empty parking lot.

Amanda Page leaned against the hood. Her hair bounced over her shoulders in a feathery curl. She'd applied a touch of makeup. She wore a white collared blouse and blue shorts revealing long brown legs worthy of any models' runway.

Sean hadn't realized until this moment just how beautiful she really was.

"Wow," he said, looking her up and down. "Just... wow."

"I was afraid I'd missed you," she said as she smiled.

"Sorry. If I'd known you were waiting, I wouldn't have taken so long."

Already, details of the past couple of days with Amanda were beginning to dim. She confessed the same condition.

They both realized, though, they had shared something amazing in its significance.

"I just wanted to let you know," she said, "I'm leaving."

"Leaving?"

"Yeah. Now that I know I'm okay, I can't stay here any longer."

"Graduation is only a few weeks away. You can't go until—"

"I have to."

"What about your parents?"

"I turned eighteen three weeks ago," Amanda said. "I can do what I want. And I'm not running away. I told them I'm going. They aren't happy about it. They know what I've been through, though. My mom's sister lives in San Francisco. They said I could stay with her and then come back and finish my requirements for graduation this summer."

"So, I'll see you this summer," Sean said. "I think I may be taking chemistry again."

"I don't think so," Amanda said. "I don't plan on ever returning to this place."

She leaned over and gave him a long slow kiss. Sean imagined how this scene must have appeared to anyone passing by—a beautiful, essentially grown woman, suffocating a skinny, awkward sophomore boy with her lips, right in the middle of a parking lot. Where were those jerks from the football team when he needed them?

He couldn't contain his grin when she finally broke away.

"Don't get any ideas." She shook her head at his lecherous smile.

"Too late," he said.

"Goodbye, Sean Brody. I wish you love and luck."

38

HE EVEN TOLD ME GOODBYE

June 3, 1994

WALKING UP MAGGIE STANFIELD'S front steps that afternoon was the most difficult thing Sean would ever do. They were supposed to go to dinner and then a movie. She greeted him with her dazzling smile that made him know how welcome he was every time he looked at her. Before he said anything, though, her smile dissolved into pain.

They shared silence while he gathered the will to speak.

"Beth wants to try again," he finally said, his voice barely more than a whisper. "And I think I have to. I think I've got to know for sure whether—"

"Please pay attention to the words you're using, Sean," Maggie said. "Beth *wants*. You *have to*. Remember, *you* get to choose this time."

He shook his head. "I know. And I think I have to choose this for now. I'm so sorry."

Her momentary anger faded. She took his hands in hers, her eyes glistening. "I'm sorry, too. But if we were ever to be together, I wouldn't want you to have any regrets. I don't want to be anyone's second choice."

She found her smile again, squeezed his hands and

kissed his cheek. "Please call me if the time comes when you can make a different choice."

Maggie retreated to the shadows of her entry room and was gone.

Sean had arranged to go to Beth's house. All day he'd been excited at the prospect. He'd waited more than a year for Beth to change her mind, to realize they belonged together. At this moment, though, going from Maggie's door to Beth's felt wrong. He would go home first. He'd call Beth and tell her he'd be late.

Sean walked into his living room. He didn't know how long he sat paralyzed by conflicting emotions. The phone's chirp interrupted his reverie. That would be Beth, wondering where he was.

"Hello."

"Yes, I'm trying to reach Sean Brody."

A woman. Sean didn't recognize the voice.

"This is Sean."

"The Sean Brody who went to Portales High School back in the sixties?"

"Yes," Sean said warily, using a tone he reserved for telephone solicitors.

"Sean, this is Mandy. Mandy Schuler ... uh Page. I don't know if you remember me or not ..."

"Amanda! Of course, I remember you. How are you? *Where* are you?"

She gave a capsulized briefing of her life after leaving Portales those many years ago, and then said, "I suppose you're wondering why I called?"

"Yes, I am." Sean and Amanda had spent a very odd but extraordinary few days together at the end of the spring semester during Sean's sophomore year. Details were vague, except Sean remembered distinctly that, late one night, she'd laughed and given him a quick flash of her breasts.

"When I was at the hospital in Albuquerque, I started writing a journal," Amanda said. "It's something I've done ever since. I have volumes and volumes of them. Every so often I go back all those years and read that very first one to revisit the ordeal that was my high school senior year. Just to remind myself how hard things can be for people who need help.

"For a few days during late April of 1969, it must have been right before I left to go to the coast, I didn't write anything, which was unusual. The only thing is a notation with big red letters and underlined twice. It says, *Call Sean. June 3, 1994.* I happened to look at that entry earlier this week. And today is June third."

"Wow, that's weird. Does it say why you were supposed to call?"

"I'm not sure," she said. "Right next to the date, also underlined in red, it just says, *Choose Maggie.* Does that mean anything to you?"

June 23, 2046

"...you haven't presented a mission profile for authorization!" protested Upton Groose. "After all the problems yesterday with the ... the feedback from the wormhole, how do you know the equipment even works ..."

"The projector is fine," Marta said. "Isn't that right, Elvin?"

"The projector is fine," Elvin agreed.

"Then, let's go."

She and Marshall removed their robes and disappeared.

Nov. 30, 2035

"Thank you for helping us," eighteen-year-old Marshall Grissom said to twenty-three-year-old Marta Hamilton when he met her at Sky Harbor Airport in Phoenix. "I hope things went better this time?"

Marta smiled. "As usual, the integration was a challenge. Once she explained, though, and I understood how much you and Sean mean to her, I *had* to help. Taking a couple of days off to fly over from Albuquerque was easy. How was your drive from Las Cruces?"

"Long and hot," Marshall said. "I had to cut a few classes. But like you said, when I understood how important it is to him..."

They made the short drive from Skyharbor to the Papago Sports Complex, where, after years of disuse, the Nashville Athletics had returned to a refurbished Spring Training facility. The lush green of a half-dozen baseball diamonds glowed at the feet of red crags, towers and swirls that were the Papago Hills at the boundary separating Phoenix from Scottsdale.

Just across the parking lot, Marshall saw open-air batting cages under the cover of a quarter-acre of metal roof. The nets that formed walls and tunnels of the cages had been lifted, like curtains, and dozens of people milled about a broad, uninterrupted artificial surface. A brief storm had just blown through, dropping enough rain to leave the parking lot shining, and rich damp smells wafting from the surrounding desert.

As they neared the cages, the desert perfume was supplanted by a sharp aroma of pecan wood smoke and pork ribs drifting from a pair of pit barbeque smokers. Almost everyone wore baseball hats. They raised toasts with beer cans or shot glasses. John Prine's scratchy tenor emanated from a sound system, singing something about *Please don't bury me* . . .

Off by a row of pitching mounds sat a coffin, where a slow line of mourners filed by, each stopping to peer inside. Marshall didn't trust his emotions enough to go there yet, but he was pleased to see a smile steal across the faces of many mourners before they moved on.

The center of activity, though, was a dozen yards away where a tall, elegant, woman with silver hair offered an amazing smile and hug to each person who approached. And among this group, Marshall heard laughter.

He'd told Marta while driving from the airport that he'd wished they could have come back to an earlier time, when Sean was still alive, so they could talk to *him*. She reminded Marshall that the logistics were impossible.

"You would be way too young," she said, "and I would be on the other side of the world. And how much harder would it be to show up only a short time before . . . knowing he was about to die?"

Hearing the laughter, Marshall thought this might be the right time after all.

They merged with the crowd. Marta grabbed a beer. Marshall settled for Dr. Pepper because he was too young to drink. And as they mingled, Marshall gathered bits and pieces of conversations being held among men and women in their eighties.

"So how many years had you guys been playing on the Cecil's Margin Service team?" one woman asked.

"Oh, shoot, I guess it must be . . . twenty? Twenty-five? This was the fourth year they've had an eighty-and-over age division at the Roy Hobbs World Series."

"Slo-pitch?" a younger man asked.

The old man's voice acquired a disdainful ring. "Not softball, sonny. Baseball."

Through jumbled bits of conversation, Marshall gleaned the details of Sean's death. He'd suffered a heart attack on the pitching mound during the seventh inning of a game at Terry Park in Fort Myers, Florida. As always, Maggie had been watching from the stands. She'd rushed onto the field to stand over Sean while a Roy Hobbs staff member shocked him with a defibrillator and performed CPR until EMTs arrived.

". . . and the EMTs kept working, but I think he was already gone."

Marta and Marshall wandered through the crowd. When the knot of well-wishers around the tall woman momentarily thinned, Marshall approached her.

"Um . . . Mrs. Brody? Maggie?" Marshall said.

The woman smiled and extended her hand.

"I . . . I . . . know you don't know us," Marshall stammered. "We knew Sean . . . in . . . another life, sort of . . ."

Marta gave him a quick little dig with her elbow.

"It's so good of you to come," Maggie said as a quizzical expression stole over her features. Then someone else demanded her attention, a man tearfully telling a story about Sean, to which Maggie gave her full attention. She coaxed laughter from the man before he moved away.

Marshall waited, and when there was another gap in the informal reception line, he touched her sleeve.

"Forgive me, please, Mrs. Brody," he said, "I have something I need to ask."

Again, she studied them, as if searching for recognition that lay just beyond her grasp.

"Do you think . . . do you think Sean was happy with his life? The way it turned out, I mean?"

"Sean loved his life," Maggie said without hesitation.

"Do you think he would have traded ten years for all this? You? These people? Baseball?"

Marshall's voice broke. Maggie put her arm through his and gave him a reassuring pat on the hand.

"Young man, Sean would have traded ten years for baseball alone."

She glanced again from Marshall's face to Marta's, smiled, and began to talk as if she'd known them forever.

"One year after Sean and I met, we came here to Phoenix so he could play in an Oakland A's Fantasy Camp. We loved each other very much, but what I saw in Sean at that moment of his life was a man increasingly bored and frustrated with his job at the newspaper. He faced some difficult questions, wondering what place the world would hold for him without his newspaper career. That baseball camp changed him. Invigorated him. Reinvested him. He stayed at the paper only another few months. Later that year, we ran into one of the retired Major League players who'd been Sean's coach at the camp. I kissed Dave

Henderson and told him, 'I brought you a frustrated middle-aged man. You gave me back a ten-year-old kid.'"

Marshall couldn't contain himself any longer. Tears streamed down his cheeks. Again, Maggie linked his arm in hers and grasped his hand. Marshall found he couldn't speak. Marta spared him the task.

"It must have been difficult seeing Sean go that way," she said.

"You'd think so, wouldn't you?" Maggie smiled. "I've suspected how it would happen for a long time, though. That's why I tried not to miss many games. And Sean, he would have been thrilled that on the last day of his life he got to play baseball."

"So . . . so it was okay?" Marshall managed.

"Well, of course, I wish he were still here. But yes. He even told me goodbye. That very morning, we were at Fort Myers Beach, watching pelicans dive into the surf and listening to the ocean. He took my hand and said, "Thank you, Maggie.' And I laughed and said, 'You're welcome. But for what?' He said, 'You saved me from an ordinary life.'"

Marshall swiped at his tears. "Thank you. We had another friend—Sean didn't know her . . . um . . . he knew her grandmother. They were both wonderful people . . . I know that doesn't make any sense to you . . ."

A spark lit Maggie's eyes.

"Sean wrote books," she said slowly, her narrowed gaze shifting from Marshall to Marta and back again. "After he retired from journalism his goal was to leave nothing to regret. He did all the things he really wanted to do. And in his sixties, he started writing again. His ambition was to write a novel. Said he didn't think he'd be complete if he didn't. Turns out he wrote several. I was his proofreader. I guess I read every one nine or ten times..."

Once again, she gave them that probing, appraising look.

"...and I got to know those characters very well. Sean said the stories came from his dreams."

An elderly man and woman interrupted with their condolences and best wishes. Maggie graciously directed her attention to them with that captivating smile. Marta pulled Marshall away.

Marshall didn't think he wanted to view the body. As they walked, though, he found himself drawn to the coffin. He approached almost fearfully, thinking with every step he should turn away. Thinking he should remember Sean as the vibrant, funny old man he'd come to know in a now-altered future at an assisted living facility here in Phoenix. But it seemed he had no choice.

Sean lay in serenity, dressed in the sort of suit he probably rarely wore in life. His face was a picture of calm. The only thing that didn't fit this careful arrangement was a piece of notebook paper resting on Sean's chest. Written in careful block letters were the words: *Good ride, cowboy. Good ride.*

Marshall smiled, recalling that Sean was a big Garth Brooks fan.

And as they walked to the parking lot, he turned one last time and found Maggie standing just a little apart from everyone else. She beckoned to them.

"I think she wants to talk to us again," Marshall told Marta.

As they reversed course, Maggie hurried to meet them.

She looked deep into Marshall's eyes and said, "Marshall..." his eyes grew wide as she said his name... "if you see him again someplace, some... time, please... tell him to find me."

Marshall and Marta both smiled and nodded goodbye.

39

TRUTH IS TOLD

MARSHALL SHOUTED into the white void during his return through the limbo. "Come on, I know you're there! You just pretend you can't talk to us on the return trip!"

Silence.

"This isn't worthy of you! You hold yourself up to be some sort of a higher, more evolved being. Tell me this whole thing wasn't about a mistake!"

"Everybody makes mistakes," *the Hall Monitor said, his voice booming with authority.* "And, apparently, history abhors inconsistency."

Marshall refused to be intimidated.

"So, history . . . or whatever it is . . . did all this for one man? Just because somewhere his life became a jumble of different outcomes in different worlds? Our discovery of time travel before we should have? Billions of dollars? Sheila, Gormly, Pratt, Lucre, Pitts, Raul, Carla . . . an entire universe, all gone? Just to benefit one guy?"

"No," *the Hall Monitor said.* "There's you and Marta Hamilton, too. And many others. There are no solitary lives, Marshall. You can't tug at a single thread without affecting many others. My guess—and it is just a guess, because I don't *know either—is that hundreds, thousands, perhaps even millions of lives were adjusted. And to my experience, history—if that's what you want to call it—is indifferent to the cost of consistency. Now go away and leave me alone."*

July 7, 2046

"Mmmmmmmmm," said Marta.

"Mmmmmmmmmmmmmmmm," agreed Marshall. "Dr. Doonaughty outdid himself that time."

"Handcuffs were a nice touch," she agreed.

"Um . . . speaking of which . . . you do have a key for these things, right?"

"There's a little button right there on the side," Marta said.

Marshall extricated himself, stretched and rolled onto his back.

Marta cuddled into the nook between his arm and his chest. "Do you feel better about things?" she asked.

"Yes. Certainly, about Sean and Maggie. I still feel bad for Amanda, though. I know it wasn't our fault. I know Gormly was responsible, but time travel wrecked that poor girl's life."

"Time travel wrecked her senior year of high school," Marta corrected. "Lots of kids have miserable lives during high school without the intervention of time travelers. I think you, of all people, should understand that."

"She had everything going for her, though." Marshall stared wistfully at the ceiling. "Smart. Beautiful. A gifted athlete. She could have qualified for scholarships to any university she wanted. But she didn't even graduate from high school. I looked it up. She left Portales right after Sean came and got Sheila. Who knows what her life would have been like if she'd just been left alone?"

"That's right. Who knows? You need to be more thorough with your research, Marshall. You only investigated her a couple of years after she left Portales."

"Right. She dropped out, moved to San Francisco, got caught in the whole hippy drug scene and got arrested."

"And that's where you stopped."

"I didn't want to go further. The whole thing reminded me too much of Samantha."

"Well, I did go further," Marta said. "There wasn't much, just a feature article in an Oakland newspaper sometime around 1994, I think. It offered some fascinating details about Mandy Schuler."

Marshall propped himself on his elbow. "Don't tell me if—"

"She *was* arrested. Not for a drug-related crime. She was arrested for protesting the Vietnam War. She hung around the hippie scene for a few months after her arrest until one day a young man wearing an army uniform happened into the Haight Ashbury District. She saw many of her peace and love compatriots assail him as a baby killer and a cog in the war machine. The young man walked away from those angry taunts, but Amanda recognized his despair and followed him. After what she'd been through, she couldn't just let him go.

"She found him despondent on a bus bench. She struck up a conversation. She listened to his story. He had not sought the war. He'd been drafted. If the choice had been his, he would have stayed home and lived the life of a typical nineteen or twenty-year old kid. He didn't have that choice, though. So, he went, and he did the best he could. She told the reporter that the young soldier had come home broken. And American society was not very tolerant of mental illness back then."

"So, what *did* happen to her?"

"She moved to Oakland and began to call herself Mandy. She helped start a clinic for people suffering from what we now know as post-traumatic stress syndrome. She became dedicated to reclaiming the mental health of people damaged by psychological trauma. One of those she helped was a man named Joe Schuler. They eventually married and had a son—Sheila's father.

"In the meantime, Amanda earned her general equivalency diploma, attended school at night to earn a social services degree and then a masters' degree in psychology. She and Joe took over the clinic and expanded it to include mental health services for homeless and disenfranchised people. She never made much money, the newspaper article said. And not many people beyond those she helped over the years knew her name."

"Wow."

"So did her encounter with Sheila make her life different?" Marta said. "Yes. Did it make her life harder? Undoubtedly. But did it make her life better or worse? That's a tough one. Mandy Schuler told that newspaper reporter she couldn't imagine doing more fulfilling work. All the people whose lives she touched were better off for it. I remember a conversation Sheila and I had one night over a glass of wine. Sheila was very proud of her grandmother."

Marshall remembered what the Hall Monitor had told

him. "*. . . only through challenge can a sentient being grow toward his or her potential . . .*"

"Okay," he said. "I do feel better."

At that moment, a harsh, unfamiliar tone sounded from Marta's phone. "Uh, oh."

"What is it?"

"I've been doing an ongoing computer search for any news stories related to Warren Pitts. I set an alarm . . ." She picked up the phone, scanned her internet alerts, sighed heavily, and turned to Marshall. "An executive jet belonging to the Hemisphere Investment Group crashed today in western Pennsylvania. All six people on board were killed. They included Hemisphere President Warren Pitts."

"Oh, my God!"

"Elvin's theory is looking better and better".

"Oh. My. God," Marshall said again.

"So, what do you want to do?" she asked.

"We have to tell them. All of it. The truth about Sheila and Jason Pratt and Gormly and Gillis and . . . and me. We can't soften any of it. We can't protect anyone. We've got to scare the hell out of them, so everyone knows they must walk away from this lunacy. Bury it right here. Make this place a tomb. And then leave it alone."

"Are you sure?" Marta said. *If Marshall was who Gillis suspected, would he really place himself in that sort of jeopardy?* "Do you want to think about it?"

"No, we have to do it now."

"Okay. I'll call that guy, Wishcamper. I had a good feeling about him. Then we'll tell the others. And assure them that I'll protect them. They were just doing what I told them to do."

"Years off our lives?" Macy asked with a shaky voice as Marshall related his conversation with the Hall Monitor. "How many?"

"He wasn't specific."

"Most of us have never come across this guy." Frank made a dismissive gesture with his hands as he paced the carpeting on Marta's office floor.

Marta nodded. "Naomi remains skeptical. She's not sure the Hall Monitor and Marshall's encounters with Sheila and Samantha were anything other than hallucinations associated with a trying environment about which we know practically nothing. Along with some wishful thinking. I haven't ever come across this guy, either. So, I don't know what I believe. I just want everyone to be informed of Marshall's concern, and assure you that I'll be taking the blame . . . The only thing I'll omit is Leonard's role in Sheila's disappearance. I'm afraid they would prosecute him, and I think he's earned a reprieve."

July 9, 2046

Marta and Marshall met with Sheldon Wishcamper in a subbasement office of the U.S. Capitol building. After talking with them for an hour, Wishcamper placed a call to Senator Mumford, who joined them. This conversation lasted another hour. Mostly, Marta talked, and Marshall fidgeted as he listened. When the time came to flesh out details of his own transgressions, though, Marshall did not hold back.

Mumford took a long cigar from his inside jacket pocket and tapped it lightly against the arm of his chair.

"Ms. Hamilton . . . Marta . . . the first thing I have to ask is whether you know Gillis Kerg's location? If you know anything, you must help to apprehend him."

"I swear to you I have no idea what's happened to Gillis. I'll take a polygraph if you want. It doesn't matter, though. Gillis will be a difficult man to find."

Mumford frowned. "And that's okay with you?"

"Yes, it is. I think Gillis was right. I think these were the people who sent an assassin from the future to kill you, Senator. I think we couldn't stop them any other way, and I think the alternative could be cataclysmic. Gillis Kerg is a hero. He made a great sacrifice in service to his . . . universe. And he ought to be left alone."

"Unfortunately," Mumford said, "Mr. Kerg's disposition won't be that simple."

"I know. I can't imagine, though, that anyone involved with this program will ever want details of what's happened over the last three years to be made public. You could just as easily decide to let him go."

Mumford's eyebrows arched. He leaned forward and pointed his cigar at her. "Are you suggesting you might—?"

"No, Senator. No. I hope you know me well enough by now to understand I'm not threatening anything. I'm just saying since there is no official record, there's no political cost to looking the other way."

"And, of course," Mumford said, relaxing one eyebrow and leaving the other to do all the work, "the same argument could be made concerning you and your whole group."

"I stand ready to accept responsibility for anything that

happened if that's what the subcommittee chooses. Everyone else acted on my direction. And I will remind you, I believe Gillis Kerg isn't the only hero of this story. Those are some remarkable people back there under the desert."

Mumford regarded her for a long time before his remaining eyebrow relaxed. "In this room, as well."

Marshall couldn't stand it any longer. "I'm ready," he said.

"For what?"

"To be arrested. Stop me before I kill again . . ."

Marta rolled her eyes.

Mumford stood. Marshall stood with him. He offered his wrists to Wishcamper. Without a word, Mumford put his cigar in his pocket and left the room.

Wishcamper motioned for Marshall to sit. "The HRI security people, not the ones on Lucre's payroll, sent me the contents of that backpack he had with him when he . . . succumbed. There were several encrypted data cards, including one with the codes to unlock them. There's no question as to what Mr. Lucre and Mr. Pitts were up to. They're both dead. We haven't been able to implicate anyone else at Hemisphere. As for the two of you, Mr. Grissom, Ms. Hamilton, you're free to go."

"So now what?" Marshall asked as they strolled across the National Mall towards the Washington Monument. "At least he didn't tell us not to leave town."

"Oh, they'll come and get us if they decide that's what they want to do," Marta said. "But I won't worry about it. Life's too short."

Marshall stopped and took her hand. "Marta, I want to follow Sheila's advice. I don't want to go back. Life *is* too short. I understand you're not sure about the Hall Monitor and my conversation with Sheila. I know it was real, though, and I believe what they told me. Between the two of us we've undergone more projections than anyone. I don't know how many years we have left to be together. I don't want to sacrifice any more of our time to the limbo. I love you. I'm sorry if that makes you uncomfortable or if... if..."

Oh my God. Who are you, Marshall Grissom? "Well," Marta said, taking a deep breath, then exhaling, "I guess I think I might love you, too, Marshall. So, what do you want to do?"

"You mean now?"

"Now, next week, next year?"

"We'll have to go back and make arrangements—"

"No. We don't. The apartment and all its artificial intelligence buddies are out to get me, and you said you didn't want to go back. So, let's don't."

"Um ... okay. Well ... where could we go?"

Marta grinned.

"I know a guy with a sailboat. He said to stop by any time."

(epilogue)

Late July 2046

IN A SHALLOW BAY ON THE Caribbean island of Grenada, a 107-year-old man nestled into a lawn chair next to an ancient ketch-rigged Tayana named *Somewhere Over China*. He and the others who made up this marina community were preparing for their evening ritual of applauding a Caribbean sunset.

The other marina denizens knew Cecil as a happy, eccentric fellow who told funny stories and had a fondness for cats. They didn't know Cecil also served as a member of a top-secret congressional subcommittee overseeing time travel. Or that he had become something of a mentor to Marta Hamilton.

Cecil had no good reason or apparent qualification for acting in either capacity. But history, it seems, has a sense of humor. An invitation meant for Cecillium Resources Ltd.—a giant Australian research organization dealing with exotic alloys—somehow found its way to Cecil's Margin Service of Spokane, Washington by mistake.

Being a civic-minded person, Cecil tried in his own small way to support worthy causes. He faithfully contributed to National Public Radio and The Society for the Prevention of Cruelty to Animals. When he learned through the mistaken correspondence that the U.S. government was soliciting corporate investment in a "cutting edge technology vital to national security interests," he was proud to have been invited and, without fail, mailed a check for four hundred and twenty three dollars every quarter.

Only later did he learn the secret project was all about time travel. When the project fell apart, other corporate entities—most of which had invested millions—cut their losses and fled. Cecil, though, remained steadfast.

On this early summer evening, Cecil was joined by Baptiste, a ten-year-old boy who haunted the marina, selling fish, relaying phone messages, performing odd jobs. Cecil lifted a pitcher from a rusty TV tray and poured himself a mojito. He drank deeply, felt the rum's warmth, and watched waning daylight assume its otherworldly sheen while sun edged closer to sea, bleeding gold into turquoise water beyond the bay.

Baptiste swigged his coke.

Raul and Fidel threaded themselves between Cecil's legs, purring their contentment.

"Hey, mon," Baptiste said, "Looks like you got company, you."

Cecil peered through long, steep shadows. He saw a tall figure and a short figure, their hands entwined.

They waved. Cecil waved back.

"Dat dose people who give me twenty dollars and let me keep my fish," Baptiste said.

With every step, Marta and Marshall began to shed their clothes. Marshall walked out of his flip flops and quickened his stride. Marta shrugged off her shirt, then trotted past him. Marshall nearly tripped as he pulled his shirt over his head. He broke into a jog and caught up when Marta paused to strip off her shorts.

By the time they reached Cecil's boat they were both at a dead run. Giggling. Breathless.

The cats, Cecil, and Baptiste watched as Marta and Marshall leapt off the dock into warm green water.

"Dem people ever wear clothes?" Baptiste asked.

Cecil cackled with laughter. "Well, fellas," he said to Baptiste and the cats, "we'd best go below and see what we got to eat. Looks like we got company for supper. Not the leftover pizza, though. Marshall's allergic to anchovies.

"Dontchaknow."

ACKNOWLEDGMENTS

As always, first and foremost, I thank Nancy for her patience and dedication to all my endeavors. Thanks to Laura Taylor, who has championed my work from the day we met at the Southern California Writers' Conference. Thanks to Shanna McNair, Scott Wolven and Elyssa East of The Writers' Hotel who have shaped my education. Thanks to Jessica Therrien and Holly Youmans of Acorn Publishing for the opportunity.

The three books that so far make up this series were written several years ago. During that time, my writing companion was Hef the Cat. She lived for twenty years but was not around to see this project through to completion. Her successor, Lumpy Cat, has bravely picked up the torch. (I would never have allowed either of them to be waxed.)

Mike Murphey Books

Tales of Physics, Lust and Greed

Taking Time
Wasting Time
Killing Time

www.mikemurpheybooks.com

AUTHOR'S NOTE

Thanks so much for reading *Killing Time*, the third book in my Physics, Lust and Greed Series. Writers write for a lot of reasons, but one of the most important is to be read. With a couple million new titles to choose from each year, believe me, it's a tough market out there. If you enjoyed this book, or even if you didn't, you can do one more thing to help. Write a review and post it on Amazon here:

http://www.amazon.com/review/create-review?&asin=B08XJZL84B

Thanks again for reading *Killing Time,* and I hope you will be on the lookout for *The Outlaw Gillis Kerg*, the fourth installment in the Physics, Lust and Greed series, appearing soon.

www.ingramcontent.com/pod-product-compliance
Lightning Source LLC
Chambersburg PA
CBHW022005050726
47499CB00002BA/309